Last Family Standing

Other books by the author

The Pastor's Wife
The Mother Road

A Wild Goose Chase Christmas, Quilts of Love series

Last Family Standing

Jennifer Allee

Nashville

Last Family Standing

ISBN: 978-1-4267-6809-5

Published by Abingdon Press, P.O. Box 801, Nashville, TN 37202

www.abingdonpress.com

Macro Editor: Jamie Chavez

Published in association with the MacGregor Literary Agency

The persons and events portrayed in this work of fiction are the creations of the author, and any resemblance to persons living or dead is purely coincidental.

Library of Congress Cataloging-in-Publication Data has been requested.

Printed in the United States of America

1 2 3 4 5 6 7 8 9 10 / 19 18 17 16 15 14

To Amanda, with love

Acknowledgments

With each book I write, I'm continually impressed by the dedication and skill of the professionals around me. Many thanks go to:

Sandra Bishop—my amazing agent and friend.

Ramona Richards—my brave acquisitions editor, who isn't afraid to push boundaries.

Cat Hoort—the savviest, most clever marketing and publicity manager I've had the pleasure of working with.

All the members of the Abingdon team, from the art department, to marketing, to sales and everyone in between. Without all your hard work, I'd fall apart!

Big thanks, too, go to family and friends who put up with me while I spend hours hunched over my laptop. You bless me every day!

1

Your daughter's on television."

"What?" I just about drop the spoon I'm using to stir my custard mixture. Is this a joke? A wrong number? I pull my cell phone away from my ear and read the ID on the screen. Nope. That's Jules's name, right under the picture of her wearing a red, white, and blue stovepipe hat at last year's July Fourth picnic.

"Monica? Are you there?"

Her voice calls through the speaker, and I slowly put the phone back to my ear. "Yeah. I'm here."

"Did you hear what I said?"

I close my eyes and shake my head, as if that will bring some clarity to my mind. It doesn't work. "I heard, but . . . are you sure?"

"Absolutely. I recorded it to the DVR so you can see for yourself."

Leave it to Jules to think of the practical answer to my questions. "I'll be right there."

"I'll leave the porch light on."

As we end the call, I look down at the spoon I'm still holding, motionless in the saucepan. Instead of creamy custard, I now have something more akin to runny scrambled eggs. It's ruined. Being a chef, I don't usually make such stupid mistakes, but I'm more than a little shell-shocked from the bomb that just fell on me. I turn off the flame, pour the contents down the disposal, then drop the pot and spoon into the sink with a clatter.

Running upstairs to grab my shoes, scenes from the past flash through my memory.

The hospital. All those white walls. The antiseptic smell. The rhythmic *squeak-click-click-squeak* of the gurney. The turtle-shaped water spot on the delivery room ceiling. The sharp cry of lungs being filled with oxygen for the first time. When I turned my head away, one nurse said to the other, "She's not keeping it. We're supposed to give the baby right to the adoptive parents."

That had been my idea. Don't give the baby to me. Why should I hold something that's not mine to keep? I thought it would be easier that way.

I was wrong.

Still, twenty-five years later, I do believe I made the right decision for my daughter. As I stuff my feet into my sneakers, I still think it was the right thing to do. For everyone. Even so, my knees feel slightly wobbly as I trot back down the stairs. My hand shakes as I grab my house keys. And when I call to my dog, Ranger, my voice shakes.

"I've got to go out."

He lifts his shaggy brown head from the couch and looks my way, no doubt thinking he can stop me with a longing look from his big, soulful eyes. But I dash right past him.

"Sorry, buddy. No walk tonight."

As I pull the front door closed behind me, a velvety breeze rubs across my cheeks, my bare arms, and my shorts-clad legs.

I've lived in the Las Vegas valley long enough to know that 100-degree weather during the day often results in the most wonderful nighttime conditions. Everyone else on the block knows it, too, and it looks like most of them are taking advantage of it tonight.

Mr. Williams raises his hand in greeting as he approaches, and I wave back. His dog, a black and white Great Dane named Caesar, tugs him along, straining at the leash. It's obvious who's walking whom.

"Where's Ranger?" Mr. Williams asks.

I motion behind me. "Hanging out at home. I'm heading over to see Jules."

The wind picks up and a gust lifts his silver comb-over and drops it on the other side of his head. Smoothing it back in place with one hand, he nods. "Have fun, then. See you—" The rest of his words are blown away as Caesar propels him down the block.

I'm thankful for the wind. It provides an excuse to keep my head down. Hands stuffed in my pockets, shoulders curled forward, ponytail swinging wildly, I speed walk the three-house distance to Jules's without having to interact with anyone else.

Just as she promised, the porch light is on and I open the front door without knocking. Inside the foyer, I kick off my shoes and call out, "It's me!" I'm immediately swarmed by tweenager John and eight-year-old twins Jerrod and Justin.

"Hey, Aunt Monica!"

"Did you bring something yummy?"

"Where's Ranger?"

Opening my arms wide, I try to hug them all at once. "Sorry, boys. Only me tonight." It's pretty rare for me to come over here without some kind of food offering.

"Guys, give Aunt Monica some breathing room." Jules leans her five-foot-nine-inch frame over the boys, bracing one hand on Jerrod's head, and plants a kiss on my cheek. Then she looks back down at her sons. "Head upstairs. Now."

The three grumble in unison, but they don't argue. It makes me wonder what Jules said to them before I got here. Did she tell them we needed to have a big-person talk? Or did she warn them there might be crying? The threat of experiencing female emotion would be enough to scare them away for at least the rest of the night. Possibly till puberty.

Jules links her arm through mine and pulls me through the house. We pass the room they use as an office, and a voice calls out. "Hey, Monica."

"Hey, Jackson," I call back to her husband. Apparently, he's also been warned about the high likelihood of hysterics.

"You want a drink?" She asks as we walk through the kitchen.

"What have you got?"

"Everything we need for killer root beer floats."

"Ooh, the hard stuff." I shake my head. "Maybe later."

When we get to the family room, my eyes immediately fly to the flat screen TV mounted on the wall, but it's not even on.

"In a second." Jules pats my back. "First, you need some details. Let's sit down."

We settle on the worn, chocolate brown sectional. I was with her when she picked it out. Chocolate was my suggestion, because I thought it would hide stains. She angles toward me and puts one hand flat on the seat cushion, right next to a big, dark spot of something. As it turns out, the antics of three young boys can't be hidden, no matter how hard you try.

We look at each other, and I realize that for once my strong, take-charge friend is at a loss for words. So I get us started. "What was she doing on TV?"

Jules tucks a piece of blonde hair behind her ear, but her hairstyle is so short, it just looks like she's stroking the top of her ear. "You know that reality show I watch? *Last Family Standing*?"

I nod. "Yeah. It's the one with the hot-but-snarky host."

She sighs, but her mouth quirks up into a grin. "Why is that the only thing you remember about the show?"

Because I only watched it once, just to please her. And since I didn't know who any of the contestants were or what was going on, all I had to concentrate on was the host. Who was pretty memorable.

"The basics are simple," Jules says. "The season starts out with eight teams made up of two family members. All the teams are dumped in a remote location and have to rough it while they compete against each other until only two family teams are left. Then the audience votes to decide the winner."

I hold my palm out to her. "Forgive me if I'm not fascinated, but what difference does it make? What does this have to do with my daughter?"

"Tonight was the season finale, and at the end, they introduce some of the contestants for the next season. She was on the show tonight." Jules looks down for a second, rubbing her finger along the edge of the cushion stain.

Now that I've had some time to process the news, questions begin to bubble up in my brain. "How do you know it's her? You don't even know what she looks like. *I* don't even know what she looks like."

"She looks a lot like you."

I immediately picture a younger version of myself: dark auburn hair, blue eyes, and an upper lip that I've always thought was a bit too thin. Does she feel the same way? Does she ever look into the mirror and give it a pouty smile, making her lips as prominent as possible?

What am I doing? I shake my head, banishing the daydream and pulling my focus back to reality.

"But that could be a coincidence. I have one of those faces, you know? People are always asking if they know me from somewhere." I sigh. That's it. That has to be it. "It's just a mistake. She must be someone else's—"

"She has your picture."

The blood in my veins immediately converts to ice water. "My picture? Are you sure?"

Jules offers up a gentle smile. "Yes. It's your graduation photo. And it has your first name and the date written on the back."

My spine seems to have lost the ability to hold me upright. My shoulders slump and I plop back against the cushions. I don't understand any of this. I chose the birth parents from a book full of hopefuls, and we even met once. But I never gave them my name, or a photo, or anything that would tie us together.

"Hey," Jules grabs my hand and squeezes it between both of hers. "Are you okay?"

"No." Only a handful of people know about this chapter of my life. Looking into the concerned eyes of my best friend, I'm glad she's one of them. "I'm about as un-okay as you can get."

She understands. The consummate nurturer, Jules also understands the importance of what we want to do versus what we need to do. She leans over and snatches the remote from the coffee table. "You ready?"

Can I ever be ready for this? Half an hour ago I was living a happy, uncomplicated life. My biggest worries were wondering if I should take Ranger to the vet for a teeth cleaning, and keeping the eggs from curdling in my custard. Now, I'm a woman with a past. A past that's about to come to life before my eyes.

God help me. Please help me. I'm so not ready.

Without waiting for me to answer, Jules pushes a few buttons, bringing the TV screen to life.

Ready or not, here she comes.

2

Seeing my daughter is simultaneously the most amazing and heartbreaking experience of my life. Jules was right; she does look like me. From the nose up, at least. Her eyes are blue, and her hair is auburn, although it's much brighter than mine. But the jawline, the chin, the lips . . . those are reminiscent of Duncan. I sure hope that's all she inherited from her father.

The young woman—who, if I've done my mental math correctly is twenty-five years, three months, and thirteen days old—smiles down at me from the wall-mounted flat screen. It's a sedate smile. A Mona Lisa smile that could mean any number of things.

I'm content.

I'm bored.

I secretly want to slap my birth mother silly, but I'm keeping that to myself until the opportune moment.

An off-screen voice blares out. "Twenty-five-year-old fashion designer Jessica Beckett comes to us from—"

The buzzing in my ears drowns out the rest of that sentence. *Jessica.* My daughter's name is Jessica.

I shake my head, and the male voice registers again. ". . . has a special reason for being on *Last Family Standing.*"

My daughter—Jessica—opens her mouth to speak. I lean forward, desperate to finally hear her, to know how her adult voice has transformed from the newborn cries imprinted on the auditory center of my brain. But she freezes, and I almost tumble off the edge of the couch cushion.

I swing my head in Jules's direction. "Why did you do that?"

"Just checking on you."

"I'm fine."

"You're whiter than an Alaskan albino."

I'm not sure why Alaskan albinos would be whiter than any others in the world, but I get her point. "I never knew her name."

"Your choice?"

"Yes." My fingernails press into the bare skin on my thighs. "I figured the less I knew, the easier it would be to let her go."

I don't know if that line of reasoning was correct or not. What I do know is that I can't imagine the whole experience being any harder than it was.

I look at Jessica's frozen face. "Where did the announcer say she lives?"

"Irvine. California."

So close. You can drive from here to there in about five hours. Did she grow up there? Has she always been just a car drive away?

"He's not the announcer."

"What?"

Jules motions at the TV. "The man talking is Rick Wolff, the host of the show."

My head cocks to the left. "Does that matter?"

She ignores the question. "Are you ready for me to hit play?"

I nod. Jules aims the remote like a gun, and my daughter begins to speak.

"I was adopted as a baby. Don't get me wrong," she waves her hands wildly, palms out, "I had a very happy childhood. No problems there."

She laughs. It sounds a bit forced, but then I don't know her well enough to judge. That could just be the way she laughs.

"My parents and I are very, very close."

Heat floods my cheeks and I swallow back something vile that tries to creep up my throat. She's close to her parents. That's good. That's what I always wanted: for all of them to be happy. There's no reason to feel like I've been kicked in the gut.

Jessica's lashes dip, as though she's taking time to compose her thoughts. When she looks at the camera, that shadow of a smile is back.

"Even though I'm happy, I think it's time I met my birth mother."

Ice replaces heat as all the blood drains from my face. "She wants to find me?"

"Keep listening," Jules says.

Jessica's face is replaced by a montage of still photos from her childhood as Rick Wolff's voice once again takes command of the program. "Jessica may want to find her birth mother, but does the mother want to be found? Jessica has located no information about the woman who gave her up twenty-five years ago. Her only clue is an old graduation photo with the name *Monica* written on the back."

There I am. My senior picture fills the screen. I was barely eighteen, excited to leave high school behind and head off to culinary school. Jessica hadn't been born yet. She wasn't even a glimmer in my eye. It wouldn't be until two years later that I'd meet her bad-boy father and lose all grip on common sense.

"Where did they get that?" I ask aloud. "I never gave her parents anything."

"They didn't get it," Jules answers. "Jessica had it when she got in touch with the show."

A moment later, I hear the exact same thing recounted by Jessica herself. The host asks her how she got the photo, and she shrugs. "It's always been on the mantel with all the other family photos. When I was old enough to understand, my parents told me it was my birth mother. They got the picture the day I was born, but they never did tell me from whom."

The mystery of how Jessica got the picture is replaced by another, far more important question. "Pause it."

Jules hits the button and looks at me.

"So she's trying to find me?"

"Yes."

"But why is she talking about it on this show?" It's a physical competition based on endurance and mind games. It's not a show that reunites families.

The corner of Jules's mouth quirks up. "Why do you think?"

I don't want to say what I think. It would be better to hear it from someone else. Maybe then it won't be real. Elbows to knees, I hang my head and wave blindly toward the TV. "Restart it."

"I can't think of anything better," Jessica's voice says, "than competing on *Last Family Standing* with my birth mother."

I raise my head slowly, just in time to see Jessica look directly into the camera, tilt her head, and grin. Good grief, it's exactly what Duncan used to do. And I never could say no to him.

Jessica's image is replaced by Rick Wolff. Wearing a khaki shirt and shark tooth necklace, he has a quasi-rugged look, like a model from a safari-wear catalog. "Will Jessica find her mother? That's yet to be seen." He crosses to a tiki torch and wraps his hand around the pole. "If she doesn't, her flame will be snuffed out before she has a chance to begin." With something resembling a coconut shell on the end of a stick, he covers the top of the torch, extinguishing it. Then he looks straight at the camera, as if he knows I'm sitting on my best friend's couch and holding my breath. "If you're out there, Monica, or if you know Monica, please call or text us at the number on the screen."

Jules aims the remote again, and the TV goes blank. "That's it. He moves on to someone else now."

Silence settles between us. I don't know what to say. A thousand thoughts are crowding my mind.

My daughter wants to meet me.

She's beautiful.

She wants me to be on a reality show.

All I have to do is call that number.

Who gave her my picture?

A reality show? Me?

Jules leans over and squeezes my knee. "Talk to me. What are you going to do?"

What am I going to do? No way I'm going on a reality show, especially this one. Jules has told me all about it. I've heard about the harsh conditions, the lack of food that drives contestants to insect consumption, the duplicity that's required in order to win. How can I willingly subject myself to that?

But how can I not? My daughter wants to meet me. *My daughter.* Jessica. For years, I've put her out of my mind. Not because I wanted to, but because I had to. It was the only way I could survive the heart-wrenching decision to let her go. And letting her go was the only way I could ensure she had a good, happy life. I never expected to see her again. But now, I can.

My daughter wants to meet me. And I will do whatever it takes to meet her.

I look at Jules, blinking hard. "Can I use your phone?"

3

What did you do?"

When Jules gave me her phone, I had every intention of calling the number on the TV screen. But halfway through dialing, a thought occurred to me. How did Jessica's family get that photo of me? She said her parents had it since she was a baby, but there was only one other person outside our little group who knew what I was doing.

"What do you mean, dear?" My mother's voice is smooth, innocent. She's obviously not a fan of *Last Family Standing* because she has no clue what I'm talking about.

"You gave a copy of my high school graduation picture to the Becketts, didn't you?"

Thick silence is followed by a long, deep sigh. That's admission enough for me.

"Mom, how could you? You know I wanted to stay out of their life."

"If you wanted that, you never should have given them your baby." She sighs again, but this time it's short and final, more like a snort. "I'm sorry. That didn't come out the way I wanted it to."

Maybe not, but it came out exactly the way she meant it. Mom has never understood how I could give up my baby for adoption, and she never agreed with my decision to cut all ties with the Becketts. If she'd had her way, we would have been one big, extended family, exchanging letters and pictures, getting together on holidays. It had almost killed me to walk away from my child when all I knew of her was the glimpse of her tiny, newborn body. How could I stand to get to know her, watch her grow, and have to leave her again and again and again? Mom's philosophy was "better something than nothing." But I knew better. It was like the one time in high school that I took a drag off a friend's cigarette. There had been something seductive about it, how it warmed my whole body. In that second, I knew I had two choices: keep smoking and become addicted, or never, ever smoke again. I chose the latter, just like I did with my daughter. If I stayed in contact, spent any time with her, I would have become addicted. I would have needed more and more of her, until I'd want her back, all for myself. The only choice, the one that would result in the least amount of broken hearts, was to go cold turkey. But Mom never got how I could quit my daughter.

"When did you even see the Becketts?"

"At the hospital, the day after she was born. I was looking at her through the nursery window, and there was a young couple next to me. It didn't take long for us to realize we were looking at the same baby." More sighing blows through the phone.

I'm not an insensitive fool. I know this whole thing has been difficult for her, too. But right now, I need information. "What did you tell them?"

"That I was your mother. That you were a good person who just lost her way. And I showed them your picture, the one I kept in my wallet."

They already knew what I looked like, and Mom knew it. But I guess she wanted them to see what I looked like before I fell into a life of sin and questionable choices. "And you gave it to them."

"Because they asked if they could keep it." Her voice has a hard edge. "And I'm glad they did. At least someone realized that sweet baby needed a connection to her real mother."

"Susan Beckett has been her mother for twenty-five years. She deserves that title way more than I do. I'm more like an after-the-fact surrogate."

"Be that as it may." Mom's dismissive tone is more than a little insulting. "Why are you asking me about this now? How did you even find out?" She gasps, sucking back in all that previously sighed-out air. "She contacted you, didn't she?"

"Not exactly."

"Have you seen her?"

"In a manner of speaking."

"Either you've seen her or you haven't. It's a simple question."

This situation is many things: bizarre, uncomfortable, thrilling, confusing. The list goes on and on. The one thing it's not is simple.

So, I tell Mom about the TV show, which I was right, is not on her list of shows-she-never-misses. In fact, she's never even heard about it, so I have to take a side trip and tell her not only what it's about but also what time it's on and which network.

"Well, that explains why I've never seen it," she says. "It's on at the same time as my cooking program. The one where they have to make a three-course meal out of whatever leftovers they find in the fridge. I never miss that show."

"Mom, focus. We're talking about Jessica."

"Who's Jessica?"

I fall back on the couch, my head lolling against the cushions. "She's my daughter." Before Mom can run off on another tangent, I tell her about Jessica looking for me to be on the show with her, and how she showed my photo on air.

"Thank the good Lord. You see, I knew I was right. I knew she'd want to find you one day."

"You still should have told me. Then at least I would have been prepared."

"Monica, your attitude is baffling. You should be thanking me for helping your daughter find you, not haranguing me for doing the right thing."

Jules comes back in the room, and through a series of exaggerated facial features, we share a silent conversation.

How's it going?

Exactly how I expected.

Oh man, I'm sorry.

There's only one way to end this phone call. "I'm sorry if I upset you, Mom. I know you only want what's best for me."

"I always have." She sniffs for effect. "When are you going to see her?"

"I have no idea. I still need to call the show."

"You haven't called them yet? What are you waiting for, an engraved invitation?"

We've gotten to the point in the conversation where Mom pulls out the clichés and platitudes. My instant response is sarcasm. "Yes, that's exactly what I'm waiting for."

She laughs, because we've done this dance enough times that she finds my dry wit, as she calls it, endearing. "Well, you got something better. You got an invitation in front of a national audience. You'd best stop chewing the fat with me and give them a call."

"Yes, Mom. I will."

We exchange the usual *I love you* and *I love you too*, and I end it.

Jules plunks herself down next to me. She's holding two bowls of ice cream. One is plain strawberry, the other is vanilla surrounded with sliced bananas, covered in chocolate fudge and whipped cream, and crowned with three maraschino cherries.

I point at the big, decadent bowl. "Please tell me that's for me."

"Of course. We've passed the point of root beer floats. Now, it's sundae time."

"God bless you." I take the bowl and dig in.

"I figured if you needed to avoid the issue for a bit, at least this is a tasty way to do it."

"I'm not avoiding anything." I give her a stern look, but there's no conviction behind it.

She laughs, and a little bit of ice cream flies out of her mouth and lands on her leg. "Of course you are. Why else would you call your mother?"

"Good point."

She swipes the ice cream from her jeans, considers her fingertip for a moment, then shrugs and licks it off. With three boys who are forever dropping food, Jules is a firm believer in the five-second rule.

The ice cream is having the desired effect. With each sweet, silky mouthful, I relax a little more, until finally, my bowl is empty, and I'm slouched down on the couch, staring at the now-blank TV screen.

"Why do you think she did it?"

Jules takes the bowl and sets it inside her own. "Because she wants to meet you."

"I get that, but why this way?" I waggle an accusing finger at the big, black rectangle. "Why on national TV? She could have hired a private investigator, kept it all hush-hush."

"Hush-hush?"

"On the down low. Nice and quiet." I press my finger to my lips. "Sh!"

"Uh oh." Jules grins. "Someone's sugar-drunk."

"Am not." But as I draw my brows down into a scowl of consternation, the buzzing in my brain grows louder. "Okay, maybe a little."

"Why don't you stay here tonight and sleep it off?"

I shake my head. "I'm fine."

"Friends don't let friends walk home while on a sugar buzz." She stands and heads for the kitchen. "But if you insist, I'll force-feed you some coffee first."

The family room is much too quiet and empty, so I follow her. While she fires up the Keurig, I grab two mugs from the cupboard, set them on the counter beside her, and then drop down on one of the barstools surrounding the island.

Jules puts one of the mugs beneath the spout and presses a button. "To answer your question, I have no idea why Jessica is looking for you on television. It could be that she's a fan of the show, and she figured her unique twist would get her on as a contestant."

"It worked."

"Or, she could be trying to shock and embarrass you."

"That worked, too." I brace my chin on my fist and sigh.

"But the only way to know for sure is to ask her."

"And the only way to ask her is to go on the show."

The coffee stops dripping, and Jules brings the mug to me. I wrap my hands around it, breathing in the rich aroma of French vanilla. As the steam rises, I blink and look up at the woman I trust more than anyone in the world. "Will you help me?"

Without hesitation, she sits on the stool opposite me and squeezes my knee. "Every way I can."

"If I do this, I'm going to need you to coach me so I don't kill myself on that show. Or worse, look like an idiot."

Jules laughs and gets up to make her own coffee. "Your priorities are seriously messed up."

"So I've been told."

She frowns at me. "You know I was kidding."

"I know." But she's also right. What kind of a person gives away her own flesh and blood? Sure, I've always said I did it so my daughter would have a better life, but is that the total truth? How much of my decision was based on what would be easier for me?

My nose starts to tingle, and I sniff it away. "Did I do the right thing, Jules?"

"You did what you felt was best at the time. At this point, it doesn't matter if it was right or wrong. What matters is that you have a daughter who wants to meet you. What are you going to do about her now?"

If I meet her, it may be the most painful, excruciating experience of my life. Or it could be the best. But if I don't meet her, then it will be like I've abandoned her all over again. There's only one thing I can do.

"I'm going to sleep on it."

4

By the time I get home, I've convinced myself that a good night's sleep is essential to the decision-making process. The fact that I'll probably toss and turn and be unable to shut off my brain is immaterial. At the very least I need to be in my bed, curled into the fetal position with my covers pulled tightly around me.

I can barely open the front door because Ranger is right there, bouncing and circling and whining.

"Back up, buddy." Sucking in my stomach, I slide through the cracked door, and shut it behind me. "You missed me, huh?"

Then the phone rings, and his actions make sense. I might have the only dog in the world who freaks out at the sound of a telephone. Ranger isn't excited I'm home; he's having the equivalent of a doggie panic attack.

"Come on." He stays so close to me he presses against the side of my leg as I walk to the phone. I'm about to answer when I notice the digital display. The phone number isn't familiar. And I have twenty-six missed calls. It's a miracle poor Ranger didn't chew his way through the door.

After the ringing stops, I dial into voicemail. The robotic female reports, "You have twenty-six new messages."

That can't be good. I sink to the floor and wrap my arms around Ranger. We both need the emotional support. He climbs over my legs until he's sitting half in my lap and half on the floor. There's a comfort to the weight and heat of another living being, because it means I don't have to go through this alone. Sure, Ranger's just a dog, but he loves me in that unconditional way only animals can. Right now, I need all the love I can get.

My back is against the wall, in every sense of the phrase. A deep breath, a few buttons punched, and the messages begin to play.

"Monica, I think I just saw you on TV! Call me. It's Wendy."

"Saw you on *Last Family*. Are you going to call them?"

"Monica. Wow, it's been a long time. Do you remember me? Tom. We had freshman biology together. Uh . . . I'll try again later."

It's a weird combination of people. Some I know now, like my pastor, who is concerned about me and makes a point of mentioning that his wife is a fan of the show, not him. Some are people who knew me in high school or culinary school. And some I haven't heard from in over twenty years. But now, thanks to the marvels of modern technology, they've all found me. It's a slightly disturbing thought. "Maybe I'm overreacting." My fingers thread through Ranger's thick, shaggy fur. "Why would anybody care about me, anyway?"

Sure. This is just a momentary blip of excitement for a few people who have nothing better to do than sit glued to their TV screens every Tuesday night, watching a bunch of emotionally vulnerable people live out an exaggerated month of their lives. Tomorrow, no one will give me a second thought.

The phone rings again and Ranger's head jerks up. If this keeps up, neither one of us will get any sleep. I turn off the ringer, then gently push him off my legs so I can stand.

"Time to hit the hay."

Ranger bounds upstairs and I follow, turning lights off as I go. Things will look different in the morning.

I'm sure of it.

Things look different in the morning, all right. They look worse. They sound worse, too, thanks to the incessant trilling of the door chimes at the obscene hour of 7:00 a.m.

I'm able to extricate myself from the bedsheets without disturbing Ranger, who's spread out on the end of the mattress. Crazy mutt. A phone call sends him into fits, but the doorbell doesn't faze him.

Slipping into my bathrobe, I shake my head. "If a thief ever broke in, you would be less than useless."

The doorbell sounds again. I hurry down the stairs, grumbling to myself that whoever's out there better have a darn good reason for being so irritating. On my way to the door, I pass the phone table. Thank goodness I decided to turn off the ringer because not only have more calls come in but also for the first time ever there's a light blinking to inform me that my voice mailbox is full.

Go figure. Your photo gets flashed on one TV show, and suddenly you're the most popular girl in school.

I yank the front door open. "Yes?"

The man on my front porch is much too chipper for this hour of the morning. His smile—which reveals blindingly white, yet not perfectly straight, teeth—rearranges the features of his face, crinkling the skin around his eyes and exposing perfect twin dimples. "Good morning, Monica."

He acts like we know each other. Even though there is something familiar about this man, I know we've never met. None of my friends have smiles like that. And none of them come with a cameraman pointing the big, black eye of a camera straight at me.

The floor is suddenly very shaky beneath my feet. "You're him."

"That's what they tell me." His laugh rumbles as he extends his hand. "Rick Wolff."

I take a step backward, as if the mere act of not shaking his hand will fix everything. "How did you find me so fast?"

An easy shrug lifts one shoulder. "Several people called in during the show last night, including a couple of your friends who provided your full name and your address."

"Some friends," I mutter.

He lets it slide. "By the end of last night's show, we were already prepping the plane to come out here."

I cross my arms over my chest, feeling more vulnerable than usual. "I was going to call in. You didn't have to fetch me."

His eyes remind me of a big jug of fresh-brewed sun tea, especially when he opens them wide. "Then you watch the show?"

"No. My friend does. She's obsessed with you. With the show." His smile shifts into a lazy grin, and I know exactly what he must be thinking. "She's married," I stammer.

He steps forward. "That's okay. She's not the one I'm interested in."

Not only is this wildly inappropriate, it's being documented on film. I've got to put an end to it. "Please, this isn't a good time. I'll call you later. When I can talk." When I'm wearing clothes.

He's about to say something, probably something smooth and charming to coerce his way into my house, when a vehicle pulls up at the sidewalk. The white van has all kinds of weird equipment on its roof, including what looks like a satellite dish. If that doesn't tell me enough, the words *My News 3* painted on the side give it away.

The man on my porch doesn't look surprised. "You should probably let me in now."

"Look, Mr. Wolff, I—"

"Rick."

"Fine. *Rick*. I can't do this now."

Something close to sympathy changes those facial features again. "Take my word for it, Monica. It will be much better if you let me in now. That news crew isn't going anywhere until they get a story."

"And how will talking to you take care of them?"

"Because after you and I talk and come to an agreement, I'll come back out here and give them a statement."

There's no denying I want to avoid speaking to the press. But there's something even more important at stake. "Will you tell me about my daughter?"

He takes another step closer. "You can ask me anything you want."

"And you'll answer me?"

"You can ask me anything you want," he repeats, with a grin that says he may or may not answer.

But there's only one way to find out.

"Okay. You can come in." I point at the cameraman, whose face I still haven't seen. "But he stays outside."

Rick shakes his head. "Sorry. Where I go, he goes. If you don't sign a release, we can't use the footage, but for now, he shoots everything."

I'd like to shoot something. Over his shoulder, I see the news van doors open and people start to pour out. Considering the postage-stamp-size of my front yard—aka, rock garden—there's no time to argue. "All right."

Once Rick and the bearer of the one-eyed monster are inside, I shut the door and lock the deadbolt with a forceful twist. Toenails click on the tile behind me, and Ranger lopes in, tongue lolling out one side of his mouth, greeting our visitors with the closest thing a dog has to a smile.

The camera is trained on Rick as he hunkers down and becomes my dog's new best friend. This is as good a time as any to make myself decent.

"I'm going upstairs to get dressed. The living room is that way." I point. "Make yourself comfortable."

Halfway up the stairs I stop, turn, and head back down, leaning over the rail to yell at them. "But not *too* comfortable. Don't dig around in my medicine cabinet or anything like that."

Back up I go, then stop, come back down again. "Not that there's anything I don't want you to see in there."

I give it one more try: up, stop, come back down. "Or anything you shouldn't see. It's just rude."

By this time, Rick is looking at me like I've lost my mind, and the camera is bouncing up and down on the other guy's shoulder, which reminds me he's recording every asinine thing I say. Clamping my lips together, I trudge up the stairs in silence. I haven't even agreed to be on their silly show yet, and already my life is a circus.

Once in my room, I go straight to my dresser, not daring to look in the mirror hanging above it to see how truly hideous I look. Instead, I open the top drawer, rummage underneath my underwear, and pull out a grainy, black and white sonogram photo. For all these years, it's been the only memento I have of my child. That and my stretch marks are the only proof I have that I gave birth to another human being.

Running my fingertips lightly across the surface, I take a deep breath. She is the reason I'm doing this. If I want to meet my daughter, I have to play along.

And I want to meet her more than anything else in the world.

5

I'm tellin' ya, Rick, we should have done it. If nothing else, it'd be hilarious."

I can hear the two men talking as I make my way down from my room. It sounds like they accepted my invitation to wait in the living room. Since you can't see the staircase from there, I stop. It's not eavesdropping, not really. More like fact-gathering. And from what I understand, I'm going to have to get used to this kind of low-class, underhanded behavior if I want to survive on that TV show of theirs.

"I've never gone through anyone's medicine cabinet, and I'm not about to start now." Rick's voice is amused, but there's an undertone of seriousness. "The woman's spooked enough. I don't want to give her any extra reasons to back out."

"You really think she'll do it?"

Silence. Is Rick whispering his response? Or is he thinking about it? Without moving my feet, I lean forward, ears straining to hear.

"I think she's too curious not to." His voice is much closer now. If I hadn't been white-knuckling the banister, the boom of it would have sent me tumbling down the stairs. He appears at the landing and grins up at me. "What do you think?"

I think this man knows how to handle people. If I'm not careful, he'll have me agreeing to all manner of ridiculous things, and then thanking him for the opportunity. Summoning the bits and pieces of my shredded dignity, I walk calmly past him. "Would either of you like coffee?"

His companion is behind him, back to being the strong, silent, camera-bearing type. Not knowing his name is driving me nuts. "What's your name?"

"Bruce." Rick answers for him.

I turn to Rick. "Is Bruce mute?"

From behind the camera comes a muttered "Hardly."

Rick laughs. "No, Bruce has quite a vocabulary. It just works better if I do the talking. And no."

"No?"

"No. To the coffee. But thank you." He motions toward the living room then leads the way in, as if he's the homeowner and I'm the visitor. Before I turn around to follow, I catch the hint of a smirk from Bruce.

Narrowing my eyes, I wag an accusing finger at him. "Careful. I'm watching you." His smirk evolves into a grin, but he remains mum.

In the living room, Rick indicates that I should sit on the couch. Then, instead of sitting in the adjacent chair, he sits beside me, angling in my direction so our knees almost touch. His proximity is a little unsettling, until Bruce squats down across from us and I realize the positioning is just so we're both in frame.

"I'm sure you've got a lot of questions," Rick says.

"When do I meet my daughter?"

"That depends on you. Are you ready to be on the show?"

"No."

"No?"

I take great pleasure in the fact that he didn't expect that answer. "I'm far from ready. But if I don't go on the show, I don't meet Jessica, do I?"

His expression softens. I'm pretty sure he feels sorry for the spot I'm in, even though he's the master puppeteer manipulating the strings.

"No, you don't. At least, not now. That isn't to say you two won't connect later some other way." When I don't answer right away, he keeps talking. "I'm sure this isn't the way you'd hoped to meet her, but if you think about it, it's really a great thing. Jessica wants to meet you."

"But why? What if the only reason is so she can be on television?"

"That's a possibility. And after thirty days on the island, you'll either hate each other or create a bond like you've never imagined. *Last Family* changes you."

The weight of his words presses down on my already hunched shoulders. "For better or worse?"

"That's up to you."

Up to me. Once again, I will make a decision that affects not only me, but my daughter, and any number of people who are now touched by the familial fingers that connect us. It's too much.

I look down at the floor, focusing on the variegated pattern of greens and browns in the Berber carpet. If I stare long and hard enough, I can block out everything: Bruce, Rick, the news van outside, the daughter I'm only barely acquainted with, the fact that I still haven't had my morning coffee. . . . Maybe, if I focus on the simple, normal, ever-present carpet, I can make it all disappear.

"Monica? Are you okay?"

Rick's voice is far off and muffled, as if he's talking through a scarf wrapped around his mouth. I try to answer, but when

I open my mouth, a sob escapes. A wave of reality crashes down, pulling me out to sea in a riptide of regret and fear. Body shaking, I curl into myself, arms crossed, hands clutching my own arms, desperate to hold my head above water.

"Turn it off." Rick cuts through the torrent of emotions. A moment later, he slides closer, puts one arm around my shoulder, and offers a consoling hug.

With a sigh, Bruce rises to his full height. "I told you we should have called first."

"Just give us a minute."

Bruce leaves the room. Rather than talking, Rick rubs his hand up and down my arm. It's the kind of contact you'd expect from a brother or a platonic friend, not from the ruggedly handsome host of a popular reality series. I wonder how many other hysterical females he's had to comfort over the years.

As the sobs subside, my body starts to relax. A tissue appears beneath my nose, and I take it with a mumbled thank-you. I wipe my eyes, thankful there's no mascara to run, and look up. Bruce is rummaging around in my kitchen.

"What's he doing?"

"I'm trying to make coffee," Bruce rumbles.

"God bless you." Now I look at Rick, surprised at how un-freaked out he is by my mini-breakdown. "Thank you."

"No problem." One more squeeze, then he removes his arm from my shoulder. "You're on a pretty intense journey. I doubt that will be your last crying jag."

Oh great. "Well, before I dissolve again, let's talk about the details."

He grins. "Then you will do the show?"

"Of course. I don't really have a choice."

Rick pats my knee, then stands up. "Let me check on the coffee and get Bruce back in here, and we'll get down to it."

He's halfway to the kitchen when he turns back to me. "For the record, you always have a choice."

Not true. I had lots of choices once, several of which led to the defining choice of my life. But right now, the path is laid out in front of me. For the next however many days, Bruce and other cameramen like him will be my new constant companions, documenting my every move, including my reunion with my daughter.

When Rick comes back, he's got a coffee mug in one hand and is holding Ranger's collar with the other. "The dog will help you come across as warm and accessible."

"I *am* warm and accessible."

He laughs as he sits and hands me the mug. "Of course you are. And we want everyone to see that."

Ranger hops up onto the couch between us and puts one paw and his head in my lap. Rick was right, having him with me is much better. On the other side of the coffee table, Bruce hoists the camera onto his shoulder and resumes his position.

"Are you ready?" Rick asks.

The question broke me moments before, but not now. I gulp in a breath and nod sharply. "Let's do this."

One more decision taking me one step closer.

6

"This is useless."

Sweat is dripping down my cheeks, rolling into my eyes, and trickling down my back. I sit back on my heels and drop the rectangular piece of flint I've been hitting with a blunt kitchen knife for the last twenty minutes.

"I'll show you again, Aunt Monica." John picks up the flint and the knife, then brings the blade down at a sharp angle a few times, producing a shower of sparks that land into the mound of dry weeds. He blows on the little pile, creating a few wisps of smoke that quickly build into a nice fire. Behind him, Jerrod and Justin cheer and clap.

The sliding glass door opens, and Jules walks out with a pitcher of lemonade and a stack of red Solo cups. "How's the quest for fire?"

"Dandy." It's bad enough I haven't been able to produce more than a spark or two, none of which resulted in a fire. What's worse is that this is the third time John has shown me how it's done. I'm being bested by a twelve-year-old.

"I'll say. That's quite a respectable little blaze." She sets the refreshments on the patio table, crosses her arms and takes in our little survival tableau. "Nice job, John."

He grins. I groan. The twins jump to their feet and run for the lemonade. Jules picks up the metal pail she's kept filled with water since we started all this, and walks across the rocky ground cover of her backyard.

"On the island, fire is essential. In Las Vegas in July, it's just redundant." She dumps the water, extinguishing the flames with a sputter and hiss.

John stands up and looks at his mom. "Can I go now?"

She nods and ruffles his hair before he runs off. "Thanks, kiddo."

I stand and rub my knees, which are pitted with gravel-impressions. "Can I go, too?"

"No way. You have three more days to learn everything you need to know about kicking butt out in the jungle."

"But I'm hot and tired and sweaty." And I'm whining, which doesn't get me anything from Jules besides a smirk.

"This is nothing. When you get out there, you'll be wishing I'd pushed you harder."

I watch the beads of condensation running down the sides of the ice-filled lemonade pitcher and feel something akin to lust. "Can we at least take a break?"

"Of course. Come into my office."

A moment later, sitting in the shade of the patio cover, ice-cold liquid sliding down my throat, I think maybe I can forgive her for the torture she's put me through. The person I should really be upset with is Rick Wolff. Apparently, because of his desire to announce the search for Jessica's mother during the live results show, I've ended up with much less time to prepare than the average contestant. Whereas most of the contestants have a couple months between the time they're chosen and the time they embark for the island, he gave me six days. And three of those days are up.

Jules fingers the napkin beneath her glass. "What's going on in that overactive brain of yours?"

What I'm thinking is small and petty. It's selfish. At least, that's what most people would say if I told them. But Jules isn't most people. She's the one person I know will listen to me without judging. Which is why the words pour out of me without hesitation.

"I think I've made a terrible mistake. I can't do this."

"Why not? What's tripping you up?"

"What's not tripping me up?" I slump down in my chair. "The whole idea of living off the land for a month scares the stuffing out of me. I've never even been camping before. My idea of roughing it is staying in a hotel where the ice machine is at the opposite end of the hall."

Jules laughs. "Just because you've never done it before doesn't mean you can't do it."

"It's all so overwhelming. Besides, you're the super-fan. This should be happening to you, not me."

"Oh no. If some long-lost relative came out of the woodwork looking for me, I'd run the other way. You're much braver than I am."

Is she serious? She's the bravest person I know. Nothing fazes her. "How do you figure?"

"Your choice of career, for one thing. You went to culinary school because of your passion for cooking, even though you knew it was a male-dominated, highly competitive industry."

That's true. While the home kitchen is most often the woman's domain, professional kitchens are exactly the opposite. It's still rare to find a female head chef, which is what I had my sights set on from the beginning.

"And after you worked your way through the ranks and made a name for yourself, you took the chance to move to a new city and start up your own business."

I shrug. "Sixty-hour work weeks got old. Starting a catering business was more of a selfish decision than anything else."

Jules leans forward, looking me straight in the eye. "Do you realize how often you characterize your decisions as selfish?"

"What do you mean?"

"You just said starting your business was selfish. And giving your baby up for adoption—you've called that selfish, too."

I slice through the air with one hand. "That's completely different."

"How so?"

I've had over twenty-five years to think about this, examine it from every angle. And it all comes down to one thing. "Because I had no idea what I was doing. All I knew was that having a baby wasn't part of the big plan."

Jules nods, pursing her lips. "And abortion was illegal then, so that wasn't an option."

"What? You know it wasn't—" Oh, she's a sneaky one. "I see where you're going. Yes, I could have done that, but no, it was never an option. Not for me."

"So you gave up nine months of your life to carry a child you knew you couldn't keep, and then gave her to a couple who had spent years praying for a baby." Her voice and her smile have both turned soft and warm. "Doesn't sound very selfish to me."

I sit up straighter and puff out a burst of air. What she says makes sense, and there is some truth to it. But it's so much more complicated. Every time I peel away one layer, I find another, like a big, stinky onion. No matter what semi-noble choice I made back then, it doesn't absolve me from my other, more questionable decisions. And it doesn't erase my guilt.

"You missed your calling, Jules." I laugh, hoping to lighten the mood and avoid further probing. "You should have been a psychiatrist."

"I have three boys and a husband. I am a psychiatrist." She pats my arm, then pushes herself up out of the chair. "Come on. You've got a fire to make before we can move on to the next lesson."

"Which is?"

"The dos and don'ts of fashioning personal hygiene items from things found in nature."

I'm sorry I asked.

It takes three hours and a blistered thumb, but I finally spark a fire. The way Jules and I whoop and holler and dance around it, you'd think we discovered the cure for cancer. By that time, she decides I've earned a break and we head inside. I try to follow her into the kitchen, but she steers me to the family room and plops me down in front of the TV.

"Not more study time." My head falls against the back of the couch. "If I watch one more episode of *Last Family*, my brain will liquefy and run out my ears."

"Thank you for that lovely visual. No, I have something different for you today." She punches a few buttons on the remote, bringing the TV to life. "I figured it was time you got a little background on Rick Wolff."

That gets my attention. "Why?"

"Because he literally runs the whole show. He's the host and the executive producer, among other things. Knowing more about him can only help you."

Hard to argue with that kind of logic, so when she hands me the remote I relax and settle in. The one-hour show takes about forty minutes to watch after zipping through commercials, but it's a very informative forty minutes. I find out that Rick Wolff is the oldest of five children, grew up in a middle-class neighborhood in the Midwest, and he's one-eighth Native American, which explains that unique last name.

The program wraps up with a montage of all the women Rick has romanced over the years, and there are a lot of them. So many, the tabloids have given them the cringe-worthy nickname, The Wolff Pack. What I find interesting is he doesn't seem all that taken with any of them, at least not from the pictures. In one, he's sitting beside a gorgeous blond, his arm slung over her shoulder. But he's still so distant. Their sides don't touch, and his hand hangs limply. When he put his arm around me, he was smashed right up next to me, his fingers squeezing my shoulder.

What am I doing? I jerk forward on the couch, grab the remote and aim it at the TV, jabbing the off button with a tad too much enthusiasm. The man offered me a little bit of encouragement while I was losing my mind. Why would I compare that to how he acts with the ladies of his pack? There's only one plausible explanation.

Sunstroke. I was out there toiling over the fire for so long, my brain fried and now I can't think straight. Before you know it, I'll be hallucinating.

"Dinner's ready!" Jules calls out from the kitchen.

I pop to my feet and hurry out of the family room, glad to get away from the image of Rick Wolff and his ridiculously dimpled smile.

7

I've never enjoyed traveling. Yes, there are beautiful parts of the world I'd love to see, but the production of getting to these places is just too stressful. Never knowing what to pack or how to get around in a new environment. It's one of the reasons I decided to open my catering business in Vegas. I figured that, sooner or later, everyone winds up here for a visit. Why not let the people come to me? That and the fact that I never want to see another Minnesota winter as long as I live.

The open suitcase on the bed mocks me. *Go ahead, fill me up. You probably won't be able to use half of it, anyhow.* The moment oozes with irony.

Jules gave me a list of things to take. And the production company emailed me a list of things not to take. A fair amount of the things on the Jules list is also on the don't-even-think-about-it list. Like sunblock. Apparently, they provide it once we arrive at the island. I suppose this is to keep the contestants from smuggling contraband protein shakes or moisturizer in their Banana Boat bottles. But there could be no sunblock for a five-hundred-mile radius, and I would still go. Not even the threat of skin cancer is going to keep me from my daughter now.

I've spent the last five days preparing myself for the game. I've watched untold hours of back episodes, so much so that I hear the theme music in my sleep. I've mastered fire, made a toothbrush out of bamboo, eaten snails, and camped out in Jules's backyard, all of which thrilled her sons far more than it did me. Right now, I'm as ready as I can be for a person who barely knew anything about this reality program a week ago.

What I'm not ready for, not in the least, is seeing Jessica. And unfortunately, that's a test I don't know how to cram for.

Not that I haven't tried. Now that I know her first and last name and where she lives, I Googled her. She has a Facebook account, but you have to be friends to view anything on it, and besides the fact that I signed an agreement prohibiting me from contacting her in any way before the show begins filming, I didn't think sending her a friend request would be a smart move. I found her in the employee roster of the company she works for, but other than her extension and company email, it didn't tell me anything useful.

Which is why I subscribed to one of those people-finder services. I'm not proud of it, but it was the only way I could think of to discover something concrete. So now, I know her address, and her parents' address. I have all their cell phone numbers. I even know how much the Becketts paid in property taxes for the last five years. But that's as far as it went. I didn't call any of the numbers, didn't drive all night to get to Irvine and camp out in front of Jessica's door. Although I did look up her address on Google Earth and saw the street view of her apartment, and then I checked the database of registered sex offenders to make sure she doesn't live next door to a predator. Which she doesn't. But that was all I did.

Except for the picture.

There was a photo of her on the *Last Family Standing* website under the "Meet the New Cast" tab. All the families are made up of two people, with their picture and a short bio. Except for ours. There's a picture of Jessica, her bio, and where my picture should be is a dark gray silhouette with a bright yellow question mark in the middle of the skull. It's the kind they use as a placeholder on sites before you replace it with your own avatar. Where my bio should be is this sensational little paragraph: *Jessica knows her birth mother only as "Monica." Will the mystery woman answer her daughter's appeal, or will she leave her hanging?*

It's ridiculous, because they know I'm coming. Yes, I understand they want to keep the suspense up until the show airs. I guess I should take it as a compliment, that folks might actually set their DVRs to see if I do right by my daughter, or if I'm a despicable human being and don't show. But it's hard to consider that kind of morbid curiosity is a good thing.

Still, I'm thankful that at least Jessica's picture was on the site. I printed it out and put a copy on the fridge.

And in my wallet.

And on my bedside table.

And in the glove compartment of my car.

Some people might consider that obsessive, but I just see it as making up for lost time. If Jessica had grown up with me, the refrigerator would have been covered with photos of her mugging for the camera, pictures she'd drawn, and school lunch schedules. My wallet would always have held the most recent school photo, the same one that would have been in a frame, sitting by my alarm clock next to my bed. And my car would have been littered with discarded scrunchies, empty juice boxes, and all the other reminders that a child had been there.

But Jessica didn't grow up with me. My fridge and my car have always been immaculate. The only things in my wallet are cash and the usual assortment of credit, ATM, and grocery store preferred customer cards. And the photo beside the bed is of Ranger and me the day I brought him home from the shelter.

So I'm not going to sweat the fact that I can't stop looking at her picture.

From his place in the corner, Ranger lets out a whine. "Poor baby." I pat an empty space on the bed beside my nearly empty suitcase. "Come on up and help me figure this out."

In two leaps he's across the room and bounding up onto the mattress. The last week has been almost as hard on him as it has been on me. I haven't spent nearly as much time with him as I usually do. He knows something is going on. I can tell from the way he follows me around.

Taking his face in both my hands, I kneed the skin under his jaws and look into his soulful, brown eyes. "I'm breaking the confidentiality agreement telling you this, but I'm going to be gone for a month." Actually, I broke that agreement when I asked Jules for help. But I didn't mean to. As long as she keeps her mouth shut, which I know she will, it won't be a problem. And Jackson. And her boys. Oh man . . . It'll be a miracle if I get through this thing without being sued.

I pull my attention back to Ranger. "John, Jerrod, and Justin are going to spoil you rotten, but I know you'll still miss me. I want you to remember, I love you, and I will come back."

He bounces on his front paws and pushes forward until he's able to lick one entire side of my face. It's a gesture made not because he understands what I said, but because he feels the love. Still, what should be a sweet moment has turned sour. Here I am, worried about how my dog will feel if I'm gone for a month, yet I was able to give my daughter to virtual strangers and walk out of her life forever. How does a woman do that? What kind of a person does that make me?

I take the picture of Jessica out of the suitcase—because of course, I put one in there, too—and stare at her bright blue eyes and her subtle smile. Will she still be smiling when we're face-to-face? More than once this week, I've prayed she'll forgive me so we can form some kind of relationship.

But how can I hope for her forgiveness when I can't even forgive myself?

8

Despite my insistence that I am perfectly capable of getting to the airport by myself, Brittany—the *Last Family Standing* contestant liaison—was equally insistent that she'd arrange for a car to come by the house. It seemed silly before, but now that the time has come, I'm glad that's one less thing to worry about.

I've spent the last hour wandering from room to room, going over mental lists of all the things that needed to be done before now. Ranger is already with Jules. The furry traitor was much less distressed than I expected once the boys got their hands on him. In my office, I flip through the date book, ensuring that I didn't miss handing off any of my catering jobs to one of my colleagues. House lights and the drip watering system in the yard are all on timers. The folks at the *Review Journal* know to donate my newspaper to a local school for the next month and a half.

A month and a half. Thankfully, I'm standing by the sofa when the thought hits me, because my knees give out and I drop down on the overstuffed cushions. What am I thinking? Obviously, I'm not thinking at all. I'm reacting. I've long thought my maternal instincts were dead, but apparently, they were only hibernating. For the first time in twenty-five years, my daughter makes a request of me, and the mother tigress inside roars to life.

Before I can follow this rabbit trail any further, my doorbell rings. That's my ride. With a sigh, I push off the couch, grab my purse and rolling suitcase, and head toward whatever scary future is on the other side of that door.

What I'm sure is the first of many surprises comes when the driver of the stretch Hummer avoids the passenger drop off area of McCarran airport and heads around to the back.

"Why are we going this way?" The window between us is open, but there's so much space between the driver and where I'm sitting, I feel I need to yell to be heard.

"Didn't Brittany tell you, ma'am?"

I growl at being called ma'am. "Tell me what?"

"You're taking a private plane. Better to keep you inconspicuous."

Is he serious? If they wanted to stay under the radar, they should have chosen a vehicle that didn't stalk its way through the streets. Still, the idea of a private plane is appealing. I can use the time—about eight hours, according to the mercurial Brittany—to think, to settle myself. If I'm lucky, I might even be able to sleep, something I wasn't able to do much of last night.

The driver pulls into a section of the airport filled with an assortment of sleek, white planes. *Small*, sleek, white planes.

"They're so tiny," I mutter under my breath.

We stop near one of them. The very tall driver opens my door and nearly folds himself in half so he can look in at me.

"Don't worry," he says with a grin. "In this case, size really doesn't matter."

That's one thing about Vegas residents: not much embarrasses us. So the man's double entendre does nothing more than make me laugh, something I desperately need.

As I climb my way out of the Hummer, he retrieves my bag from the trunk, then carries it to a man wearing a bright orange vest. The two exchange a few words. The driver points at me, vest-man looks at me and nods, then takes my suitcase and stows it in an open compartment in the side of the plane.

"Have a good flight, ma'am." With a quick, two-fingered salute, he ducks back into the driver seat. A moment later, the Hummer is gone and I'm staring at the steps leading up into the plane.

Now what? Am I supposed to wait here? Should I go up and make myself at home? Is there still time for me to turn around and run?

Vest-man shuts the cargo hold door and turns. When he sees me, he looks confused. "Do you need something, miss?"

I want to hug him for calling me miss. "I, uh, I just wasn't sure if I should board the plane or wait out here."

He shrugs. "Up to you. We won't be leaving for about half an hour. Might as well go on in and get comfortable."

Well, if he insists . . .

There are only four seats inside the airplane, two rows of two, facing each other to form a little conversation area. My heart sinks a bit when I notice someone is already sitting there. I can see the top of a head over the back of one seat. So much for a quiet, contemplative trip.

As I try to maneuver my way through the small space, I accidentally slam my purse into the back of the person's seat. Yeesh, what a great way to meet someone.

"Sorry. I didn't mean to—"

"No problem."

That deep rumble cuts me off as the person stands and a moment later I'm face-to-face with Rick Wolff.

"What are you doing here?"

He laughs. "Nice to see you, too, Miss Stanton."

Way to go, Monica. First you bang into his seat, then you're rude. "I'm just surprised. I didn't expect to see you again until I got to the island."

"Normally, you wouldn't. Please, sit down." He motions to the empty seats across from him.

I sink into it, impressed with the soft leather, the leg room, and the cup holder in the arm rest. "Wow. This is going to ruin me for the next time I fly coach."

"The way I see it, if you're going to buy a jet, you may as well get a comfortable one."

My eyebrows go up. "You own this?"

He shrugs as if it's no big deal. "When you fly as much as I do, having a plane makes sense."

"Uh huh. Well." I shift in the seat, enjoying the creak of the leather. "Thank you for giving me a lift. Although I'm still confused."

"I'm not surprised. Let me try to explain."

"Excuse me, Mr. Wolff?" The pilot stands behind Rick's seat. "Are you expecting any other passengers?"

"No. Our party is complete. Feel free to leave whenever you're ready."

The pilot nods. "As soon as we get tower clearance, we're out of here."

As the pilot moves to the cockpit, I smile at Rick. "Won't Bruce be joining us?"

"No, he's already on the island, getting some candid shots of the other contestants."

"They're all there?" And by that I'm really asking if Jessica's there. I'm sure he understands my code, but chooses to ignore it.

"Yes, they are. Except for you, of course." He leans back and crosses one ankle over his knee. "You're making this season a little more complicated than usual."

"Me? I'm the one having my life turned inside out. How can I be complicating things?"

"It's not your fault," he says. "But I can't let any of the other contestants see you until we officially start the game."

In other words, they—my daughter, in particular—can't see me until the cameras start rolling. "You want the look of shock on Jessica's face to be real."

"You make it sound so calculated."

"Because it is."

"It's also the whole point of the show. Real emotions, real reactions. That's why they call it *reality television*. Jessica knew what she was getting into. And by now, you should, too."

There's a little pop as the sound system turns on. "Please fasten your seat belts, folks. We're cleared for takeoff."

Rick's foot thuds to the floor as he sits up straight and snaps the buckle. "I realize this is a very emotional situation for you. Frankly, when we received Jessica's audition tape, my first impulse was to reject it."

"Why?"

The boyish smirk that seems to always hover around his lips disappears. He hesitates, as though he really doesn't want to reveal his thought process. But then something clicks, and he starts talking. "Because your story transcends making good television. You and Jessica are real people, with real families and real lives."

I'm not sure what he's getting at. "Aren't all the contestants real people? As you said, it's a *reality* show."

"Yes, of course. But they're all family members who already know each other and have outrageous elements to their relationships. We've never had a parent and child meet for the first time on our show." He runs a hand through his hair, mussing it more than it already was. "The next thirty days will change your life, and not just because you'll be on television."

"I see." The seat shakes with the revving of the jet engines. "What made you change your mind?"

"Jessica. I couldn't stop thinking about her. About how honest she seemed when she said this was her only chance to find you."

My eyes sting and I blink hard to keep the water works at bay. As my emotions try to overtake me, Rick's eyes narrow as he determines it's time to change the subject. He slips back into his slick, TV host persona and the smirk once more plays around his lips. "Besides, you're going to be pure ratings gold."

I snort out an unladylike laugh, and the feeling that I'm going to cry abates. "How do you figure?"

"You're a mystery, and everybody loves a mystery." He leans forward and winks. "Including me."

I didn't fall off the proverbial turnip truck yesterday. I know this thinly veiled attempt at flirting is meant only to distract me and perhaps throw me off balance. Still, there's something about this man that makes my mouth go dry and chases most coherent thoughts clean out of my brain.

The plane jerks forward. Rick laughs and points at my lap. "You'd better do what the man said. Buckle your seat belt, Monica."

After shifting and squirming, I find both ends of the belt. And the only thing that comes to my head is, *Buckle your seat belt, Monica. It's going to be a bumpy month.*

9

Rick Wolff snores. I wonder what the gossip rags would pay to know that?

We hadn't been in the air twenty minutes when he put his seat back, closed his eyes, and fell asleep. That was two hours ago.

On one hand, I'm glad, because it means I don't have to worry about making small talk, or worse, trying to avoid conversation as we sit across from each other. But then there's the other hand . . . the one that wants to toss a pillow at him, blame it on turbulence, and then grill him for all the information I can get.

I'm pretty sure that grilling him would be useless, so I do everything I can to distract myself. Nothing works. Not going through the list of 556 books on my e-reader, not playing Angry Birds, not even writing in my journal. It's a beautiful book, spiral bound so the pages are easy to manipulate, and a leather cover so soft that sometimes you want to just rub your fingertips across it. Jules gave it to me last night when I dropped off Ranger. "So you can record all the insane, wonderful, terrifying thoughts that bombard you," she told me.

What a fabulous, thoughtful idea. The only problem is, she didn't realize there'd be so many insane, wonderful, terrifying thoughts filling my brain that they'd clog up in a bottleneck somewhere between my head and my hand. I open the book, sit it on my lap, and think. And think. My pen hovers over the blank page, until finally, it begins to move, releasing my innermost brilliance.

I doodled a flower.

Staring down at it, I try to convince myself that this isn't just any flower. This is a pictorial representation of my state of mind, kind of like a reverse Rorschach test. Except I don't buy it. Not for one moment do I feel like a sunny, optimistic flower.

A few more strokes of the pen, and a tiny stick figure man emerges. Next, I give him a pair of huge scissors which he uses to cut the flower's stem in half. Not about to sit back and allow this act of flora-cide, I send out a group of chubby garden gnomes. My pen moves faster, and I start making little *pew pew* noises, because apparently my gnomes are armed with lasers.

"I think you killed him."

The chuckled words make me jump. I was so engrossed in my newly created world, I didn't notice that Rick had stopped snoring. Now he's leaning forward, craning his neck to see the journal.

Slamming the cover shut, I glare at him. "It's not polite to sneak up on people."

"Who's sneaking? This plane is hardly big enough to stand in, let alone sneak."

Good point. "I was just trying to distract myself."

He grins. "Sorry I fell asleep. I hate to think what other entertaining things I missed."

"That was the most exciting thing. Promise." I make and X over my heart with a fingertip.

With a nod, he sits back in his seat and stretches his legs. "Are we there yet?"

"I wish."

"Where's a transporter when you need one?" He mutters as he leans over and pushes up the window shade.

Did I just hear him correctly? "Did you say *transporter*? As in *Star Trek*?"

"Sure." He looks a little confused by the question. "Or a stargate. Anything to get us from point A to point B in the blink of an eye."

I point at him, wiggling my finger. "You're a sci-fi nerd!"

"Guilty as charged."

"So am I." Finally, something we can gab about to fill the time that won't affect the integrity of the show.

The rest of the flight is much better. We discuss our favorite shows. Mine is the short-lived *Firefly*, his is *Farscape*. He questions the wisdom of making episodes one, two, and three of the *Star Wars* series and I agree that, with the exception of giving me another opportunity to watch Ewan McGregor, it was a bad move.

"Seriously, the first three—"

"You mean the second three," he interrupts.

I roll my eyes. "You know what I mean. Episodes four, five, and six, which he made first. Those three movies were so groundbreaking, why mess with them?"

"Like changing the older movies with new digital effects. There are some things you should leave alone."

The excitement of the conversation drains away, and I'm right back where I started, worrying that I'm doing the wrong thing by changing the parameters of my relationship with Jessica.

Picking up on my obvious mood swing, Rick nudges the sole of my sandal with the toe of his tennis shoe. "Movies are totally different than real life. Most things in life require a little messing."

"I hope you're right." I sigh and try to smile. "Of course, I haven't had any contact with my daughter for the last twenty-five years. It couldn't get worse than that, could it?"

With the pinging of a bell, the Fasten Seat Belts signs light up. We both buckle up and Rick points at the window beside me. "Take a look."

As the little jet starts its descent, it breaks through the clouds. Below is the ocean, crystal blue and amazing. "I've never seen it from overhead before."

"Spectacular, isn't it?"

"I'll say." I push closer to the window until my nose nearly touches it. Down below are several islands. "Is that where we're landing?"

"Yes, on the biggest one. And from there . . ." He pauses until I look over at him, then he grins and finishes with a shrug. "Well, you'll have to wait and see what happens. The same as everybody else."

The land masses below, round but with uneven edges like big ink blots, are lush and green. From up here, it looks like we're heading to paradise. Like the Garden of Eden before the Fall.

I just hope this garden isn't hiding any snakes.

It's the smallest airport I've ever seen. Actually, I don't think it really classifies as an airport. There's one runway, a rickety tower with glassless windows on all four sides, and a single-wide mobile home that I think is the terminal.

"Gee, you guys don't spare any expense, do you?"

Rick undoes his seat belt and stands. "We work with the habitat as it is. I'm just happy when we find a place that has an actual runway."

"That would help, I'm sure."

I follow him through the small cabin. As soon as we step outside, I'm hit by two things: heat and humidity. The moisture in the air is so thick, it takes a concerted effort to pull it into my lungs.

"Please tell me this is an unusually moist day," I gasp.

Rick laughs and shakes his head. "Sorry, but this is where you and I part ways."

As if on cue, two vehicles pull up. One is a black BMW that I'm sure has the air running full blast. The other is a battered Jeep with no doors and open-air windows. Naturally, he goes to the BMW.

"Next time I see you, the game will be in full swing. Good luck."

He waves and ducks into the car. A moment later, I'm coughing from the debris that's kicked up as they speed off. There's a thud beside me and I turn to see that the pilot has deposited my bag by my feet.

The driver of the Jeep twists in his seat and jerks his thumb over his shoulder. "Just toss it there."

With a sigh, I hoist my suitcase and wrestle it into the back. I try to blow my bangs off my forehead, but they are now so damp and sticky, the hair won't budge from my skin.

As I climb into the passenger seat, I smile at the driver, hoping to get on his good side. "Hi. I'm Monica."

"I know." He puts the car in gear and we jerk forward.

Only digging my fingernails into the roll bar keeps me from falling out the door opening. I feel blindly along the edges of the seat, but apparently this vehicle isn't equipped with seat belts. As we bounce along the uneven road, I make another attempt at conversation.

"Do you live here, or are you part of the TV crew?"

The man doesn't take his eyes off the road. "I'm not allowed to talk to the contestants."

"Oh." I haven't been here five minutes and already I'm hitting my head against a wall of rules. "Can you at least tell me where we're going?"

"To base camp."

My heart quickens. "Are all the other contestants there?"

His only response is a scowl and a quick, sideways eye flick. I'm fairly sure that he aimed for the next rut we bounce through.

After I land with a thud and a yelp, I pinch my lips together to refrain from saying anything else. I get it. All information from here on in will be on a need-to-know basis. And right now, nobody thinks I need-to-know much of anything.

10

Base camp is exactly what it sounds like. It's a large clearing swarming with people and trucks full of equipment. All around the perimeter are the most elaborate tents I've ever seen. The one in the middle could easily hold a family of five.

As we drive past, the canvas door on the tent opens and Rick Wolff walks out, followed by three other men in some variation of t-shirts and shorts, all talking animatedly. Rick's head is down, hands stuffed in the pockets of his khaki shorts. He doesn't seem to be paying any attention to the heated discussion going on behind him.

He glances up as my jeep drives by, and I have a weird urge to wave at him, but I resist. Surely, any kind of interaction between us now is taboo. There's a tiny spark of recognition in his eyes when he realizes it's me in the truck, then he immediately looks away. Just as I expected.

At the opposite end of the camp the driver jerks to a stop in front of a tent that looks positively miniscule compared to the others. I jump out of the vehicle and walk around to the other side on shaky knees. A woman is already approaching, a broad smile cutting a bright, white swatch through her coppery skin.

"Welcome!" She tosses her long, black braid over one shoulder and extends her hand. "I'm Kai, and I'll be your shadow for the next twenty-four hours."

I laugh and shake her hand. "Monica. But then you already know that."

With a nod, she pulls my suitcase from the back of the jeep as if it weighs no more than a purse. "See ya later, Dan." She tosses a wave at the driver, then leads the way into the tent.

It's Spartan: an air mattress in one corner, a collapsible camping chair beside it, and a little table with a battery operated lantern on top. Kai moves the lantern and replaces it with my suitcase, which she immediately rifles through.

"This is the mandatory luggage search they warned you about." She pulls a canvas drawstring bag from where it was tucked into her belt. She keeps up a constant chatter and every now and then she stuffs something into the bag, although I can't see what's going in there. I must have let some contraband slip through by accident.

"Sorry." While apologizing, I try to look over her shoulder. "I tried to follow the guidelines."

"No problem. Everybody does this." Kai holds up a t-shirt, examines the front and back, then stuffs it in the bag.

I frown. "I thought I got that one right."

"You did." She turns, still smiling, and hands me the canvas bag "This is the stuff you get to take to the island with you."

She can't be serious. "That's it?"

"Yep." She points at my purse. "I need that, too."

Clutching it to my side, I feel a moment of panic. "But my ID is in here."

"I know. Which is why you want it in a safe place."

If I argue the point, I'll just lose. So I let the straps slide down my arm and hand the purse over. Kai takes it with a smile and puts it inside the suitcase.

I catch one last glimpse of my e-reader, my cell phone, my toothbrush, and about a dozen extra pair of underwear before she zips the top shut and hoists the suitcase again. Then she laughs. "It says right there in plain English: *Five pairs of underwear.* But everyone tries to bring more."

I knew about the limit. But with clean underwear on the line, it was worth taking the chance.

"Leave your canvas bag here. Let's hit the chow tent."

She doesn't have to tell me twice. I toss the bag on the mattress and follow her out. We haven't gone ten feet when a gal who looks about sixteen but I'm sure is much older, bounds up to Kai and takes my suitcase.

"With the others?" The way she asks while in mid-turn indicates the question was merely a formality.

"Thanks," Kai calls after her. Then she looks over at me. "Don't worry, it's going to a very secure spot. It's joining all the stuff the other contestants brought and weren't allowed to keep."

At the mention of the other contestants, I scan the area. If it were possible for my head to rotate 360 degrees on my neck, it would. As it is, I hear a couple vertebrae crack as my head snaps back and forth.

Kai shakes her head. "Sorry. You're the only one here." She jerks her thumb over her shoulder. "The others are all on the game island already."

"They're already playing?"

"In a manner of speaking. They've met each other. But the challenges won't start until you get there."

"Lucky me."

With a snort, Kai ushers me into another, bigger tent. "The good news is, you're getting one more night alone to mentally prepare yourself."

"And the bad news?"

"They're starting to make bonds. By the time you get there, you'll be the odd man out."

Nothing new there. But then a thought occurs to me. "What about Jessica? Does she think I'm not coming?"

For the first time since I've been with her, Kai's smile slips. "I have no idea what she thinks. But what would *you* think if you were the only person without a partner?"

The same thing I thought when Freddie Boswell accepted my invitation to the eighth-grade Sadie Hawkins dance and then didn't show. That I'd been stood up. But this is much worse than not having a date for a dance. My daughter thinks I've abandoned her. Again.

Fingers wrap around my upper arm and Kai pulls me forward. "Come on, Momma. The best thing you can do for your kid now is to eat up and get a good night's sleep. Tomorrow, you'll be the strongest person on the island."

I wish I had just a fraction of her conviction. But right now, with my legs shaking and my stomach doing flip-flops, it's hard to believe I'll be good for anything tomorrow other than collapsing into a jelly-spined lump.

In the meantime, I'll spend tonight grilling my shadow. Not that I expect her to spill anything more than she intended to tell me, but I can try.

You'd think a woman screaming at the top of her lungs would bring everyone running. It doesn't. Eventually, it brings Kai shuffling in. Through half-closed eyes, she watches me jumping from one foot to the other as I carry on and smack the mattress with a palm frond.

"Bug?" she asks calmly.

Bug is an understatement. That thing was big enough to put a saddle on and ride back to the airstrip. And that's not the worst of it. "It was on my face."

She cocks her head to one side. "Did it bite you?"

"I don't think so." I run my hands over my cheeks. "No."

Pivoting back around, she dismisses my panic with a wave of her hand. "When one bites you, then you have permission to scream. Until then, go to sleep."

"Kai, wait." I run up behind her. "What if it comes back?"

She laughs and shakes her head. "Honey, you're spending a month in a jungle. You'll get to know bugs and critters you never knew existed. Better get used to it."

I stand near the opening of the tent long after Kai leaves. Get used to it? How can I get used to having heaven knows what kind of multi-legged, grotesque, possibly poisonous *things* ready to attack me at any moment? There's no way I'm laying back down so close to whatever is crawling around on the ground. But I can't stand here all night, either.

Grabbing the lantern off the table, I leave the tent. The camp is quiet. You'd never know from looking at it that I was shrieking like a banshee just ten minutes earlier. Two men sit near a fire burning in a big metal drum. They must be on guard duty, although what they're guarding the camp from, I couldn't say. It's not like any hoodlums will stumble across our group. One of the men looks up and sits a little straighter when he notices me.

I wave and point in the other direction. "Heading to the bathroom," I call out, then walk toward the Porta-Potties.

A thump off to one side brings to mind the scene in *Castaway* when Tom Hanks's character is spooked by falling coconuts. Stopping short, I close my eyes and listen. What seemed like vast silence is actually filled with sounds. Warm breezes blow through the palms, creating a rustling harmony to the melody of the ocean's rush and retreat. The cry of a bird, high-pitched and anxious, cuts through the night. I look up and see that the sky is filled with them, flying low, their wingspans enormous.

"Wow." I'll never forget this moment.

"Amazing, isn't it?"

I gasp and jump, dropping my lantern at the same time. It stays on, casting an eerie glow up on the grinning face of Rick Wolff. How did he sneak up on me?

"Didn't your mother teach you any manners?"

"Sorry. I didn't realize it was rude to share an appreciation of nature." He picks up the lantern and hands it to me.

"You just scared me. What are you doing out here?"

"Something woke me up." One corner of his mouth twitches. "Sounded like a howler monkey."

There's no good way to respond, so I scowl and change the subject. "I thought you weren't allowed to talk to me anymore."

"Technically, no. But we ran into each other while taking a stroll. To ignore you would have been plain *rude*."

I can't help but laugh. "Touché."

He points up. "There's some incredible wildlife out here."

"You must have seen a lot."

"I have, but it still fascinates me. That's one of the reasons I still do the show after all these years."

Another flock appears in the sky. "Like that," I say, pointing up. "I've never seen birds with wings like that."

He nods, hands on his hips. "That's because they're bats."

The blood rushes from my face. "What?"

Smiling calmly, he looks me in the eye. "Those are bats."

Instinctively, my hands fly up and wrap around my neck. It's silly, I know it is. Bats don't bite your neck, and even if they did, it would only be vampire bats, and I'm fairly sure vampire bats don't hang out in the tropics. Still, I've seen too many of a certain kind of movie, and the need to protect my neck is heavily engrained in my psyche.

"Excuse me." My voice drops to a whisper and I take a step backward. "I'm going back to my tent."

Rick leans in and drops his voice to match mine. "They can't hear you."

"Good." As I run off, his deep laugh joins the other jungle noises.

This is crazy. When I thought they were birds, they were tranquil. Now, all I want to do is run from the bloodthirsty predators in the sky. But run where? Back into my tent with the mutant insects?

Back home. I want to run back home, where the only wildlife I have to deal with is Ranger and the occasional lizard that scurries out from under the flowering lantana. I want to be in my bug-free bed and wake up in the morning ready for another day in my normal, well-ordered life.

I look behind me. Rick is walking toward the men at the fire barrel. If I begged him to take me back home, would he? Probably not. I did sign a contract, after all. But even if he would, it's not an option. No matter how miserable and scared I am, I can't ignore the reason I'm doing this. Jessica is waiting. If I have to brave bats and bugs to get to her, then so be it.

Besides, it probably won't be as bad as I'm imagining. It's only thirty days. A person can stand anything for thirty days. Right?

11

I can't stand it."

How can it take this long to get from one island to the other? I knew I shouldn't have eaten so much this morning, but Kai had been adamant that food wouldn't be easy to come by anytime soon. So I ate, despite the nervous tension already tumbling and churning in my stomach.

Now, leaning over the rail of the boat as it bounces and skips through the waves, all I want is to get rid of my breakfast. Either that, or die. I'm not picky.

"Breathe slowly. Out through your mouth, in through your nose." Kai rubs my back while she coos the instructions to me.

I groan. "Oh, something's gonna come out through my mouth."

"No, it's not. You'll be fine. We're almost there."

"Promise?"

She squeezes my shoulder. "Have I ever lied to you?"

"No. In the day I've known you, you've never lied." I've had relationships with men that I couldn't say that about. Not that I'd bring that up now.

Instead, I listen to Kai's voice, squeeze my eyes shut, and I breathe.

"Atta girl. You just keep breathing."

Perched on the edge of the hospital bed is, a volunteer in a blue smock, hair pulled back in a fluffy blond ponytail. Her strong fingers surround my hand, the one without the IV needle invading the skin.

Another contraction. Pain cuts me in two. "I can't. I can't."

"Of course you can. Your body is made for this."

She leans forward, eyes clear and certain, and I believe her. I can do this. And I keep breathing.

"What did I tell you? Here we are."

Kai's voice cuts into the memory. Even before I open my eyes I can feel that we've slowed down. I look over the bow, and there it is. Land.

The boat stops a fair distance from shore. "Why are we stopping here?" I ask.

"Because running aground is bad." As usual, Kai gets right to the point.

A small motor boat pulls up beside us. Kai crooks her finger at me. "Grab your bag. That's our ride."

I follow her across the deck, wondering again how she can move in a straight line when all I can do is lurch in a wobbly zigzag like a drunken poodle. After snatching the canvas bag of my meager belongings, I follow Kai to the railing and look over. "How are we supposed to get down there?"

Her answer is to smile and unfasten a rope ladder. As it unfurls and the end splashes into the water, I weigh my choices. I can make my way down the questionable-looking ladder, possibly slipping on a damp rung and falling to a watery death. Or, I can stay on the boat. There really is no choice.

I slip my head and one arm through the drawstrings of my bag and shift it until it hangs on my back. Then I step around Kai and make my way down. The plastic buckles of the bulky, orange life vest they made me wear catch on each rung I pass.

Every time I pull back and the buckle pops free, I tense up, anticipating the fall. Finally, the motorboat is right below me. The captain of the little vessel is standing there, his arms up in the air, as if he intended to catch me upon my inevitable fall. I'm so glad to see him there, I don't even mind when his hands close around my waist and he helps me off the ladder.

"Thank you." I try to step away, but the deck bucks beneath my feet. The only thing that stops me from going over the side is the captain's hand that shoots out and grabs my upper arm.

"We best get you off your feet." His voice is like gravel in a garbage disposal, but his eyes are bright and from the way his skin crinkles at the corners, I'd say he's amused by my lack of sea legs.

A thump sounds behind me as Kai jumps from the bottom of the ladder to the boat. Her fingers close around my other arm, and she grins at the captain. "I'll take her from here."

He nods, gives a mock salute with two fingers to his forehead, and moves to the outboard motor. Once Kai's got me settled on a hard seat of molded plastic, she pats me on the head like I'm a five-year-old girl. "You'd better hold on. The trip to shore will be quick, but pretty choppy."

"It can't be worse than that thing." I glare at the ship I've just abandoned.

Kai shrugs. "Don't be so sure. The smaller the boat, the rougher the ride." The motor revs and we shoot forward, confirming what she just said.

Groaning, I double over and clutch the sides of the seat. "I'm on the voyage of no return."

"I've heard it called worse." The captain bellows to be heard above the noise.

Thankfully, it doesn't last long. A few minutes later, Kai jumps out of the boat and into the water, then crooks her finger at me to follow.

Pointing down, I shake my head. "I don't want to get my shoes wet."

"Might as well get used to it. What with the ocean and the rain and the mud, dry shoes will soon become a distant memory."

Why do I question anything anymore? It seems the whole theme of this adventure is *Jump first, ask questions later.* As I slosh through the surf, I manage to keep my bag above water, but my athletic shoes will never be the same again. Clumps of sand cling to them, and water squishes out the sides as I walk farther up the beach.

"Where is everybody?" The same assortment of people are here that were on the other island. They're like busy little drone bees, ID cards dangling from lanyards and bouncing on their chests as they hurry from one place to the next. But these aren't the drones I'm looking for.

Stumbling through the sand, I catch up with Kai. "Where are the other contestants?"

"They'll be here soon, which means we have to get you out of sight."

I'm beginning to wonder if this whole thing is one gigantic April Fool's joke. Will I ever really get to see my daughter, or will they keep shuttling me from place to place in increasingly uncomfortable modes of transportation?

If ever there was a time to assert myself, it's now. I stop short and jam my fists on my hips. "I'm not taking another step until I see Jessica."

When Kai turns to me, she's not smiling. "Come on, Monica. You knew how this was going to play out." She keeps her voice low and even, moving slowly to my side like a cop trying to talk a person off a ledge. "You can't just be standing here when Jessica arrives. There's a whole big reveal planned."

I know that. So when she threads her arm through the crook of my elbow, I let her pull me along with her. "Sorry. I'm just so tired of waiting."

"Of course you are. Let me give you a little tip."

"Are you allowed to do that?"

"It's common sense stuff. The same thing any fan of the show would tell you." Her head swivels from side to side, then she looks back at me and smiles. "Besides, if no one overhears you give advice, did you really give it?"

Who am I to argue? "What's the tip?"

"Most people think the physical challenges are the hardest parts of the show. But they're not. What's really tough are the mind games. Enough people will be trying to psych you out and undermine your confidence. You don't need to do it to yourself."

"It's just . . ." A big puff of air bursts from my lungs as I prepare to speak aloud what's been bothering me for the last week. "It doesn't seem real. It feels like the time will come, but she won't be there. I'll be alone."

"I can promise you this. You'll see her."

My eyes open wider as I grasp Kai's unspoken message. "You've seen her, haven't you?"

She nods and pats my hand. "No more talking, now."

We've reached a thatched hut with a door, but no windows. The inside is much less rustic. From the looks of it, I'd say it's soundproof.

"Wow, they're really serious about the surprise factor."

"You have no idea." She points to a plastic water bottle on a collapsible snack table. "I suggest you down that while you have the chance."

She sits cross-legged on the ground and I do the same. As I chug-a-lug the last fresh, clean water I'm liable to see in a month, Kai explains exactly what's going to happen. How the other contestants will be brought here, to what is considered the Home Island, and how Rick will welcome them. And after that, he'll bring me out of the tent and I'll join Jessica . . . and everyone else.

I suck the last drop from the bottle, then crush the plastic. "This is my last private moment, isn't it?"

"Yep. From here on in, the cameras will watch everything you do."

"Everything?"

She grins. "Well, not *everything*. There are lines even reality folks don't cross."

That's good to hear. But after the hours and hours of back episodes Jules forced me to watch, I'm pretty sure their lines are about a mile farther out than any of my lines. Not that it matters now. I'm committed to following this through, no matter what.

"Are you a praying woman, Kai?"

She shrugs and tilts her head so that her shoulder nearly touches her ear. "Sometimes."

"If you think about it over the next month, send one up for me now and then."

Kai nods, and I really hope she's serious. Because I'm pretty sure that divine intervention and a few well-placed miracles are the only way I'm going to make it to the other side.

12

Tom Petty was right. The waiting really is the hardest part.

How long has it been? With no windows, no watch, no clock, there's no way to tell. I've done everything I can think of to pass the time. I've gone through my bag and shaken out each item to make sure no bugs stowed away. I've gotten up and paced in a circle, sat back down on the ground, and gone through the bag again. Still, it feels like hours, but for all I know it's been twenty minutes.

I've never been good at waiting. My tendency to charge forward without thinking has gotten me into trouble more than once, including that one time with Duncan McAllister. And that little misstep had me waiting nine months.

The door opens and I jump, almost expecting to see Duncan standing there. Of course, he's not. It's Kai.

"They're ready for you."

I pull in a breath, but it stutters its way into my lungs. Maybe the waiting wasn't so bad after all. Sure, the waiting was boring and irritating, but it didn't come with fear that nails my feet into the ground.

"Come on." She waves me to her. "Time to get in the game."

This is it. I sling the canvas bag over my shoulder again and make my feet move, one in front of the other, trying not to think about the fact that once I step through that door, my life will never be the same.

Who am I kidding? My life hasn't been the same since Jules summoned me to her house that night. The only chance I have of making things right and getting back to some semblance of normal is to go through with this.

Once I'm standing outside with Kai, she smacks me between the shoulders twice, slides her hand down to the small of my back, and pushes me forward.

"Remember, none of them is any better or any worse than you." The more she talks, the faster we walk. "You're all here to play the same game."

"I'm not really here for the game," I say in a hissing whisper, not wanting to be picked up by the boom mics I see several men holding. "I'm here for my daughter."

Kai narrows her eyes and gives me a quick scolding look. "Yes, and she's here to play the game. If you want to get close to her, then concentrate on doing what you have to do to win. Or at least to not get kicked off first."

Good grief, she's right. Until now, all I'd thought about was being here with Jessica. I never stopped to think that the amount of time we spend together is directly tied to how well we do in the game. I have to put my all into playing this thing, whether I want to or not.

Kai pulls me up short right where the palm trees end and the open beach begins. "When Rick calls you, you're going to walk that way." She points to the left.

"I don't suppose I can take you with me?"

She gives a sad little head shake. "Wish I could. But you'll be fine."

"How can you be so sure?"

"I've been with this show since episode one, season one. We haven't lost a contestant yet."

"There's always a first time."

"It would definitely be a ratings booster."

I frown at her and she rolls her eyes at the fact that I might begin to believe she was serious. Then she puts a finger to her lips and turns her attention back to the beach.

From where we're standing, I have a partially obstructed view. A boat similar to the one that brought us here is anchored off shore. Several steady-cam operators are scattered around as well as at least two stationary cameras. Rick isn't in view, but now that I'm not talking, I can make out his voice.

"Welcome to season twelve of *Last Family Standing.*"

Cheers erupt, and I imagine them bouncing up and down in the sand, pumping their fists and clapping. That's how all the seasons I watched started. By the end, they'll hardly have enough energy to stand, let alone do a fist pump.

"Jessica."

As soon as I hear Rick say her name, I hold my breath and strain to hear what else he has to say.

"You're standing by yourself. I'm sure you're anxious to know if we heard from your mother."

She must have answered him, but I don't hear anything.

"Let's not make you wait any longer. Monica Stanton! Are you out there?"

Kai nods, gives me a thumb's up, and pushes me toward the beach.

I can do this. I can do this. It plays over and over in my head, my own personal mantra to avoid doing something embarrassing, like passing out or throwing up.

I come out from the trees and into the open. And there they are. On the right is one large group of people, but the way they're standing, you can make out the family pairs. And on the left, standing by herself, is Jessica.

My daughter.

Clapping and other assorted noises come from the group, but I'm really not interested in them. I drink her in, memorizing the moment, even though it's being captured on film by at least six different cameras. Jessica whips her head around to look at me, sending her auburn ponytail swinging like a pendulum. Her eyes widen, and as I draw closer I read the surprise there. She really didn't expect me to come. But then, why would she?

Rick's talking, saying something about how they found me, and how it's a first for the series. About six feet separates me from Jessica and I have been struck mute. It's not that I don't have anything to say. I have too much to say. What comes first? How do you greet the child you haven't seen since the day she was born? *How've you been?* No, that's all wrong. *What's new?* How did I ever think I could do this?

Jessica takes the initiative. "Hi."

Her first word. Something melts inside me.

"Hi, Jessica."

For some reason, she flinches when I say her name. The response makes me want to take her in my arms, so I step forward, but she takes a step back and to the side. Despite the embarrassment burning in my cheeks, I cover by moving beside her and looking at Rick.

Let the games begin.

On TV, *Last Family Standing* moves at a rapid pace. In real life, it's as slow as, well . . . real life. We're given a map and told to hike around the island to the place we'll call home for the next month. Unfortunately, I think that Bob, the man who grabbed the map and claimed he had an excellent sense of direction, overestimated himself because a one-mile walk has taken about an hour. And we're still not there.

If we hadn't been expressly instructed not to interact with them, I'd ask one of the camera dudes for directions. They've got to be as tired of walking in circles as the rest of us. But other than a grunt now and then, they've kept their feelings to themselves.

Bob is examining the map, holding it up at shoulder level, his eyes darting back and forth between it and the vegetation. He squints, turns the map ninety degrees, and grunts. "Ah, there we go."

"You had it turned the wrong way?" Marcy, a fiftyish woman with super-short, bleached blond hair, sun-dried skin and muscle tone that speaks of a lifetime in the gym, tries to grab the map from him. "Let someone else take charge, you moron."

"Don't talk to my dad that way."

Bob's daughter, whose name I didn't catch, waves a finger in Marcy's face, only to have Marcy's twin sister—the equally buff, equally blond Maxie—join the fight.

"Who do you think you are, pointing your finger in her face?"

I should do something, but what? The last thing this argument needs is more people getting involved.

Jessica doesn't feel the same way. She steps forward, her palms up in a friendly gesture of neutrality. "I don't know about you guys, but I'm hot and tired and I just want to get to camp and work on shelter before the sun completely vanishes."

It's the most I've heard her say since meeting on the beach. Her voice is deeper than mine, but that just makes her sound confident and soothing. I'd follow her anywhere, and it looks like the others are considering the same thing.

She smiles at Bob. "Would you consider giving someone else a shot with the map?"

He looks like he's trying to decide which is more important: defending his honor or finding our camp area before we all pass out. Thankfully, his honor loses. "Sure. But how do you know anyone else will do better?"

Jessica faces the rest of the group. "Were any of you ever a Scout?"

One man and two women raise their hands. Jessica carefully removes the map from Bob's fingers and hands it over to them. "Why don't you three work on this together?"

As our Scouts examine the map, Jessica wanders a few feet away from the nucleus of the group and leans against a tree. I walk over and stand beside her.

"That was impressive."

She crosses her arms and shrugs. "Somebody had to do something."

"Jessica, I—"

"Jess. *Nobody* calls me Jessica. It's Jess."

If I'd been in her life all these years, I'd know that. But I don't, which makes me a nobody. I get it. At least she's inviting me to call her by her preferred name. Maybe one day, I'll move my way up and become a somebody.

"We've got it!" One of the female Scouts calls out. "It's this way." She points in the opposite direction than how we'd been going, then the three of them take the lead.

One of the twins mutters, "Let's hope this one knows what she's doing."

"Amen," the other twin mutters back.

Bob and his daughter glare at them.

I smile at Jess, hoping to share a laugh with her, but her face is devoid of emotion. She shifts her canvas bag to the other shoulder and trudges past me.

This is going to be the longest thirty days of my life.

13

As it turns out, it's much easier to follow a map when it's turned the right direction and you determine where north is. Our three former Scouts must all have earned merit badges in cartography, because twenty minutes later, we arrive at our destination.

Eight identical crates are scattered around the clearing. Off to one side is a wooden pole with a flag bearing the LFS logo whipping in the wind. In the middle of the pole is a spike with a battered metal bucket hanging from it.

Bob, most likely hoping to make up for his map blunder and do something useful, peers into the bucket and pulls out a scroll. "We have pail mail."

This is no great surprise, as every episode shows someone, at some point, going to the bucket to retrieve the "pail mail." It's the non-tech island version of texting. We all gather around as Bob pulls the end of the twine bow, unrolls the paper, and reads out loud.

"Congratulations. You've reached your new home and completed your first challenge."

Bob pauses for a smattering of half-hearted applause.

"But don't get comfortable now. There are eight crates in your camp, one for each team, containing identical items. Will you work together or will you look out for your own team and no one else? The choice is up to you."

Nobody says anything. Bob rolls the paper back up and drops it in the bucket. As far as I'm concerned, working together sounds like the smartest thing to do. We can build a stronger, bigger shelter, and build it faster, if we all pitch in. And then I can take off these terrible, still damp, still sandy shoes, and we can all get some sleep.

Emboldened by Jess's earlier intervention, I speak up. "I think we should work together."

"Oh, you'd love that, wouldn't you?" Maxie has her hands on her hips and is staring me down. "I can just see it now. Half of us will end up doing all the work, and the rest of you get to take advantage of it."

"No. That's not what I had in mind at all."

"Maybe not, but it's what would happen." Marcy jerks her head toward the crates. "My sister and I will fend for ourselves."

"Us too." Bob and his daughter pick a crate and drag it under a tree.

Trevor, one of the Scouts, pulls his wife away. "Come on, before all the good spots are taken."

Another male/female team walks away, leaving Jess, myself, and six others.

My shoulders drop in defeat. "That was a dismal failure."

"Not necessarily." A tall, African American man who could have stepped out of a modeling portfolio, looks over his shoulder at the teams struggling to open their crates. "I think you may have just separated the troublemakers from the team players."

I hope he means what I think he means. "Do you want to work together?"

"Sure. Look at us. We're like a UN delegation. Let's set a good example for the world."

Now that he mentions it, we are a diverse group. Between the eight of us, we represent the African American, Asian, Hispanic, and Caucasian communities. The song "Jesus Loves the Little Children" pops up in my head, but I refrain from singing, mainly because, as well-meaning as it is, some people might find it offensive. "Red and yellow, black and white" . . . nobody *really* has skin in any of those colors.

We quickly agree to join forces and drag the remaining four crates into a lopsided semicircle. I turn to ask a question and find my face inches away from the unblinking eye of a camera. The crew has been so quiet, I forgot they were there, which is a dangerous thing. If I don't want to come off like a total idiot, I have to remember that everything I say and do is being recorded, and any of it could appear on television. Trying very hard not to commit the cardinal sin of the island—acknowledging the man behind the camera—I turn away and join Jess at our crate.

As we get to work cutting bamboo, the eight of us introduce ourselves and share some personal information. There's Sal, whose full name is Guillermo Salvador, but as he says, "Hardly anyone can get Guillermo right. It's just easier to go by Sal." He's playing with his daughter, Gracie. She's about the same age as Jess, and has an inviting, bubbly personality. Her long, silky black hair hangs free down her back, and my fingers itch to braid it for her before it becomes a mess of snarls and tangles.

Evelyn Cho, the Scout who took the lead and finally got us to camp, is a widow in her fifties. Her sister, Jasmine Goldstein, is ten years younger and lives with her stockbroker husband in Upper Manhattan. "He's Jewish and I'm Buddhist," Jasmine jokes. "When people ask about our kids, we tell them they're Jewdists!"

And finally, there's Malcolm Carter, the man who put our little band together. "I had no desire to be on this show, but Layla begged me. I even tried to bribe her out of it. Told her that she could either have a car for her twenty-first birthday, or she could write my name down on the application and see what happened. Seemed like a good idea at the time. Got me out of buying a car, and the chance of us being picked was miniscule. Guess the joke was on me."

Layla grins as him. "Dad just forgot what he's always telling me: have faith. Good thing I had enough faith for both of us."

"Oh, I had faith, all right. My faith was just leaning in the other direction." He winks at his daughter and picks up a palm frond. "We're going to need more of these once we get to the roof. Why don't you go gather some?"

"Sure. Hey, Jess." She bounces over to Jess, who's taken the one-pound bags of beans and rice from each of our crates and combined them in one. "Come help me hunt for palms."

A hesitant smile creeps onto her lips. "Okay."

It's a surreal moment, watching my newfound daughter with her newfound friend, each carrying a machete as they stroll into the jungle. I might be worried if I didn't recognize the cameraman following right behind them. From the stocky build and unruly hair, I'm fairly sure that's Bruce.

Malcolm laughs. "I wouldn't admit this to her, but I actually was praying that we'd be chosen."

"So you really did want to be on the show?"

"Oh no, I really didn't. But I knew how much it meant to Layla. If we'd gotten a *no*, she would have been crushed." He moves over to the pile of bamboo logs and looks for the right size to add to our structure's floor. "It's just one of those sacrifices a parent makes for his child. But then you know all about that."

I stare after him as he walks off to find more vines, or whatever it is he's using to lash bamboo together. What did he mean by that? Was he serious or was he being sarcastic? Should I be touched or offended? Before I can spend any more time tying my emotions in knots, Sal calls us into a group huddle.

"Evelyn was just saying our shelter should be up off the ground."

"Because of the rain," Evelyn interjects. "When it rains, and it will rain a lot, we don't want our floor to be submerged."

Sal nods. "I agree."

Gracie looks from her dad to the shelter currently in progress. "It's a great idea, but how do we get it off the ground?"

"We need to cut more bamboo." Evelyn's suggestion is met with a groan from her sister.

"I can't chop anymore." Jasmine holds up her right hand. "I have a blister."

Evelyn snorts. "You'll have a lot more than blisters if you have to sit in water for days on end."

Gracie points toward the horizon. "We don't have much daylight left. There isn't time to cut more bamboo and raise the shelter."

"I think there's another way." I'm almost afraid to mention it, because it might be really stupid. Then again, it could save us a lot of time. "What about the crates?"

We all turn and look at the crates together, and I wait for someone to laugh.

"That's perfect," Sal says. "Four crates, four corners of the shelter. Let's get to it."

"Should we wait for the others to get back?" Jasmine looks in the direction that Layla, Jess, and Malcolm went.

I shake my head. "Gracie was right. We need to finish this quick. We're not changing anything about the structure, just getting it off the ground." Then I look over at the other four teams, the ones who have already finished their individual shelters. Some look sturdier than others, but each and every one of them sits squarely on the beach. "Do you think we should tell them?"

Sal shakes his head. "No point. One crate won't do them any good. Besides, they all chose to go it on their own. Now they'll see if they made the right choice."

Without another word, we get to work. I take the beans and rice out of the crate Jess just put them in, and pile them on the stack of crate lids. Malcolm had mentioned something about trying to make a table from them. That's an even better idea now.

Evelyn, Sal, Gracie, and I each take a corner of the almost complete floor and lift it up. Then Jasmine maneuvers the empty crates underneath. Even though it's made of bamboo, which is lighter than other types of wood, it doesn't take long for the floor to get heavy.

"Uh, Jasmine, do you think you could hurry?" Sweat rolls down the side of my face and into my ear.

"I want to get these positioned right."

"This is no time to worry about feng shui," Evelyn growls. "Just get them under there."

"Okay, okay." Jasmine putters for another minute, then backs away. "Set it down. Gently."

We do, and then we step back and hold our breaths, as if any sudden movement might make the floor disintegrate. But it holds its shape. And we finally breathe.

"What are you doing?" Malcolm's voice booms as he trudges toward us, dragging a long bamboo pole beneath each arm, and a bunch of vines hanging around his neck.

Uh oh. Layla and Jess are behind him, arms loaded with palm fronds. They don't look any happier than Malcolm sounds. I stop breathing again.

Sal takes over and explains what we did and why we did it. Malcolm lets the bamboo fall to the ground, then he squats beside the raised floor and looks beneath it. When he stands, he's smiling.

"That's the way to do it. Good job, everybody. Now let's get this thing finished."

As Jess walks past me with her load of ceiling fronds, she gives me a smile just slightly larger than the Mona Lisa look she usually sports. "Good thinking using the crates."

My ability to breathe is restored. "Thanks."

I want to run after her and strike up a conversation, but I hold myself back. There will be plenty of time to talk. Right now, we're working together to complete something. Malcolm's words come back to me, about how important the game is to Layla, which makes it important to him. It's the same with Jess. Not only did she choose to play this game, she chose to play it with me. There's no way I'm going to let her down.

In the meantime, I'm actually enjoying myself. As the shelter takes shape, my sense of accomplishment grows. Finally, we're done. And it's beautiful.

"That's the saddest thing I've ever seen." Jasmine shakes her head.

Evelyn pokes her in the shoulder. "You won't think that when it keeps you dry tonight."

Gracie doesn't look convinced. "Do you really think we'll all fit in there?"

"Sure we will," Jess says. "Like eight cozy sardines."

"That's another thing you'll be thankful for," Evelyn says. "Once the sun goes down, so does the temperature. The close quarters will keep you warmer."

Not once while we were building the shelter had I stopped to think about actually using it. Of course we would all cram in there to sleep. But who would sleep where? What would we use for pillows or blankets? There were several useful items in each crate—a machete, bags of rice and beans, a canteen, a cooking pot—but no bedding of any kind.

Before I can bring up my concern, Bob walks up. "Nice shelter," he says.

From the look on his face, it's obvious he wants something, but really doesn't want to ask for it. His daughter bounds up beside him.

"Can we borrow a machete?"

Oh, now they want to share. I bite my tongue to keep from saying all the sarcastic thoughts struggling to be set free.

"There should be a machete in your crate," Sal says. "Why do you need to borrow one?"

The daughter rolls her eyes. "Dad broke it."

"What?" Malcolm crosses his arms over his chest and leans forward slightly. "Those things are nearly indestructible. How did you manage to break it?"

Bob really doesn't want to share. But finally, he says, "Trying to open a coconut."

"It was a rock."

"No it wasn't."

"I think I know the difference between a rock and a coconut. It was a rock."

"Tracy!"

More eye rolling from Tracy. "Whatever. Tarzan here broke the machete and you guys have, like, four of them. We just need to borrow one."

Bob glares at his daughter, but doesn't call her on her rude behavior. The dynamic between those two is seriously messed up. Not that I have room to judge parent/child interactions.

Malcolm and Sal look at each other, apparently deciding that since they're men, they're also in charge of any tools we may have. After some silent communication, they turn to Bob and say together, "No."

"Dude, seriously?" Tracy's voice is a high-pitched whine. "We'll give it back."

Evelyn cocks her head. "In how many pieces?"

Tracy looks like she still wants to argue, but her dad cuts her off. "Don't waste your breath. They won't help us."

They start to walk away, but then Bob stops and spins around. "You think you're a happy little team right now, all working together. But only one family can win this. Sooner or later, you're all gonna turn on each other. Wait and see."

Jasmine bristles as we watch him stomp off. "Ooh, I'd like to loan him my machete, right in his—"

"Down, girl," Evelyn says. "He's just trying to psych us out. Ignore him."

Easier said than done. As we return to work, getting things ready for our first night on the island, the atmosphere of happy camaraderie is gone. In its place is a strained quiet, and I'm pretty sure we're all thinking the same thing. Even if we stay strong and work together to beat the other four teams, eventually, we'll have to compete against each other. The closer we become now, the harder it will be when it's every man and woman for themselves.

Jess is collecting rocks to put around the fire pit that Sal and Gracie are digging. I haven't even spent twenty-four hours with these people, and the idea of turning on them already makes me nauseated. But Jess is my main concern. I came here for her, and I want to win this for her.

Problem is, I'm not the only one on the island who feels that way. I may not have known them long, but it's been long enough to know this: nobody is going down without a fight.

14

Our first night is miserable.

One conspicuously missing item in the crates is flint. Despite the fact that we all give the rubbing-two-sticks-together approach a try, the closest we get to fire is a few puffs of smoke and some hot wood. It makes me feel a little better that the Singletons, as Layla has started calling the other teams, don't do any better. But having no fire is bad on many levels. There's no way to cook the beans or rice. There's no warmth and no light. In the end, we fumble our way into the shelter cold, hungry, and ready for the day to be over. Then the rain comes, just as predicted. And while our raised shelter keeps us from lying in water, it doesn't do a thing to protect us from the holes that show up in our palm frond roof.

Now it's morning. We're cold, wet, exhausted, and facing a terrifying reality.

There is no coffee.

Across the camp, Trevor stamps out of his shelter. "This is ridiculous. How can they expect us to live in these conditions?"

His wife, who I finally found out is Wendy, runs after him. "It's not so bad, Honey. Besides, even if we had coffee, we don't have a fire to brew it over."

"Not helping!" He growls and disappears around the trees, with Wendy right behind.

Meanwhile, back in our shelter, I'm the only woman awake. Now that the rain is over and the roof has stopped dripping, the rest finally fell asleep. Sal and Malcolm are already leaning over the so-far-incorrectly-named fire pit, attempting to spark a flame by magnifying the sunlight through the lens of Sal's glasses.

Hunkering down between them, I squint at the pile of kindling they've assembled. "Any luck?"

"Tons," says Malcolm. "All of it bad."

"While you conquer fire, I'm going to see if I can find something edible in the jungle."

Sal waves one hand without looking away from his task. "If you find a Starbuck's, I'll make you the Island Queen."

Laughing, I stand up and go to the crook of the tree where we put the machetes to keep them semi-dry. I grab one, start to walk away, then stop. Something isn't right. I go back to the tree.

"There are only three machetes." Really, I was talking to myself, but the guys overhear and a second later are standing next to me.

"How did they sneak over here and grab the machete without anybody noticing?" Sal glares over at the Singletons.

"All the rain last night would have covered the noise." Malcolm looks at the ground. "And washed away any footprints. I really don't care how they did it. I want to know *who* did it."

After the scene last night, Bob is the obvious suspect, and the men look like they're about ready to go over there and tear into him. But the last thing we need is to start day two with a fistfight.

"Guys, why don't we let it go?"

They look at me like I've announced I'm defecting to the other side. "You can't be serious," Malcolm says.

"Yes, I am." I sigh and cross my arms tightly over my chest. "Look, if we only had one machete and it had gone missing, I'd be right there with you. But we still have three."

Sal frowns. "And that gives him the right to take one?"

"No, of course not. But it gives us the opportunity to stay out of a confrontation. We've got more important things to deal with than fighting over a big knife."

They don't say anything at first. Then Sal snorts and moves back to the fire pit. "He's probably broken it by now anyway, trying to chop his way into a boulder."

"Thank you," I say to Malcolm.

He shakes his head. "I'm not promising I won't say something eventually, but for now, I'll leave it alone. Happy hunting."

Malcolm joins Sal. One of the girls rolls over in the shelter. I have a sudden desire to be alone, so before they all wake up and want to know what I'm doing, I hustle my way into the jungle, with my own personal cameraman hot on my trail.

"I found bananas!"

Stumbling out of the jungle, my prize held aloft, I expect to be received back with hurrahs like a hero. Instead, Jess storms up to me, hands on her hips, eyes narrowed in a glare.

"Where have you been?"

What kind of question is that? We're on an island. There are only so many places I could go. "I went to look for food."

"You look like you've been wrestling a cat."

I look down at the scratches on my arms and legs. "Climbing a tree is harder than it looks. I slid a few times."

"You need to be more careful." Jess takes the machete from me, as if I might accidentally chop off my foot while we talk. "It would be terrible if anything happened to you now."

A warm glow spreads from my neck to my toes. She cares about my well-being.

She obviously noticed my silly grin and realizes how I interpreted her words, because she rushes to set me straight. "If you break a leg or something, you'll be off the show, and I won't stand a chance at winning."

Silly me.

Before I can wallow in my misery, Gracie bounds up to me. "Bananas. Cool!" She takes them from me and I follow her over to our still-fireless fire pit.

Layla wrinkles her nose. "They're kinda green."

"They were the best I could find." Truth is, they were the only ones I could get to, and that had been iffy for a while. "Once we get the fire situation figured out, I can come up with different ways to cook things. For now, anything we eat has to be raw."

Layla's eyes are wide. "Please tell me you're a chef."

"I'm a chef."

"Woo hoo!"

The prospect that I might just be able to prepare bananas and coconuts in unique ways sends Layla hurrying from person to person, sharing the news. For the most part, the hearers look impressed.

It seems my island-cred just went up a little.

"Has anybody noticed something missing?" Jess asks.

Sal nods. "Yeah, we discovered the machete this morning."

"No, not that. *That.*" She points across the beach. "Where are the Singletons?"

Not in their camp of single-occupancy shelters. Uh oh. "Shouldn't we have gotten mail today?"

Simultaneously we break into a run. Evelyn is the first to reach the pail. When she looks inside, she mutters and pulls out a curled piece of paper. "They didn't bother telling us about this." Without waiting to be asked, she reads aloud.

"You've made it through your first night. Now it's time for your first competition. If you win, tonight could be your first comfortable night on the island."

"They can't start the challenge without us, can they?" Jasmine's hands are clasped together in front of her, and she looks about ready to crumble.

Malcolm offers her a consoling rub on the back. "I'm sure they won't do anything until we get there. This is just a way for the other teams to get under our skins. But we're not going to let them." He looks us over. "Everybody ready?"

A chorus of "Yes!" is his answer. Then we race-walk to the challenge area.

It doesn't take us long to reach the right spot, but by the time we do, most of us are huffing and puffing. I seriously hope this challenge doesn't involve running.

"Nice you could finally join us." A perturbed Rick Wolff sits in a director's chair beneath a shade umbrella. He makes a point of looking down at his watch.

Sal waves at Rick. "Would have been here sooner, but we were never informed there was mail." Then he zeroes in on Bob. "But we still managed to get here, even without a *map*."

Bob takes a step toward Sal, but Rick stands up and gets in front of him. "Is that true? You didn't share the mail?"

"Hey, don't blame me." Bob waves a finger at Trevor. "It was his idea."

"Way to roll over and play dead," Trevor says. "I just suggested it, kinda like a joke, you know? But then everyone else wanted to do it."

Now that Trevor has given them all up, the Singletons begin yelling at each other. Rick calls for order several times, but they completely ignore him. Finally, he pulls a chrome whistle from the pocket of his khaki shirt and puts it to his lips.

Not only does the shrill blast get their attention, it scares some birds out of the trees. Instinctively, I duck at the same time I look up to verify they really are birds. When I look at Rick, he's smiling at me, but he immediately pulls his attention back to the Singletons.

"Apparently, there's some confusion about the purpose of pail mail. It's to give information to *everyone* at camp. There aren't a lot of rules in the game, but this is one of them. If it happens again, there will be consequences." He pauses long enough to slowly look down the line, making eye contact with every contestant. Then he claps his hands together and grins. "Let's get to it."

Now that the scolding is over, I have a chance to take in the challenge area. It's about the size of a football field. Stationary cameras are set up all around the perimeter, and about half a dozen steady-cam operators are taking directions from a petite woman sporting the biggest pair of headphones I've ever seen. In the middle of all the commotion is the play area. It's filled with poles of different colors, and each pole has a bag tied to it.

Jess sidles up beside me. "What do you think?"

I look over at her and wonder if she realizes our shoulders are touching. *Be cool, Monica. Just a simple strategy session.* "The colors have to mean something."

She nods. "There are eight different colors on the poles."

"And three poles of each color."

It doesn't take long for us to figure it out. The poles are arranged so that no two like colors are beside each other. We'll need to go to the poles with whatever color we're assigned and untie the bag from each one. What we don't know is what's in the bags and what we have to do with it.

I lean so close to Jess's ear that her hair tickles my nose. "Memorize it."

"What?"

"Try to memorize the course."

I saw a lot of different challenges during my week of cramming with Jules. And if this challenge is the kind I think it is, memorizing it will give us an edge. I want to tell this to the others in our alliance, but we probably don't have much time. So Jess and I stay where we are, burning the course into our minds.

Sure enough, just a few minutes later, a production assistant directs us all to one side and has a rep for each team draw a colored ball out of a box. Jess draws an orange ball, which is now our official team color.

She wrinkles her nose and hands me one of the orange bandanas the PA gave her. "The worst color possible."

"Not really." I motion toward the course with my chin. Several of the colors, particularly yellow and green, tend to blend into the background. Orange is probably the easiest of them all to spot.

Jess gets my point, because her nose relaxes and she almost smiles.

Once all the rocks have been picked and bandanas handed out, the PA has us stand on mats that match our team colors. Then Rick stands in front of us and off to the side, next to a big lump of something covered in burlap. Here it comes. He's going to start talking in his TV host voice. It has a very specific cadence, and I've noticed he slips into it whenever the cameras are nearby. It's not as warm and casual as the way he talked at my house or on the plane or in the jungle, but it's effective for the purpose it suits.

After some general exposition for the home viewing audience, he gets down to the rules of the challenge. I'd been right. Each team has to get to all three of their poles and remove the bags. The bags contain puzzle pieces. After the team has all three bags, they start working on their puzzle. The first team to finish is the winner.

"Ready to know what your prize is?"

We make the appropriate, affirmative shouts to his rhetorical question. Then he pulls a burlap cover from the lump beside him.

"Everything you need to make life a little more comfortable. A tarp, rope, hammer, and nails. And most important . . ."

Please be flint. Please be flint.

He holds it up. "Flint."

I can't help myself. I shriek and clap and jump up and down, just like most of the other women. Amazing what one cold, hungry night can do to you.

Rick grins. "Before we start, there's one other twist you need to know."

Darn. I should have known the challenge was too straightforward.

"Only one member of each team will retrieve their bags from the poles. And they'll be wearing one of these." He pulls a black eye mask from one of the roomy pockets of his cargo shorts. "The other team member will be the caller, positioned on the perimeter of the course. The caller guides the blindfolded person by shouting directions at them."

Amidst the groans and fist pumps and smack talk, Jess bumps her shoulder against mine in what I take as a silent version of "atta girl." Memorizing the course had been a good idea, in theory, but there was no way to tell where we'd start from, or if the blindfold would go on before or after we were positioned at the course.

"This challenge requires clear communication between the caller and the seeker. It's a true test of how you work together as a team." Rick puts one hand in his front pocket, then looks down at the fat, black watch on his other wrist. "You have five minutes to strategize. Starting now."

The chatter begins, and Jess turns to me. "Are you better at yelling directions, or at following them?"

That's a loaded question. In my line of work, I am forever issuing orders: to wait staff, to sous-chefs, to prep cooks. Owning my own business makes it even more important that everyone who works for me does their job quickly and correctly. Still, Jess isn't my employee, she's my daughter. The daughter I've just met. I can't stomach the idea of screaming orders at her.

"I'm better at listening," I say.

"Cool. I can scream like nobody's business."

Great.

Ten minutes later, we're all in position. There are four platforms on either side of the course. The callers stand on them, and the seekers stand in front of them on the edge of the course. Our blindfolds are adjusted.

"Ready?" Rick calls out.

As ready as I'm going to get.

"Go!"

It's pandemonium. I take one step forward and, even though I was standing right in front of the course before the blindfold went on, my mind goes completely blank. All the callers are yelling, and I can't distinguish Jess's voice. Hands out, I take another step and run into someone.

"Watch it!" Bob's voice yells.

Frustration takes over, and I yell back. "I'm blindfolded. I can't watch anything!"

"Monica!"

Finally, I hear my name. I turn my head toward the sound of her voice. "Where do I go?"

"Take three steps forward. Then turn left."

Got it. One step. Another step. One more—"Ouch!"

I collide with another body. The impact spins me sideways and knocks me off my feet.

"Oh no! I'm sorry. I'm so sorry. Who did I just run into?"

That's Gracie. I struggle to stand and turn in what I think is her direction. "It's Monica."

"Man, I'm sorry. Are you okay?"

Before I can answer, I hear Sal bellowing. "Gracie! This isn't a cocktail party. Get moving!"

"Good luck," I say. Then, since I have no idea where Jess is now, I tilt my head back and yell into the sky. "What now?"

Jess gets me back on track. I make it to our first pole, but not without running into three other people, and having my foot stepped on so hard, I'm pretty sure the toenail will fall off. I feel around the pole until I find the bag, and then discover how hard it is to untie a knot when you can't see it. When I finally get it free, Jess guides me back to her and I toss the bag up on the platform. From the grunt, I may have hit her with it, but if I did, she doesn't say so. She just sends me back out into the fray.

The entire time, Rick is making like he's on ESPN, commenting on our progress, who's ahead and who's falling behind. Mostly, I've tried to ignore him in order to concentrate on Jess, but now he gets my attention.

"Wendy's doing a great job guiding Trevor. He's got his second bag and is heading out for the last one."

No. If I can't win, it needs to be someone in my alliance, not one of the Singletons. "Jess!" I yell. "Let's go!"

The girl wasn't kidding when she said she was a good screamer, although I doubt she'll have much of a voice left by the time this is over. Getting to the second pole takes much less time than the first one, as does untying the knot. In fact, I'm feeling a little smug when I get back to the platform.

"Trevor's still fumbling with the last bag," Jess says quickly.

"Be my eyes, Jess. Let's win this."

I push myself, moving faster than I thought I could. Now that I can pick her voice out of the cacophony, I'm much more secure. We're going to do this.

"Dad, stop!"

"Mom, stop!"

Mom? I turn my head, even though I'm still moving forward. Did she just call me—

A solid body mass barrels into me with such force that I turn in a complete circle. Stumbling, I throw out my hands, desperate to break my fall. And I do, only it's not with my hands. It's with my face.

My forehead makes contact with something hard. Light explodes in my eyes, which isn't right, since I'm still wearing a blindfold. Next thing I know, I'm on my back, and Rick is shouting.

"Everybody stop! Stand where you are and don't remove your blindfolds."

Stand where you are. But I'm lying down. Should I stand? I want to raise my hand to ask, but it's so heavy, I just give up. Lying down is good. I'll stay here.

There's a commotion beside me, people kneeling, talking. Something goes around my upper arm and squeezes. I sure hope a python isn't eating my arm.

"Monica, just relax. We're going to take off your blindfold."

"No, no, no." I make my arm move and bat at their hands. "Blindfolds stay on. Rick said."

A deep laugh rumbles by my other side. "You have permission to lose the blindfold."

"Rick, it's you." I push the side of the mask up, and peek out at him with one eye. "I fell."

"Yes, you did."

He slowly pushes the mask up and off my face. Someone immediately swoops in, waving a light back and forth in front of me. I scrunch up my face, because it's really annoying, but the person holds my eyelid open with a finger. Foiled again.

When the strobe-light wielding medic takes a break, Rick looks up at him. "Is she okay to keep playing?"

"Those are two different questions." Everything about the man, from the way he tilts his head to the tone of his voice, makes me think he's posturing for the camera. Sure enough, hunkered down a few feet away is my old buddy, Bruce.

I break out a big smile and wiggle my fingers at him. Even though I can tell he's trying to stay serious, he lifts his pinky from the camera and wiggles it back at me.

The medic is still talking. "She may have a mild concussion, but I doubt it's serious. We'll need to watch her for the next few hours, keep her awake. But I wouldn't recommend sending her out on this course again."

"Can we move yet?" At the grumbled question, I notice that the other seven seekers are standing around the course. Rick yells back that they should sit down where they are and keep the blindfolds on.

I look at Rick. "That's Bob," I hiss at him. "He's cranky."

"Seems that way."

"And he stole our machete."

His eyebrow lifts. "We can talk about that later. Right now, we need to get you off the course."

No, that won't work. If anything happens to me, then Jessica can't play. Jessica. There's something important I need to remember.

"Wait." I gasp and grab Rick's wrist before he can stand. "Jessica. She called me Mom. Did you hear?"

An easy smile takes over his face, exposing his dimples and crinkling the skin around his luscious amber eyes. "I heard."

A sigh puffs out of my lips. "You have such pretty eyes."

Everybody in the vicinity laughs, including Rick. "Okay, time to get you out of here."

He walks away and the medics move in. They keep up a constant chatter, telling me that they're moving me to a stretcher, that they'll give me fluids through an IV, yadda, yadda, yadda. Meanwhile, Rick is explaining what happened to everyone else, saying that the challenge will continue with the seven remaining teams.

"Sorry, Jess," he says. "That means you're out of this one."

My heart sinks. I wanted to win for her, and instead, I got her thrown out of the challenge. No second place, no parting gifts, no nothing.

Day two on the island is shaping up to be worse than the first. I hate to think what will happen on day three.

15

The medics take me to what is essentially a tent with open sides. I'm propped up against a bed roll, then they get an IV going and give me a cold pack for my forehead. Jess comes over a few minutes later and plunks herself down on the ground beside me.

"I'm supposed to keep you talking so you don't slip into a coma or something."

She looks mad enough to spit fire, which would really come in handy back at camp, but right now it just makes me feel worse. "I'm so sorry, Jess."

Her brows draw together. "For what?"

"For letting you down. If I wasn't such a klutz, we might have won the challenge."

She snorts and looks back at the course. "It wasn't your fault. It was that big guy on the brother/sister team. He's built like a linebacker. I can't remember his name."

"It's something that sounds like it should be in a sci-fi novel. Ronan? Conan?"

"Payton!" She snaps her fingers. "That's it. He ran right into you."

What do you know? She doesn't blame me. She may even have been worried when it happened, which is why she called me *mom*. On the other hand, she may have yelled out "Mon" and I misheard. I want to ask her, but I'm not quite sure how to bring it up. Then she starts laughing.

"What's so funny?"

Jess covers her mouth with her hand until her giggles are under control. "You told Rick he has pretty eyes."

I drop the cold pack from my forehead because there's no need for it anymore. Suddenly, my entire body is frozen. "I did what?"

"It's okay." She waves her hand as if she's shooing away a mosquito. Then she slaps her arm, and I realize she really *was* shooing away a mosquito. "Everybody knows you were talking crazy from your knock on the head. I'm sure he's already forgotten all about it."

Except that now I remember Bruce was right there with the camera, which means my ramblings were caught on film forever. Without a doubt, that's one bit that won't end up on the cutting room floor.

"Hey, they're starting again."

Jess is pointing at the course. All the seekers are standing, the callers are poised and ready. When Rick gives the call to resume, they start yelling and scrambling. Being able to see the seven people stumbling and fumbling their way around the course makes me want to bury myself in the sand.

"Did I look like that?"

Jess purses her lips, then nods. "Pretty much."

Two days in and I've already abandoned any dignity I might have had. I have to remind myself that it's worth it. My daughter is counting on me and I can't let a little thing like the fear of looking stupid stop me. After all, it can't get much more embarrassing than this.

In the end, Evelyn and Jasmine win the challenge. They were the last team to collect all three bags, but as it turned out, that was less important than puzzle-solving skills, which they have in abundance.

The medics clear me to return to camp, so I walk along with the others. The Singletons are so ticked that none of them won, they leave as soon as Rick releases us, nearly race-walking away. Jess bounces up to Gracie and Layla, and the three of them start whispering and giggling. Evelyn and Jasmine laugh and talk about winning the first challenge. Right behind them, Sal and Malcolm carry the basket of prizes between them. I bring up the rear, taking it slow and steady.

"Who'd have thought the puzzle would have been the hardest part of that challenge?" Sal says. "Way to go, ladies."

Evelyn gives a little bow as she walks. "Thank you very much. And thank you for carrying the basket."

Malcolm smiles. "Our pleasure. Thank you for deciding to share it. Guess that'll show the people who decided to go it on their own."

"Did you see how fast they took off?" Jasmine huffs out a breath. "What are they rushing back to? It's not like the beach is going anywhere."

A terrible thought crosses my mind. "Does it bother anybody else that they're alone at camp right now?"

There's a quiet pause and everyone looks back at me. Then the three girls sprint ahead with Evelyn and Jasmine hot on their tails. Sal and Malcolm walk faster, but the basket is heavy and awkward, so they don't get too far ahead of me.

When we come around the bend in the path and walk onto our beach, the scene is worse than I expected. With the exception of the floor and the crates, our shelter has been leveled. There's more yelling going on now than there was during the challenge, and all the voices start to sound alike.

"How could you do something so awful?"

"We didn't do anything. It was like that when we got back."

"Oh sure, the wind came in and only knocked over our shelter."

"You calling me a liar?"

"What does it sound like I'm calling you?"

My head throbs. No, no, no. This isn't right. First the machete, now this. The Singletons couldn't really be that devious and underhanded . . . could they?

A high-pitched scream overhead brings a halt to the accusations and we all look up to see several lanky monkeys swinging from tree to tree.

"They did it." A red-faced Trevor jabs his finger in the air toward them.

Sal takes a step closer. "Really? That's your excuse? The monkeys did it?"

"Well, we sure didn't do it."

"Why would they mess with our shelter, but none of the others?"

Uh oh. "Bananas."

Sal and Trevor turn to me and speak together. "What?"

"We had bananas. Maybe they were hungry."

Sal grumbles what I think is something not very nice in Spanish. "There's a whole jungle full of bananas. Why would they need ours?"

"No idea." My shoulders lift in a shrug, which is immediately followed by a pain shooting through my head. "I need to sit."

I go straight down, legs crossed, elbows on knees, head hanging like a bobble-head dog with a broken spring. All around me, the fight goes on, but now they all sound slightly muffled, and I've stopped caring about the outcome.

Jess kneels next to me and hands me a canteen. "You need to stay hydrated."

"I had fluids." I hold up my hand, showing off the band aid and the bruise that bear evidence to the IV they stuck in me. "I'm the most hydrated person here."

"Maybe, but nobody else just fell headfirst into a big wooden pole. Now drink."

She waves the canteen under my nose, and I can hear the water sloshing inside. "Okay." Turns out I was thirstier than I thought. After taking a few swigs, I swipe the back of my hand across my mouth. "What do you think?"

"About the fight?" She makes a face that tells me exactly what she thinks. "We're wasting time arguing about it. There's no way to know what really happened."

"There is one way." I jerk my thumb to the camp perimeter. "You know a camera guy was here the whole time. One of them knows exactly what happened."

Jess's eyes narrow. "You're right. But they won't tell us anything."

"True. Guess we'll have to wait till the show airs to find out what really happened. Come on." I try to stand, but my legs are a little wobbly, so I end up moving to my hands and knees and pushing myself up from there.

"What are you doing?"

That's a loaded question. In the grand scheme of things, I have no idea what I'm doing. All I know is that I want to have a semi-dry place to sleep tonight, and not monkeys or the Singletons or anything else is going to keep that from happening.

"You and I are going to start repairing the shelter." My hope is that, once the others in our alliance see us working, they'll abandon the argument and join us. At the very least, it will give us something to do other than take part in a screaming match.

As we pull away the scattered palm fronds that used to be the roof, I make two interesting discoveries. One, the bananas truly are gone. And two, the missing machete is back. Either those are some super-smart monkeys, or the Singletons are lying.

The old adage "cheaters never prosper" goes through my head. They may not prosper, but they can sure make life miserable while they're trying.

It's amazing how much easier it is to start a fire when you have flint. It only takes Evelyn five minutes of striking it with the blunt side of a machete to produce a little shower of sparks that catches in the dry kindling. A cheer goes up as she blows on it and adds more fuel until it becomes a respectable blaze.

Because I'm the chef, everyone thinks I should be in charge of cooking. "It's not like we have lots of choices." I hold up two bags. "Beans or rice?"

Rice receives the majority vote. I set up a cooking pot and put on some water to boil. Sal and Malcolm are working together to stretch the tarp over our newly repaired roof.

Gracie sighs. "It will be so nice to stay dry tonight."

"And warm," Layla agrees. "If we can keep the fire going."

"Unless we get another storm, it'll keep going. But if it does go out, we can always start a new one." Evelyn holds up the flint before stuffing it into the pocket of her shorts. "Nobody's getting their hands on this baby."

I'm trying to decide how much rice to make. Yes, we'd all like a big portion, but we only have four pounds. Even with the beans, that isn't going to last for thirty days. The idea is for us to find our own food—like fish, coconuts, the infamous bananas, or possibly a wild island chicken, which isn't a real thing except in my imagination.

A commotion on the other side of the beach catches my attention. Payton stands with his feet planted and arms crossed tightly in front of him, which emphasizes muscles that look like they were carved from granite. That's the body that ran into little old me. It's a miracle I was able to maintain consciousness.

Bob is standing opposite Payton, poking his finger toward his face. Bob is about a head shorter than Payton and not nearly as well built. The fact that he's being so confrontational speaks to his bravery. Or his stupidity.

"I don't know how anybody so big can be so clumsy. You run into her," Bob waves his hand vaguely in my direction. "Then you run through my fire. You're a menace."

Payton glares at him. "You didn't have a fire, you had smoke."

"That would have turned into a fire if you hadn't stomped on it."

"Look, I said I was sorry."

"You're sorry, all right."

"What does that mean?"

I can't stand it. The yelling and the near certainty that one of them is going to slug the other are making me so tense I want to scream at nobody and everybody. Instead, I call Evelyn and Jasmine over, and tell them what I want to do. They aren't crazy about the idea at first, but as the Bob/Payton fight escalates, they start to see it my way. Finally, they give me their blessing, and I ask Jasmine to keep an eye on the rice.

With a broken tree branch clutched in one hand, I stomp over to the quarreling men.

"Here." I thrust it at them, making the flame on the end dance and quiver.

Their eyes widen to the point that I can see the fire's reflection flickering against the irises.

Payton speaks first. "What's this about?"

"It's fire. It keeps you warm. You can cook with it." I move closer to him. "Take it."

He reaches for the piece of wood, but Bob stops him. "Wait. This could be a trick."

My eyes roll skyward before I can stop them. "You caught me. This is my special piece of exploding wood."

Bob and Payton look at each other. It's as if this simple act of kindness has short-circuited their brains.

"Look, I can't take all the strife wafting from this side of the camp. If it takes the gift of fire to make the arguing stop, then so be it." I look Payton in the eye, because he seems the more reasonable of the two. "But if your fire goes out and you start arguing again, don't come looking for more. This is a one-time thing."

"Okay." Payton takes the fire. Bob snorts and says thanks in a decidedly unthankful tone.

As I march back to my side of the beach, seven sets of eyes stare at me. Their expressions run the gamut from shocked to angry to pleased. Before anyone else has a chance, I start talking.

"I had to do something to stop the arguing. Anyway, the fire came from the flint Evelyn and Jasmine won, and they said it was okay."

The faces start to relax, coming closer to calm resignation. No one really wants to argue. After all, we're the good alliance. If they handed out hats in this game, ours would be white.

Malcolm nods. "It was the right thing to do."

"They're going to get flint tomorrow, anyway," Layla says. "What's one day early?"

The crisis is over. I go to the fire and thank Jasmine for keeping the rice from sticking to the bottom of the pot. On the other side of the shelter, Jess and Gracie are gathering canteens to make the final water run of the day. They head to the path, but Jess stops and looks at me. She smiles, not the Mona Lisa smile but a genuine, unmistakable, lifts the corners of her mouth and makes her eyes crinkle kind of smile. Then she turns and she and Gracie move into the jungle.

That smile could have meant a lot of things: *I'm proud of you. Thanks for stopping the fighting. Man, you are one naïve woman. How could I have come from such stupid stock?* The possibilities go on and on. But with the mood I'm in, I need to believe it meant something positive. Naïve or not, I assign a meaning to my daughter's beautiful smile.

And as I stir the rice, I smile, too. Because right now, if nowhere else than in my head, my daughter is proud of me.

16

The rain starts again overnight and it puts out the fires on both sides of the beach. But this time, the roof on our community shelter doesn't leak, thanks to the new tarp. The mood in camp overall is much better than yesterday. Even the Singletons seem a bit mellower. Of course that could be because they just don't have the strength to be feisty. They couldn't have gotten much sleep last night, and without fire, they're heading to the next challenge without any breakfast.

We're having beans for breakfast, just to mix things up. Jess hunkers down beside me where I'm doing my best to scoop equal portions onto big, green, semi-clean leaves.

"How are you feeling?"

"Other than the ice pick jabbed between my eyes, I feel great."

"I'm not surprised you have a headache." She pushes my bangs back with one finger and grimaces. "That is one nasty bruise."

The notion that my daughter just touched me, even in such an innocuous way, overwhelms me. Rather than say something ultra-mushy and embarrass us both, I turn my attention back to the beans, putting an extra scoop on Jess's leaf. I'll balance it out by taking less for myself.

"Thanks." She takes the leaf and starts eating with her fingers. "Will you be up to competing today?"

"You bet. I just hope we get to see where we're going for this one."

Jess laughs, then she gets up and joins Gracie and Layla. The way they're sitting on the edge of the shelter, their legs dangling, they look like three teenagers enjoying a week away at camp. I wonder if she ever did that. There are so many things I don't know about her, so much I want to learn. But the time has to be right, and I'm pretty sure she's the one who needs to determine when that right time is. So for now, I'll just keep on cooking bland food and fumbling my way through challenges. Eventually, my daughter will initiate a meaningful, heart-to-heart conversation.

I hope.

An hour later, we're ready for another challenge. But this time, we're on the beach about half a mile from our camp. From the looks of the course, which starts on the beach but extends out into the ocean, it will involve swimming. Great, today I have the opportunity to avoid drowning.

Rick explains the rules, and this time, two of the staffers run the course to show us how it's done.

"One team member starts here, on the platform. You'll go across the balance beam to the next platform. Then across the rope bridge."

The rope bridge looks simple, until we see both the staffers fall off when the thing twists around.

Rick grins. "Not as easy as it looks. From the second platform, you'll swim to the buoy and dive down to untie a bag. Once you have the bag, swim back to the start, and hand it off to your teammate."

They sure do love two-part challenges. I really, really hope Jess is a good swimmer.

"In each bag is a key that unlocks a chest. Inside that chest is a slingshot and ammunition." He points farther up the beach where rows of clay pots are set up, three in each team color. "The last two teams to break all their pots will be up for elimination this evening. I'll give you time to strategize."

This shouldn't be so bad. All we have to do is come in somewhere between first and sixth.

"How are you with a slingshot?" Jess whispers.

"I have no idea. I've never used one."

"Me neither."

"But I have good aim."

She nods. "I'm pretty good in the water. And after yesterday, I don't think we want you doing anything that requires balance."

"Sounds good."

I watch the other teams as they decide who does which leg of the challenge. For the most part, lighter, more agile people are chosen for the water portion: Jess, Layla, Gracie, Jasmine, Maxie, Tracy, Wendy, and the gal whose name I still don't know. Of the ones manning the slingshots, I'm the least muscular, but that won't matter too much if I'm the most accurate.

Finally, the cameras are ready, including two crews in the water, on their own platforms on either side of the course.

Rick raises his hand. "Families ready . . . Go!"

Those of us on the beach can't keep from screaming and cheering on the ones in the water, even though it's doubtful any of them are paying attention. Jess, and most of the others, cross the balance beam quickly. Only Maxie and the nameless one fall off and have to start over.

The rope bridge is an entirely different animal. No one makes it across the first time, which means they all have to go back and start over. When Jess gets to the second platform, she stops on her hands and knees and looks to her right and her left. I wonder if she's too scared to go on, but then I understand what she's doing. She's looking to see how the others approach the bridge to figure out what works the best.

"Smart girl," I murmur to myself.

She slowly inches forward, one hand on either side of the bridge, her weight evenly distributed. When it begins to wobble she stops and centers herself. Then she moves on. It takes her a while to get across, but even so only Layla and Wendy made it ahead of her. The rest of the course is cake. Spongy, soggy cake.

She swims to shore with the small bag clenched between her teeth. I run to meet her, and when she hands off the bag, she gasps out, "You've got this."

I've got this. Oh boy, I hope I've got this.

Malcolm and Trevor already have their bags open and are taking aim at the pots. I take my spot, which, judging from the colors of the mats, will be in between Bob and Marcy when they get here. Tuning out the noise all around me, I put a heavy glass marble in the slingshot, pull it back, aim, and let it fly.

Only it doesn't fly. It plops to the ground about three feet in front of me.

There's a learning curve, no doubt about it. The mats are filling up as people finish the water course, but still no one has broken a single pot. I relax, take a deep breath, and try again. Nothing breaks, but I get a lot closer this time.

A crash sounds. Rick calls out in his excited voice, "Evelyn breaks the first pot!"

It's time for a personal pep talk. *You can do this, Monica. Aim, pull back, aim again, and let it fly.*

This time, my aim is high and the marble sails over the pots. But that's good. If I just bring the next one down a little . . . *Crash*!

A shriek explodes from me as an orange pot shatters. Then another pot is hit.

Rick is almost as excited as we are. "Monica and Malcolm have both broken pots. We have a race going now!"

On my left, Bob is beyond frustrated. He pulls back on the slingshot, his arm shaking. "Why won't this thing work? It's got to be broken."

On my right, Marcy lets out a sound reminiscent of an angry bear. "It's not broken. You just can't aim worth squat."

"I haven't seen you hit anything." He turns toward Marcy, which unfortunately means he turns toward me at the same moment that he loses control of the slingshot.

It's one of those moments when time slows way, way down, and you're able to cram a thousand thoughts into one little second. There's a big, stone-sized, solid glass marble shooting toward me. I imagine it hitting me in the temple. If I was lucky, it would kill me straight out, but more likely, I'd end up in a vegetative state and the only people who would come to see me after several years in that condition would be the midnight cleaning crew at the full-time care facility. Oh no, I'm not going out that way.

I cover my head with my arms, but I get hit anyway. Smack dab in the elbow. Needles of pain radiate up to my shoulder and down to my fingers as I scream and do a most unflattering dance.

"Everybody stop!" Rick makes his way to me while Marcy and Bob continue yelling at each other.

"Look what you did, you big klutz," Marcy yells.

"What I did? That never would have happened if you'd kept your big mouth shut."

Doubled over and holding my elbow, I say through gritted teeth, "I wish you'd *both* keep your mouths shut."

Rick is beside me now. His lips are twitching like he doesn't know whether to be concerned or amused. "Do we need the medic?"

"No. No medic. I am not dropping out of this challenge." Not again. Because if I drop out, that automatically puts Jess and me in the bottom two teams, which is totally unacceptable.

Not looking at all convinced, Rick wraps his fingers around my wrist and supports my elbow with his other hand, then unbends my arm. "Does that hurt?"

Can he see that I've broken out in a cold sweat? "A little. But it's getting better. Really."

He looks closer at my skin, then whistles. "It's already bruising. Keep this up and you'll set the record for most injuries by one person in one season."

That's a record I'd rather not hold. "I'll be fine."

"Okay." He claps his hands and goes back to his place.

Marcy and Bob have finally stopped bickering, but I notice that neither one of them apologized to me for what happened. That's fine. I flex my arm, working the elbow until the pain is more like a dull throb. When I win this competition, that will be thanks enough.

It's more difficult to hold the slingshot now, so the first few shots go astray. All around me, it seems they've figured out the trick of making contact. Except for Bob, who is still convinced he has a defective weapon. Finally, I manage to break my second pot. There are four of us who are down to the final pot. Rick keeps up his commentary until finally he congratulates Trevor and pronounces him the winner.

"Don't stop," Rick says. "Remember, the two teams that come in last are up for elimination tonight."

There's no stopping me now. Aiming, shooting, I clear my head of everything but the last orange pot. For good measure, I imagine Bob and Marcy's faces on it. Three shots later, it's over. I've cracked all our pots.

My hands shoot up in the air, and I emit a simultaneous victory yell and cry of pain.

"Monica and Jess finish second and are safe from elimination!" Rick shouts.

I drop the slingshot and turn, right when Jess runs up and tackles me in a bear hug. "I can't believe you did it!"

She can't realize that her arm presses right against my sore elbow, and there's no way I'm telling her. So I force a smile. "Didn't think I had it in me, huh?"

"Not after you got beaned in the elbow."

We get to the spot where the contestants are gathering and watch the rest of the challenge. It's impossible not to cheer them on, especially when it gets down to three men: Payton, Bob, and Sal.

"Sal has to win," I whisper to Jess, who nods in agreement.

But he doesn't. Payton is the next to break his last pot. Which mean that either Bob or Sal will be out of the game by tonight.

17

The mood around camp is tense. Twelve people are relieved to be safe, and four people have no idea what the outcome of tonight will be.

Evelyn is sitting by the fire pit with Sal and Gracie, tutoring them in the best way to start a fire. We have no idea what the challenge will be tonight, but it will pit the two teams against each other. At least once every season, it's been fire starting. Since the other team has no flint to practice with, our guys will have a definite edge. If fire is the challenge.

But we won't know that until we head to the final challenge area, and that won't be until after dark, which is several hours away. I can't sit around doing nothing until then, so I grab one of the machetes. "I'm going to hunt for food. Anyone want to come?"

"I'll come," Malcolm says.

I was hoping Jess would volunteer, but she and Layla are taking turns braiding each other's hair. Having company is better than going out alone. Not that we're ever alone, but the camera men take the "no interaction" policy so seriously, they're worse company than mute introverts. In fact, if I was alone in the jungle with a cameraman, and I fell and broke my leg, I doubt he'd do anything to help. It would be just like those wildlife documentaries, where the person behind the camera keeps on filming, even when the cute little baby wildebeest is being gobbled up by the hyenas.

Malcolm grabs another machete and we head through the trees and vines. "What are we looking for?" he asks.

"Anything edible." I poke at a clump of plants. "I'm really not picky."

"Funny, we've only been here two days, and we're already desperate for real food."

"Imagine how it'll be in a week."

Malcolm sighs and shakes his head. "You know, there are people in the world who never know where their next meal is coming from. It's how they live every day of their lives. Those bags of rice and beans we have would be a feast to them."

He's right. As a chef, I'm extremely familiar with the plight of the hungry in America and abroad. I've participated in charity cook-offs and auctions to raise money for organizations like The Brown Bag Gang and Goats for Ghana. But I've never attempted to empathize with the people we were feeding. I've never been really, truly hungry. The next time I'm asked to participate in one of those fund-raisers, I'll have a much better appreciation for what I'm doing. But that doesn't make me any less hungry now.

"I hope you know the difference between what's edible and what's not," Malcolm says.

"For the most part. If I don't know what something is, I wouldn't suggest we try eating it."

He salutes. "You're the chef."

"Yes, I am. And what are you?"

"What do you think?"

Twenty questions isn't my favorite game, but in this instance, I'll go along with it. "Well, your talk about the hungry people in the world makes me think you're involved in some type of humanitarian work."

"You could say that."

When I first met him, I thought he looked like a model, but now I rule that out. "Do you work full-time?"

"Oh yes. Actually, I work a lot of overtime."

"How does your wife feel about that?"

"My wife died four years ago. Ovarian cancer."

I want to rip my tongue out. "Malcolm, I'm so sorry."

His smile is melancholy, but sincere. "It's all right. Viv's in heaven now, so she's happy about everything."

As soon as he mentions heaven, I remember how he and Layla talked about having faith, and it clicks into place. "You're a pastor."

"Very good." He squats down beside something growing low to the ground. "If this is the plant I think it is, our information packets said the roots are edible."

Squatting beside him, I poke into the dirt around the base of the plant. "You're right, it's taro. They'll make you sick as a dog if you eat them raw, but cooked they're fine. They'll make the rice and beans go farther."

After digging up about a dozen, we decide to head back. "But keep your eyes open for coconuts," I say. "If I boil these with coconut milk, it will enhance their natural nuttiness."

We walk in silence, but then I can't stand it anymore. "Can I ask you something personal?"

"Knock yourself out."

"I'm just wondering how a guy like you feels being on a show like this. I mean, the competition gets pretty cutthroat."

"You mean, what's a nice pastor like me doing in a place like this?"

I laugh. "I guess so."

"Like I said before, it meant a lot to Layla. But just the fact that we were chosen . . . it makes me think we're meant to be here for something bigger than the game." He scratches the back of his neck and looks away from me. When he finally speaks again, his tone is serious. "I think part of the reason Layla and I are here is because of you and Jessica."

"Me and Jess?" I stop short and lift my arms, clumps of dirt falling from the taro roots in my hands. "Why?"

"How do I say this?" He glances past me for a brief moment, and I realize that what he really means is, How do I say just enough so you'll understand, but not so much that it ends up on television?

"You're in a difficult situation. Not just playing this game, but getting to know your daughter. There may come a day when you need to talk or pray with someone. And maybe God put me here for that reason." His serious mood vanishes as quickly as it came when he spies something under a tree. "Look. A coconut!"

He jogs over and snatches it up, as if it might disappear if he takes too long. Obviously, we're done with our conversation, which is fine by me. I'm not ready to discuss my relationship with Jess, not even with a man of the cloth. But it is good to know he's around . . . just in case I change my mind.

The final challenge area is designed to make a statement. Tiki torches surround the playing area, which is a large, round sand pit. On one side, two tiers of roughly hewn bench seats are meant for those of us who will watch. On the opposite side is a raised, black platform.

We file in, first the audience filling the benches, then Bob and Tracy, and Sal and Gracie move into the middle of the sand pit. Rick jumps onto the platform, grinning like the head frat boy at a hazing.

"Welcome to the proving ground. This is where we find, after one simple challenge, which family will stand and which will be out of the game."

Everything I can cross, is crossed: fingers, toes, arms, legs. If it wouldn't make my head hurt worse, I'd cross my eyes. *Please, oh please, let it be making fire.*

Rick makes the announcement, and my heart plummets. The challenge that night is an old-fashioned egg toss.

Sal and Gracie look terrified. Bob and Tracy are their usual smug and sassy selves, making me wonder if they hold some kind of father/daughter egg toss title.

Beside me, Jess hangs her head, looking down at her folded hands. "This isn't good," she mumbles.

No, it's not, but rather than agree out loud, I bump her shoulder with mine. "They still have a chance."

But not much of one. As it turns out, Gracie is scared of raw eggs. More specifically, she's scared of raw eggs breaking in her hands and sliming her. The first couple of throws are okay, but after every one, Rick orders each person to take a step backward. The farther away Sal gets, the harder he throws. And the harder he throws, the stiffer Gracie becomes, until finally, that thing she most feared happens.

She stands there, staring at her father, hands out, palms up, egg yolks and whites oozing through her fingers. Sal smiles and tries to console her. "It's okay, *mija*. We did our best."

Meanwhile, Bob and Tracy are being poor winners. Tracy jumps up and down in a circle, then jabs her finger at them and yells, "We owned you! You're cracked, just like your egg!" I want to slap her.

Rick puts an end to their victory party by telling them to sit on the benches. Then he comes down from his podium and stands between Sal and Gracie, laying a hand on each of their shoulders. "I'm sorry, but you will not be the last family standing. Grab your things and go."

It's an abrupt, unceremonious dismissal, but it's the same one Rick gives to every team when they leave. Then he turns to the rest of us. "As you see, anything can happen. One thin eggshell could stand between you and victory." He claps his hands together. "Make your way back to camp."

We stand up and are almost out of the play area when Rick stops us.

"I almost forgot." He grabs a small burlap sack from the edge of the platform and tosses it to me. It's heavier than it looks, and I'm pretty sure I break one of my already short nails as I catch it. "A flint for each team. Pass those out when you get back to camp."

As we head back to our shelters, the mood is mixed. The Singletons are thrilled, going on and on about how they'll be warm and now they can cook. But the rest of us, the white hats, are quiet. We've lost two allies, but more importantly, two very nice people have been sent away because of an inability to throw and catch raw eggs, a skill that people in real life never, ever need. The randomness of it is beyond depressing.

"How are you holding up?" Malcolm comes up beside me, looking as serious as I feel.

I shrug. "I'm sad."

"Imagine how I feel. Now I'm the only man in our group."

Even though I keep my eyes on the ground, his comment makes me smile. Then Layla bounds up and links an arm through her dad's.

"Cheer up," she says. "We all knew this would happen sooner or later. At least we didn't have to turn on each other like the Singletons were hoping we would. And now there's more food to go around and more sleeping space in the shelter."

Malcolm's booming laugh echoes through the jungle. "That's my little ray of sunshine, always looking for the positive."

"Dad." Clearly embarrassed, she jogs away and claims Jess's elbow.

"She's a great girl."

The pride is so evident on his face, he doesn't need to say a word. Watching our daughters looking so carefree and happy, I wonder if I'll ever be as comfortable in my role as a parent as Malcolm is. Sure, he's been with his daughter her whole life. It stands to reason they'd have a close relationship. What kind of a relationship can I hope to create with Jess? It's only been a couple days, but so far, we haven't talked about anything important. My strategy of waiting for her to start a mother/daughter conversation is obviously flawed. I guess it'll be up to me to spot the door crack when it opens up and jam my foot into it before she can slam it closed again.

18

Handing out flint made me the most popular girl in camp last night. But I knew it wouldn't last. Sure enough, the sun is up and, thanks to a rain-free evening, the fires are still burning. It's a new day, and I'm back to being boring old Monica.

The morning pail mail informs us that today is a free day. It stretches out like a long, deserted road. Twentyish hours of making nice and finding ways to pass the time. Which makes today the perfect opportunity to visit the confessional. I've seen others walk in that direction, but between my near concussion after the first challenge, and all the excitement of yesterday, this is the first time I've gone.

It's a bit of a walk, so by the time I get there, I'm starting to have second thoughts. What am I going to say, anyway? I really don't want to talk about anybody back at camp, because I know how those things get twisted. But this is something we're all required to do. Maybe, I can just talk about Sal and Gracie, how nice they were and how sad I was to see them go.

The confessional setup is pretty bare bones: one stationary camera and two women. They're having a heated conversation about sushi, of all things, but as soon as I walk up, they go silent and the brunette moves behind the camera.

"Welcome to the confessional." The one with the blond ponytail points at a log on the beach. "Have a seat there and get comfy."

There's really no way to be comfortable on a hard, dry log, but I do my best to look like I am. I cross my arms, uncross them, cross my legs, uncross them, face the camera full-on, then turn slightly sideways.

"That's great," she says, making a movement that tells me to hold still.

I stop fidgeting. "Now what?"

"Now, you just tell us what's on your mind."

Right now, my mind is wishing this log was padded. Shoot, I had this all figured out. What was I going to talk about? "Sal and Gracie!" I'm so glad I remembered, I almost forget to say anything else. "I really miss them."

Ponytail waits for me to say something fascinating, and when I don't, she frowns. The surf behind me has just gotten really, really loud.

"They were nice." Oh man, now I sound like the island idiot.

"You know, sometimes it helps if we treat it like a conversation." Ponytail speaks slowly and sweetly, as though that will help me understand. "Just pretend you're talking to a close friend. Okay?"

Just like I'm talking to Jules. I can do that. "Okay."

"Great. You've had a few injuries already, haven't you?"

I laugh. "You know, I'm usually not accident prone. I work with knives on a daily basis, and look," I hold my hands up, fingers spread. "Haven't cut one of them off yet."

Once I start talking, it just keeps flowing. I lift my bangs and stick out my elbow, showing off my war wounds. I talk about the shelter, and how we have our doubts whether it was knocked over by monkeys. When I finish the fire sharing story, Ponytail seems impressed.

"I don't know that anyone has shared their fire before."

"It was kind of for a selfish reason," I admit. "My aching head couldn't take anymore yelling."

She nods. "How are things going between you and your daughter?"

The abrupt change of subject nearly knocks me off my log. Jess and I haven't even had a heart-to-heart yet. What makes Ponytail think I want to talk to her about it?

"You know, I'd better get back to camp before they think I've run away." I hop up before she can stop me and jog back the way I came. There aren't many things that would send me running back to that group. Asking me about the most important, nearly nonexistent relationship in my life is one of them.

Dinner that night is taro root and rice in a coconut milk reduction. It turns out better than I expected, but I won't be adding it to my catering menu anytime soon.

"Well." Jasmine pokes at her portion with one of the crude bamboo spoons Malcolm spent the afternoon whittling. "This is very . . . interesting."

Evelyn frowns at her. "There's not a thing wrong with it." She turns to me and nods sharply. "We need to stretch out the rice, and you found a way. Kudos."

"And don't forget the coconut," Malcolm adds. "No scurvy for this group."

Jess wrinkles her nose. "Doesn't citrus fruit prevent scurvy?"

We look from one to the other, but I don't think anyone really knows for sure.

"We could ask one of the Singletons," Layla says.

Even if one of them knows, I doubt they'd tell us. Still, I look over at their side, with their individual fires burning in front of their individual shelters. They're sitting in pairs, but no one is talking, and they certainly aren't laughing. I suppose, from a game play standpoint, they're being smart. By avoiding personal relationships, they can strategize and play a cutthroat game without guilt. Even so, I can't help but feel sorry for them.

I'm pulled out of my musing when a flash of lightning cracks the sky, followed by a rumble, and the rain begins to fall. We scramble for the shelter, taking our possibly-scurvy-preventing dinner with us.

"I wish we had a way to keep that from happening." I point to the fire, which is now a slightly smoking heap of wet wood and ash.

"At least we have more than one flint now. Which reminds me," Evelyn waves her bamboo spoon around, "everyone needs to practice starting a fire."

Layla sighs. "Maybe we should hunt up some eggs and take turns tossing them to each other."

"There's really no way to know what's coming next." Jess takes a swig out of her canteen. "Do you think we'll have a challenge tomorrow?"

Malcolm nods as he eats his last few grains of rice. "We should. A reward challenge."

"Ooh, what do you think the reward will be this time?" Layla leans forward, and even in the darkness, her eyes sparkle. "Maybe pillows and blankets. Or food. I hope it's food."

Evelyn shakes her head. "I hope it's something to catch food, like fishing gear. That's what we really need."

"Like that old saying." Jasmine taps her lip with one finger. "Give a man a fish, he'll eat for a day. Teach a man to fish—"

I hold up my spoon with authority. "And he'll find a woman to clean them all."

All the women laugh. Malcolm hangs his head in mock shame. "I apologize for my entire gender."

I pat his shoulder. "Apology accepted. Personally, I hope it's a gentle challenge. One that involves padding. Or sitting in a chair."

"Or a pillow fight," Jess adds.

Everybody has an idea of what kind of challenge I might get through unscathed, each one more ridiculous than the other. Before long, we're laughing so hard no one can speak.

It's such a light-hearted moment, I choose to ignore that these people are my competitors, just like the Singletons. Right now, with the rain pattering against the tarp and collecting in puddles beneath our raised floor, I choose to be thankful that I found camaraderie and humor in such a bizarre place. Tomorrow, we compete. And tomorrow, I'll agonize over when and how to have a serious talk with Jess.

But tonight . . . tonight we laugh.

19

The challenge the next day is the exact opposite of gentle. It's a physical obstacle course that includes scaling walls, crawling through mud beneath a low wooden structure, and swinging from one rope to another like Tarzan.

That's bad enough, but then Rick delivers the twist: team members will be tethered to each other. The only way to win this is through extreme teamwork.

Oh no. Absolutely nothing can go wrong with this.

A production assistant gives us what we need. There's a leather belt with padding on the inside. We're told to buckle it loosely around our waists. Then we connect ourselves together with a three-foot length of rope that snaps onto D rings on the side of each belt.

Jess looks down at her waist. Her eyes follow along the rope, to my belt, and then up to my face. "This is a very bad idea."

I don't blame her for being afraid. With my track record, who knows what calamity I'll drag her into?

With an awkward pat on the shoulder, I attempt to encourage her. "I'll do my best to stay out of trouble. Promise."

She doesn't look convinced. If we weren't literally attached at the hip, I'm pretty sure she would have walked the other way. Instead, we stand on our orange mat, waiting for Rick to start the challenge.

But there's one more thing. Rick reveals the reward we're playing for.

"Something to stretch out that supply of dry goods. Fishing equipment."

Evelyn pumps her fist, making it clear just how much she wants that prize.

"And, to make island eating a little more interesting, there's this." Rick holds up another basket full of jars and bottles. "A selection of cooking oils, spices, and utensils."

My heart actually jumps when I hear the word *spices*. "We are so winning this," I whisper to Jess. Her only reply is to cover her eyes with one hand and shake her head.

"Families ready!" Rick calls.

I crouch slightly, weight on my back foot, ready to spring forward when the word is given. Jess is in for the surprise of her life. We're going to win this thing.

We come in dead last. Although technically, I don't know if you're considered last if you have to stop in the middle of the course.

It started out so well, too. If not for those stupid rope vines, I'd be taking inventory of the spices. Instead, Payton is carrying the prize back to camp, and I'm having my ribs wrapped.

"I seriously doubt you fractured anything," Mr. Medic says. "But this will give you support and lessen the pain for the next few days."

When he's finished, I try to take a deep breath, but the bandage keeps my lungs from totally filling. "I feel like a sausage."

He pats my shoulder. "Great. Then I did it right." He looks next to me. "How's our other patient?"

"Peachy." Jess grumbles.

A female medic is at Jess's ankle, wrapping it up. "It's just a little sprain," she says. "You'll be fine."

"I'm so sorry, Jess."

She turns her head slowly and glares at me. "You promised you'd stay out of trouble."

"I tried." If I thought it would help, I'd go on about how having the rope obstacle right after the mud crawl was a really bad idea, and how it really wasn't my fault that I couldn't hold onto the rope with all that mud on my hands. Maybe, if everyone had fallen, that line of reasoning would help. But they didn't, so it won't. So I stop talking.

A shadow crosses in front of the sun as Rick walks up to the medic canopy.

"How are the two patients?"

"We'll live." Jess pushes herself up on her elbows and juts out her chin. "Rick, correct me if I'm wrong, but in the history of this show, I don't think anybody has managed to get hurt in every single challenge, have they?"

His lip twitches. "No. Monica here is a first." Then he looks at me and shakes a scolding finger. "It's a streak I hope you break soon."

"Yeah, before I break my body beyond repair." My other two injuries were painful and embarrassing, but this is the worst. Because this time, I took Jess down with me.

By the time Jess and I limp and hobble our way back to camp, everybody has adjourned to their regular places. Payton and his partner—I really need to find out her name—are off trying out the fishing equipment. The rest of the Singletons are grumpy and probably wishing they had the kind of alliance where people shared what they won. Back at the big shelter,

Malcolm is chopping a branch into fire-pit-size pieces while Layla and Jasmine are weaving together strips of something.

Malcolm notices us first. "The wounded warriors have returned."

I groan and collapse on the shelter floor. Jess limps past me and joins the other women.

"What are you guys making?" she asks.

Layla grins. "Blankets. Kinda." She goes on excitedly about how they decided to weave together palm fronds into large rectangles. "They won't be the same as real blankets, but they might help a little."

Jess nods. "Cool idea. Want help?"

As she joins the weaving bee, Malcolm leans the machete against the side of the shelter and sits next to me. "You're getting a reputation, you know."

My eyes narrow as I look at him. "Is that right?"

"They're starting to call you Hurricane Monica."

"Excuse me? In what way am I like a hurricane?"

He laughs. "Because you breeze in leaving a trail of destruction in your wake."

"Oh brother."

"Hey, I defend you." He raises his hands in surrender. "I remind folks that all the damage you've done has been to yourself."

I glance at Jess. "Until today."

He looks at her now, too. "She doesn't seem any worse for wear."

No, she doesn't. Laughing and chatting while she wrestles palm fronds into submission, she's once again settled into an easy camaraderie with someone other than me. And I really don't want to start talking about that, because if I do, I think I may cry.

"Where's Evelyn?"

Malcolm tilts his head, and I know he recognizes my desire to change the subject. Thankfully, he goes along with it. "She was so irritated about not winning the fishing equipment, she decided to make her own. She whittled a point on the end of a stick and went off to stab something."

"Uh oh. Payton better watch his back."

"I'm sure he can take care of himself." Malcolm stands and stretches. "Would you like me to take over dinner duty?"

"No, I'd still like to cook." So far, making a meal is my big contribution to our group. It's the one thing I've been able to do without hurting myself or others. "Do you mind?"

He dismisses my concern with a wave of his hand. "Not at all. I'd probably burn it if I tried. I just wasn't sure if you were up for it."

My side still hurts, but not nearly as much as it did when I hit the ground. Cooking—if you can call what I'm doing cooking—will help take my mind off of other things. Like how my daughter always finds a way to spend time with someone else and avoids talking to me.

A quick inventory of our food supply tells me it didn't magically multiply and diversify while I was gone. We still have three bags of beans, two bags of rice, six tubers, and two under-ripe bananas. It won't take long until all the beans and rice are gone. I wonder how long our happy, can-do team attitude will last once we're all starving to death?

"Monica."

I could have sworn someone just said my name, but nobody's looking at me. I'm about to go back to cooking when I hear it again.

"Monica!"

It's a hissing sound coming from the jungle growth on the edge of camp. I hiss back. "Who is it?"

"Payton. Come here."

What does Payton want? I struggle to my feet and walk toward the voice. There he is, on the other side of a palm tree, eyes darting back and forth as if he's an agent on a covert mission.

"We have to stop meeting like this." I hope he appreciates dry humor.

Whether he does or not is a mystery, because he ignores the joke and holds out a canvas bag. I start to open it, but he stops me.

"This is just because of the fire. And because I nearly gave you a concussion." With a sharp nod, her turns and walks into the jungle.

"Payton, wait!" He looks at me over his shoulder, and I feel silly for asking this, but it may be my only chance. "Who is your teammate?"

"My sister. Rhonda." And then he's gone.

I open the bag and laugh. Inside is one fish and a spice bottle labeled *garlic salt*. Well, what about that . . . I've always heard the way to a man's heart is through his stomach. Who knew fire has the same affect?

20

The next day is sunny and dry. The perfect day to send another family packing.

"Here you go." I join Jess on the edge of the shelter and hand her a canteen. "I filled it for you."

"Thanks." She sets it down beside her.

"How's the ankle?"

She straightens her leg and moves her foot from side to side. "Not bad. It still hurts some, but I'll be fine."

"Great."

She glances at my waist, but doesn't ask about my injury. Instead, she looks away from me. For a minute, I expect it to be like any other day when she acknowledges my presence, but doesn't interact beyond a surface level. But then she turns back, shoulders hunched, hands grasping the edge of the shelter floor.

"You're not married, are you?"

"I'm . . . um . . . no. I'm not married."

"Have you ever been?"

My cheeks are burning. It's no secret I wasn't married when I had her. Why else would I have given her away? Still, having this conversation, knowing it's being filmed and any part of it might show up on TV, makes me more than a little uncomfortable.

"Nope." I take a shot at being breezy. "Never have."

"Why?"

"No one ever asked." That's true, but there's more to it. No one ever asked because I never let any man get close enough for the question to come up.

"Not even my father?"

The shock of the question squeezes like a fist in my gut. I can't talk about Duncan. But I can't ignore her question, either.

"No," I say, unsuccessfully trying to keep my voice from shaking. "He never asked me, either."

Jess chews on her bottom lip, but before she can say anything else, someone calls out that we have pail mail. She hops down from the shelter, careful to land on her good foot, and heads to the pole where everyone is gathering.

My legs shake as I move to join them. The first personal thing she asks me, and it's about *him*. If I wasn't such a stupid, self-centered idiot, the question wouldn't have thrown me like it did. Of course she wants to know about her birth father. How could I think getting to know me was her only goal?

She'll ask me about him again. I know she will. And then what do I do? How can I tell her about her father, when I never told her father about her?

The closer we get to the challenge, the more I hope it's something really, really physical. Maybe something that involves running with scissors so I can put myself out of my misery once and for all.

No such luck. This particular challenge is about solving a series of puzzles, which makes it all about mental acuity.

Unless I think too hard and give myself an aneurism, chances are good I'll get through this one unscathed. Makes me think maybe the powers that be decided the medics were working too hard. So, since it appears I can't get myself a medical leave, I may as well do my best to keep us out of the bottom two.

I may not be good at untangling my personal life, but I'm pretty darn good at solving puzzles. Jess and I come in second, about a hair's breadth behind Bob and Tracy, whom I'm quickly coming to think of as our nemeses. Standing behind our last completed puzzle, I feel myself tense up as one after another, the Singletons finish their puzzles. Finally there are three teams left: Maxie and Marcy, Jasmine and Evelyn, and Malcolm and Layla.

And then, Maxie and Marcy complete their last puzzle.

"No way." Jess gasps through her hands, clenched into fists and pressed up against her mouth.

I know exactly how she feels. Tonight, people who've become friends will compete against each other, and another team in our alliance will be leaving.

The rain starts as we walk back to camp. By the time we reach our shelters, everyone is soaked through. There's no fire, no way to get dry, so we huddle together under our relatively watertight roof.

Arms wrapped around my knees, which are pulled up to my chest, I try to keep my teeth from chattering. My body starts to shake, but I don't think it's entirely from the cold. The longer I sit there, staring out at the pounding rain, the angrier I'm getting. Finally, I can't keep quiet anymore.

"How could this happen?"

"We're in the tropics," Evelyn says. "Rainstorms are the rule, not the exception."

I shake my head so hard that water flies from my hair. "No. I mean that the four of you have to compete against each other tonight. We're the good guys. We work together. Why are we dropping like flies?" Zeroing in on Malcolm, I expect him to have an answer. "Well?"

"Don't look at me," he says. "I rarely understand why things work out the way they do. I just trust that everything will work out. Eventually."

"At least you didn't hurt yourself today," Jasmine pipes up.

"Or anyone else," Jess mutters.

Jasmine nods. "That's a step in the right direction."

"If you say so."

Malcolm smiles. "There you go. Let's look at what's going right. No injuries. And we have a sturdy roof to keep off the rain."

Right then, as if to prove him wrong, the wind shifts. Now, the rain is blowing into the shelter. We look at each other, but no one has anything left to say. I lay my forehead on my knees and brace myself to wait out the storm.

When it's time to go from camp to the final challenge area, the rain has died down a bit, but it hasn't stopped. As we trudge over to the benches, I realize that the area is covered. For the first time in five hours, we're not being pelted. It's the only reason I can think of to be grateful for coming here tonight.

Rick takes his spot on the podium. His hair is dry. His clothes are dry. His fingers don't look like ten pale, wrinkled prunes. I just might hate him a teeny tiny bit.

He welcomes us, then announces the final challenge. Tonight, it really is building a fire. Jess and I look at each other. All four of them practiced with the flint, so they should be equally matched. But Evelyn is a former Scout. She's the type of woman who whittles herself a spear to go fishing. If I had to guess which one would get their fire going first, I'd pick her. As much as I like the sisters, I really want Malcolm and his daughter to win. Layla and Jess have formed a friendship, so I know she'd be sorry to see her go. And I enjoy Malcolm's company. Besides, if God really did put him here to give me support, he's not allowed to go anywhere.

The four of them take their places. Rick calls for the challenge to start. And it's over in about a minute.

Layla, the person who paid the least amount of attention during the fire-building lessons, managed to get a spark on her second try. Then she fed it just enough tinder and gave it just enough oxygen that it bursts into a nice, respectable flame.

Rick sends Layla and Malcolm to the stands, where Jess immediately grabs the other girl in a bear hug, and Malcolm sits beside me, his face a mix of emotions. Then Rick stands between Evelyn and Jasmine to deliver his signature good-bye.

"I'm sorry, but you will not be the last family standing. Grab your things and go."

Before they leave, the women turn to us and wave. Jasmine is stoic, keeping her composure. But Evelyn is visibly upset, the firelight bouncing off the tears running down her cheeks.

Rick looks at our group. "Fire means life, especially in the jungle. Today, fire saved one team's life in the game, and ended another's. Head on back to camp."

Walking back, I watch Jess and Layla, arm in arm, heads bent toward each other as they whisper about who knows what. If Layla had gone home tonight, would Jess talk to me instead? Would she link her arm through mine for moral support? Highly unlikely. It's good she has a friend here, but with competition heating up how long will it last?

I walk faster and catch up to Malcolm. "We have to make sure we beat the Singletons next time."

He looks down at me in surprise. "So you're serious about playing the game?"

"For Jess, yes." I point at our daughters. "Look at them. I want them to have that as long as possible."

"You know, they can still have that after the show is over. There's no reason they can't stay in touch and remain friends."

"I know that. But they need each other now." I look around to make sure no one else is close enough to hear me. "To be honest, I'd like to see your team and my team be the last ones standing at the end."

Slowly, he nods his head, as if chewing over what I just said. "I'd like that, too. But then we'll have to fight to beat each other. We wouldn't have a choice. How would you feel about that?"

"Not good, but it's the lesser of two evils."

"Ouch." He fakes a grimace. "You know, part of my job is convincing people to stay away from *all* evil, not how to choose one."

That makes me laugh out loud. "If you wanted to stay away from evil, you shouldn't have come on this game."

It's an exaggeration, of course. I don't think any of the Singletons are truly evil, but they haven't put their best selves forward to show the world. And the longer we're all here on this island, the uglier it's going to get.

The wind begins to gust, and Malcolm leans into it as we walk. "Tell you what. I promise to give my all to every challenge, and play with sportsmanship and integrity."

"Haven't you already been doing that?"

He hesitates. "Yes."

"Then I guess I can't ask for anything else. Thank you."

When I signed on for this game, I didn't care about the winner. All I cared about was being here for Jess. But now, it's become very important that the winner is someone who deserves it. I honestly don't care if it's my team or Malcolm's, just as long as none of the Singletons take home the title, or the big fat check that goes along with it.

21

For the next four challenges, I manage not to sustain or cause any injuries. And while Jess and I don't win, we don't lose the elimination challenges. Two more teams have left the island: Payton and Rhonda went first, followed by Maxie and Marcy.

It's our fifteenth day out here. My bumps, bruises, and scrapes have mostly healed, just in time for Island Ball, another challenge that promises to knock me off my feet.

There are four baskets, the kind used in basketball, one on each side of a square playing field. Instead of balls, we have coconuts. The idea is for each team to get the coconuts in their own basket, while stopping the other teams from getting them in theirs.

"If football and basketball had a baby, it would be Island Ball," Rick jokes. "First team to three wins. And . . . go!"

Jess and I have a definite disadvantage, since our team is the only one without a man. Bob, Trevor, and Malcolm barely have to do more than stand in front of the person they want to block to be effective. As Jess runs with the coconut, my job was supposed to be stopping Tracy or Wendy from making a basket. But when I see Bob barreling toward Jess, my objective changes. I may be smaller than the guys, but I'm a mama bear.

And when mama bear clicks into protection mode, everybody else in the jungle had better watch out.

Bob is right on Jess's heels when I charge into him at full run, catching him off guard. He goes down, and I go with him, attempting to do the shoulder tuck roll I learned in high school gym class a thousand years ago. Instead of tucking and rolling, I may have dislocated my shoulder.

"A nice tackle from Monica!" Rick is doing his announcer thing. He sounds impressed that I was able to take down Bob. Truth is, I'm kind proud of me, too.

Bob is just ticked. He scrambles up and glares at me. "What do you think you're doing?"

"Playing to win."

I stand up and rotate my shoulder, which is painful, but still in the socket. Then I run to the coconut basket on the opposite end of the field, grab another one, and meet Jess halfway.

Her look is a cross between shock and admiration. "Thanks for protecting my back. Let's go."

Oh, baby girl, I think as I run behind her, I've been trying to protect you since the day you were born

Now that Bob knows what I'm capable of, he's changed his tactics. Now he's going after Layla.

"Bad idea, Bob."

Ignoring the twinge in my side, I sprint toward him. Just as his hand reaches out to grab Layla's arm, I get hold of the back of his shirt and tug him off balance. He doesn't fall this time. Instead, he yells and turns on me. For a moment, I'm afraid he might hit me, but then Tracy starts screaming because Trevor is blocking her.

"This isn't over," he growls at me, then he runs off to help her.

Whatever. Where's Jess? I look toward our basket in time to see her send our second coconut through it. Good girl.

Running back to the basket, Malcolm is coming in my direction. As we get close, he winks and lifts one hand. We high-five each other without breaking stride. When I pick up the last coconut, I'm grinning like a fool. When it comes to sports, I've always preferred things like swimming, running, or horseback riding. Things I can do by myself, and only have myself to depend on, with the exception of the horse, but in my experience, they're pretty dependable. I've never been part of a team. This feeling that I'm an important part of a winning effort . . . it's very new, slightly odd, and completely wonderful.

Before I can reach Jess with the coconut tucked under my arm, I'm blocked by the twin wall that is Bob and Trevor. I'm thinking there's no way they would tackle a woman. Even though they're running straight at me, I expect them to stop short before they hit me, or run around me. But there comes a point when I realize they won't stop, because the whole point is to tackle me, and I have to do something to get this stupid coconut to Jess before they mow me down. So I throw the coconut over their heads.

Except my aim is really, really off.

The coconut nails Bob square on the forehead, then bounces off and rolls back to me. Bob goes down on his knees, holding his head and screaming some words I've only heard a few times in my life. Apparently afraid that I might do the same thing to him since I'm armed again, Trevor breaks right and runs away from me.

If Bob was seriously hurt, I'd stop and help. But if he's coherent enough to string all those words together, then I'm not that concerned. I run around him, toss the coconut to Jess, then watch as she makes the last basket with no interference whatsoever.

We won. We actually won something. The shock nearly knocks me over. When Jess runs up and throws her arms around me in excitement, I'm even more shocked.

"An amazing victory by Monica and Jess!" Even Rick is shocked.

"She cheated!" Tracy stalks past her father, who has stopped swearing but is still on his knees with a hand to his forehead. She stops in front of Rick, hands on her hips. "She threw a coconut at my dad. That's not fair."

"No, I didn't mean to. I was trying to throw it over his head."

Tracy throws her hand up in a dramatic gesture. "Now she's lying."

Rick moves closer to Jess and me, probably so the cameraman can get all four of us in the same shot. "When a play is in question, I'm the referee. And I'm confident that Monica didn't try to hit Bob. Her team wins."

Tracy stomps her foot and walks off in a huff, but she still doesn't go to her father. It makes me think her indignation is more an act for the camera than the result of genuine concern.

"Thank you," I say to Rick.

He grins. "No need to thank me. I call it as I see it."

"How can you be so sure she didn't mean to hit him?" Jess asks.

"Because if she did, I think she would have aimed for a different spot."

He walks away, laughing to himself. I'm pretty sure that's one sound bite that won't make it onto television.

Rick gets our attention, then motions us closer. "Everybody gather around. You probably want to know what Monica and Jess won."

Only Malcolm and Layla respond, but I notice even they aren't very enthusiastic. Uh oh.

Rick goes on. "The winning team is being taken by helicopter to a very special, picturesque spot on the other side of the island."

Jess gasps in shock. Groans come from the others.

"Once there, they can take a shower, get clean clothes, and feast on a barbecue dinner."

Even louder groans.

"But there's one more thing. To make the dinner a real event, we've chosen a special person from each of your lives and invited them here to join you."

Some swearing mixes with the groans, and even Malcolm and Layla are frowning. Everybody knows that the only way to have our special people here right now was to have everyone's people here. Which means that, somewhere in the jungle, their mothers or sisters or fathers or brothers or best friends or whoever, are being taken away from the challenge area. So close, but no way to see them. If I hadn't won the challenge, I'd be upset, too.

Rick ignores the dissent and speaks directly to Jess and me. "Are you ready to meet your guests?"

"Yes," we say together.

"Monica, we've brought you someone who's very close to you. The person who knows you better than just about anyone else. Here she is, your best friend, Julia."

I can't contain my squeal of joy as Jules bounds out of the jungle. We run to each other and simultaneously hug and jump up and down. "I can't believe you're here," I say.

"Neither can I. This is so cool!"

Jess is watching us, her look unreadable. She looks at Rick, waiting to find out who they brought for her.

Rick nods. "Jess, it wasn't easy, but we found a very special person for you. It's someone you've wanted to see for a long time. Here he is . . . Duncan McAllister, your birth father!"

All warmth flees my body. My face, chest, hands, feet, have all turned to ice. The foliage rustles, and out walks the biggest mistake of my life. He hasn't changed much in the last twenty-six years. Dark brown hair a little too long and hanging in waves that brush his shoulders, cheeks and jaws covered with a shadow of stubble, and eyes as dark and decadent as devil's food cake. A slow, easy smile lifts his familiar lips. If Jules wasn't right behind me, that smile would have knocked me over.

"How?"

That one, rasped word pulls me out of my self-centered daze. *Jessica*. Her eyes are huge, and her cheeks are totally drained of color.

"Turn off the cameras." I march up to Rick. "So help me, if you don't turn those things off right now, I'm going to start heaving coconuts."

Tracy jumps up and points at me. "See! I told you she did it on purpose."

"Knock it off, Tracy," Bob says, and my opinion of him goes up just a bit.

Rick's eyebrows draw together. "The cameras are always rolling. You know that."

"I don't care. How could you do this?" My eyes burn, my nose tingles. I'm so angry, my whole body buzzes with electricity. "How did you even find him?"

"Does that really matter now?"

"Of course it does. I never told anyone about him except . . ." My heart plummets to my toes. *Mother*. "Oh no."

Rick nods, a hint of sympathy in his eyes. "That's how we found out." He leans closer, and says so quietly that I almost don't hear him, "And that's why I made sure we got Jules here."

He did that for me? The warm fuzzy moment is fleeting. No matter how sweet a gesture it was to bring out my friend, they still brought Duncan here for the sole purpose of ratings.

"It's good ta see ya, Nikki." That Scottish brogue is as deep and charming as the first time I heard it.

"Duncan."

He looks from me to Jess. "This is your daughter, then?"

My throat closes up as the realization hits. They didn't tell him about her. He has no idea that he's a father, and *this* is the way he'll find out. No matter what happened between Duncan and me, he doesn't deserve this.

Jess looks at Rick. "I thought you said—" She walks up to me. "Is that man my father?"

"Father?" Duncan comes closer, joining our dysfunctional family tableau. "Am I her father, Nikki?"

"You didn't tell him?" Jess demands of Rick, then turns to Duncan. "Why did you think you were coming here?"

"They told me it was ta see Nikki."

I can see Jess working through the puzzle of information in her head. Then, as the last piece falls into place, she points at me. "And she never told you about me?"

Duncan shakes his head. "No, Love."

Rick puts a hand on my shoulder and I jump at the unexpected touch. "Monica, you might want to introduce them."

No, no, no. I don't want to introduce them. I want to go back in time and lose the challenge. I want to let Bob and Payton plow into me and destroy any chance we had of winning, because this is the worst prize ever. It's not even a prize, it's more like a punishment. But wishing for something that's impossible won't help. I can't put this off any longer.

"Duncan, this is my daughter, Jessica. And yes, she's your daughter, too."

"Jessica. A beautiful name for a beautiful lass."

Her dam of self-control crumbles and she sobs, and when Duncan opens his arms, she walks into them. He enfolds her, and she wraps her arms around his waist, clutching fistfuls of the back of his shirt. The sounds coming from her are muffled against his chest, and I can't tell if she's crying or talking. But one word comes through loud and clear.

"Dad."

22

It's my first time in a helicopter, and all I can think about is how unfair life is.

For the last two weeks, I've been hungry, uncomfortable, mosquito bitten, and usually waterlogged. All this in order to get to know Jess, even though she's mostly avoided any interaction with me beyond competing in the challenges. So it really raises my hackles that all Duncan has to do is show up, and the two of them are huddled together in the backseats, laughing and talking like long-lost friends.

Jules leans over and squeezes my knee. "Enjoy this," she yells over the noise of the rotors.

She's obviously taking her own advice, and I can't blame her. When will she ever again fly over a beautiful, tropical island in a private helicopter? When will I?

There's nothing I can do now about the situation with Duncan, so I try to concentrate on the scenery below. Living on the island, I hadn't truly grasped its beauty. From up here, the sea is clear and blue as a sapphire, the vegetation lush as emeralds. Jess's hearty laugh pulls me from my moment of nature appreciation. My heart is hard as granite, and I'm jealous of this easy relationship they've fallen into.

We land in a clearing on the other side of the island and are met by smiling natives dressed in colorful, traditional garb. Duncan and Jules are led in one direction, while Jess and I are taken in another. Jess looks over her shoulder, obviously not wanting to let Duncan out of her sight.

One of the women smiles and lays her hand gently between Jess's shoulder blades. "We will bring you back together for your meal. But first, you get clean."

We go around the corner, and there is one of the most fabulous things I've ever seen: two side-by-side showers. And not a camera in sight.

Thirty minutes later, we're being escorted to the dining area, and Jess can't stop touching her hair.

"It feels so good to be clean." She runs her fingers through her ponytail, which is hanging over her shoulder. Then she holds a piece of the hair to her nose. "And it smells so good."

Her enthusiasm is contagious. "My favorite thing was using the loofah. I think I exfoliated about a pound of dead skin."

"That too." She runs her hands up and down her arms. "You don't know how wonderful some things are until you don't have them."

"Or until you do."

She turns her head sharply, but doesn't respond.

We walk on, and the silence becomes heavier by the second. Finally, I can't take it anymore. "We're going to have to talk eventually, you know."

"I know."

What is Jess thinking? She's obviously hesitant to really open up and share her feelings. So why did she search me out in the first place? I was perfectly fine, living my quiet, normal life. I thought I was happy and well-adjusted. But she had to bring me here and shake me out of my denial. She had to show me how isolated and lonely I've really been, and that there's a hole in my life that won't be filled unless she's in it.

Maybe it's time for me to stop acting like a woman who wants to be her friend, and start acting like her mother. It's time for me to take the lead.

"He left before I knew about you."

She looks at me, confused. "What?"

"Duncan. Your father. We met at culinary school."

"He's a chef, too?"

I shrug. "I have no idea what he is now. But he was working toward that when we met. Anyway, he left the school before I knew I was pregnant. That's why I didn't tell him."

Our guide turns and walks backward for a moment. "We're almost there."

We both nod. The rest of this conversation will have to wait, but at least we've taken the first step.

When Rick said we'd be eating barbecue, I envisioned a rough-hewn picnic table and a gas grill. I never expected the gorgeous setting we walk into. There's a square table covered with a silk cloth and set with china plates and flatware. A canopy covers it so we'll be dry if it rains. And the whole thing is set up on a bluff, giving us an amazing view of the sun setting behind the ocean.

Duncan and Jules stand close by, talking and sipping on drinks with little umbrellas in them. Jules notices us first and raises her glass. "Hail the conquering heroes."

"I can't believe this." My fingers trail along the back of a chair, and I think how great it will be not to sit on the ground.

Two waiters come to the table to seat us and pour our water. As the ice clinks into our glasses, Jess lets out a sigh. "Ice."

"And look. A real fork." I hold one up as if I've discovered a sacred relic.

Duncan's eyebrows lift. "How long have you two been out here?"

"Two weeks," we say together.

More waiters come to the table now, carrying enough food to feed a small country. Platters of barbecued beef, chicken, and pork. Bowls of salad, fruit, roasted potatoes, and grilled vegetables. Baskets of rolls and plates of butter. The aroma of all these dishes is enough to make me slightly woozy. My stomach doesn't just growl, it barks, demanding to be fed.

Jules must have read my face, because she raises a hand in warning as I reach for a roll. "Pace yourself. If you eat too fast, all that food will just come right back up."

The first thing I bite into is a succulent beef rib, slathered in barbecue sauce. There's no way to hold back my groan of joy as my taste buds start doing a happy dance. Protein, how I've missed you.

Jules is eating with almost as much enthusiasm as if she'd been starving along with us the last two weeks. But she slows herself down long enough to make conversation. "Jess, I'd love to know more about your family."

Her mouth stuffed with bread, Jess looks at me and Duncan. "Which one?"

Jules chuckles. "I already know all about your birth mom, here. In fact, I could tell you some stories—"

"Don't you dare," I say, brandishing a rib bone.

"Killjoy." Jules looks from me back to Jess. "I want to know about your parents. You know, the ones who raised you."

If my fingers weren't coated with sticky, red barbecue sauce, I'd give Jules a big bear hug right now. Her choice of words was perfect, and being a fairly objective observer, she can ask the question I couldn't.

Jess blinks, swallows her mouthful of food, then smiles. "My parents are awesome." She stops, and her eyes dart in my direction.

This could go one of two ways: I could be hurt that she's so close to the people I gave her to. Or, I could be thrilled that she's so close to the people I gave her to. Until this moment, I honestly didn't know how I would react to hearing her talk about them. Maybe it's the fact that she seems to care how I feel right now, or maybe it's just because I'm in a state of euphoria from eating real food for the first time in fifteen days. Whatever the reason, the only emotion filling my heart is happiness.

I smile and encourage her to continue. "I'd love to hear more about them."

"Okay." She takes another scoop of potatoes, then sips her water before she talks. "My dad is an engineer. He specializes in designing bridges. And my mom was a photographer."

"Was?"

Jess hesitates. "She used to have her own studio, but now she's doing . . . other things."

"An engineer and a photographer." Jules is understandably impressed. "What a great combination of analytical skills and creativity."

Jess nods. "Mom says that's why I got into fashion design, because it requires both sides of your brain."

I'm still happy. Even though my smile feels like it's been carved in stone, I'm still happy. And why shouldn't I be? Her mother is a photographer. Imagine the amazing pictures they must have. Albums and albums full of Jess at every stage of life. And her parents have been such a positive force, they even influenced her career path. That's just great.

Duncan leans forward, elbows on the table. "You had a happy childhood, then? They treated you well?"

"Very well. Except for that pony I asked for every Christmas until I was nine but never got, my childhood was great."

"When did they tell you that you were adopted?" Jules asks.

Jessica's fork clatters onto her plate and she jumps from the table. "What? I'm adopted?"

All three of us look at her in shock. And then she starts laughing.

"Sorry, I couldn't resist. Oh man, you should see your faces." She sits back down and looks at Jules. "They never kept it a secret. But they officially told me the whole story when I was seven. That's when I found out who the woman in the picture was."

She's known about me for eighteen years. For some reason, that detail squeezes my heart. What does a seven-year-old girl do when she finds out her mother gave her away?

Again, Jules asks the question for me. "How did you feel when you found out?"

Jess shifts in her seat. "It really didn't change my life, you know? My parents were still my parents, they still loved me, I still loved them." She spears a potato with her fork, and it seems she's done talking. But she's not. "It wasn't until I hit my teens that I started thinking it was a big deal."

A big deal? Was that good or bad? I hold my breath, willing her to keep talking, but then the servers come back and clear away our dinner plates. They're followed by more servers, carrying trays of sweets: mini crème brûlée pots, thickly frosted brownies, fruit tarts, and an amazing variety of pastries.

"Oh goody. Dessert!" Jess claps her hands and, for just a second, I get a glimpse of the excited little girl she must have been.

This is the perfect time for chocolate.

As we're digging into the sweet treats, one of the native women comes to our table. "There is one more special surprise."

We all turn in the direction she points, and there's our surprise. Rick Wolff walks up, his 100-watt smile bracketed by dimples, wearing his trademark dark blue safari shirt, khaki pants, and shark's tooth necklace.

"Hello, family." He lifts his hand in greeting.

Beside me, Jules is trying to keep herself calm by digging her fingernails into my thigh. I lean over and whisper to her. "Relax. He's just a guy."

"Just a guy, my elbow," she says.

"And you're married."

She snorts. "I'm married, but I ain't dead. Besides, I'm just looking."

I laugh, because I know my best friend. Her husband has nothing to worry about.

Rick rests his fingertips against the edge of the table. "You're probably wondering why I'm here. Well, I have one more surprise for you."

Oh no. His last surprise was bringing Duncan out of the jungle. What's next?

"A reunion like this is too special to end in just a few hours."

Oh no, no, no.

"So Duncan and Julia will be going back to camp and playing the game with you until the elimination challenge."

NO!

"Yes!" Jules is obviously not in sync with me on this one. Neither are Duncan and Jess, who grin and lean across the table to high-five each other.

In the category of "worst-case scenarios" I'm sure something ranks higher than spending the next two days with the man who broke my heart while he bonds with our daughter. But nothing comes to mind. There's only one way to deal with this right now.

"Pass the brownies, please."

23

We cause quite a ruckus when we walk back into camp. Questions zing at us like arrows, and Jess and I struggle to answer all of them. After we explain that Rick sent two more people back to camp, and why, I put a stop to it all.

"Look, it's late and, miracle of miracles, it's not raining. Personally, I want to get some sleep while I'm still dry. We'll make introductions tomorrow."

As I head to the shelter, Jules is right beside me. "Wow, you've gotten downright forceful out here."

"What can I say? Living off the land changes a woman." Smiling, I nudge her shoulder with mine.

Malcolm and Layla meet us at the shelter. "Since we'll be bunking together, it might be good to make introductions now." He holds out his hand. "I'm Malcolm, and this is my daughter, Layla."

"Duncan. And you already know my daughter." He shakes Malcolm's hand, then Layla's.

Before Duncan can work any more of his charm on them, I step in and introduce Jules. Malcolm is polite to our guests, but I sense tension between him and me. He may be a pastor, but I imagine it's difficult to be loving and generous when you missed out on dinner and you've hardly eaten for two weeks. But I think I have a remedy for that.

"We brought you guys something." I hand him my bandana.

"What? Your laundry?"

"Open it and see."

To the casual observer, I wanted it to look like I held my bandana wadded up against my stomach. But really, it's carefully wrapped around a selection of goodies I smuggled from the dinner table.

As Malcolm opens the bundle, his eyes widen. Layla looks over his shoulder. When she sees what he's holding she squeals.

We shush her as a group, then look to make sure the remaining Singletons didn't notice.

"There was no way to bring enough for everybody," I whisper. "But I had to bring something to you two."

Malcolm's face softens, then he shocks me by bending down and kissing my cheek. "Thank you. You have no idea what this means."

"I know what it means. You're a saint." Layla grabs the food from her dad and sits on the edge of the shelter.

Shooing him away with a wave of my hand, I motion with my head toward Layla. "You better hurry up if you want to get some."

"You two seem close," Jules says after Malcolm moves away.

"We're just friends. Really, we've only known each other for a couple weeks."

Duncan moves closer, arms crossed loosely over his chest. "If I remember, Nikki, you only knew me for a few weeks before we—"

"Went to the beach. Yeah, I remember." Boy, do I. And I don't want him sharing the facts with the entire world.

Jules taps me on the shoulder. "Sorry to interrupt, but is there a latrine around here?"

"Sure. I'll show you."

As we walk away, I hear Jess say, "I'll fill you in on how we sleep, Dad."

The weight of her easy, casual acceptance of him presses down on me, hunching my shoulders and bowing my head.

"That's gotta be hard," Jules says.

"It is." We trudge along, and I want so badly to spill my guts. But the camera man trailing us is like a gag. Right before we get to the Porta-Potties, I turn to the man and wave my finger in front of the lens. "You stop here, my good fellow."

Without lowering the camera, he responds with a silent salute and holds his ground.

"Are those guys around all the time?" Jules asks as we go down a slight hill.

"Yep. And they've always got those heavy cameras on their shoulders. Makes me wonder how they walk straight once they put them down."

I give Jules a quick introduction to the island facilities. When she comes out, we pump sanitizing lotion from a jug onto our hands. But when she turns to go back, I stop her.

"I need to talk to you."

She looks around. "Here?"

"It's the only place where there aren't any cameras."

"Got it." With that, she plops down on the sand near one of the latrines and I drop beside her.

Being with someone I trust, out here where there are no cameras, has stripped away the protective armor I didn't even know I'd been wearing. Suddenly, my heart is exposed, my nerves raw, and every emotion I've felt for the last fifteen days is magnified a thousand times. I wrap my arms around my drawn up legs, drop my forehead against my knees, and sob.

Jules lays her arm across my shoulder. The weight of it is comforting, assuring me I'm not alone. But she doesn't say a word. She lets me cry until there are no tears left.

Finally, I lift my head and swipe the back of my hand across my eyes. "I'm such a mess."

"Yes, you are," she agrees. "But you're entitled. This is a pretty intense situation."

Intense doesn't begin to describe it. "I don't understand how she could bond so quickly with Duncan. She only talks to me when she has to, but they're getting on like old buddies."

"Maybe she empathizes because neither of them had any say about the adoption."

"I hadn't thought about it like that." Of course, she's right. Jess probably would have reacted differently to Duncan if he'd been involved in the decision to give her up. But he never knew about her, which makes him blameless in her eyes.

I stare out at the dark, rhythmic dance of the ocean. Moonlight glints off the waves as they creep up the beach, wet fingers clutching the sand, trying to dig in and rest, but they lose the battle. Some greater force pulls them back, returning them to the sea, until the next time they try and make their escape. The ways of nature are a mystery to me, much like the relationship between a mother and a daughter.

"I don't know what to do," I say. "I want to talk, answer her questions, find out who she is. But now *he's* here."

"Only for two days."

"Two days too long. Jules, what am I going to do?" I let myself fall backward so I'm lying face up on the sand, staring at a velvet black, bedazzled sky. So much beauty being wasted on me.

"All you can do is take each day as it comes. Right now, she's got two days with her birth father. Let her have that. When he goes, then you'll be there to step in and fill the hole."

"I hope so."

"Don't worry. Everything will work out the way it's supposed to." She lies back, too, and sighs. "You don't see stars like this in Vegas. And so many birds out flying at night."

"Those are bats," I say in the casual way of someone who's become accustomed to them.

"Really?" Jules pushes up on her elbows, as if doing so will give her a better view. "Cool."

I laugh. "That's why you do so well in a house full of males. You appreciate stuff like that."

She nods. "God puts us where we need to be."

"Do you really believe that?"

"Oh sure. Sometimes it takes us awhile to get there, but most people do."

"And what about the people who don't?"

Jules laughs and sits up all the way. "If I knew that, I'd be God, and we *know* that's not the case." She stands up and brushes sand from the back of her jeans. "We should get back before they send out a search party."

"You have no idea how true that is." I scramble to my feet. "A few days ago, Trevor went missing. It caused quite a stir."

"But he was here?"

"Yep." Leaning close, I whisper in her ear, even though no one's around. "He must've gotten a bad piece of fish or something."

It's funny how easy it is to find humor in someone else's gastrointestinal distress. But as we walk back to camp, laughing and holding our sides, I'm thankful for that bad piece of fish and whatever else can take my mind off my own troubles.

I wake up on one side of the shelter. Jules is next to me, Layla and Malcolm are in the middle, with Duncan and Jess on the other side. When it came time to figure out who slept where last night, I made no secret about wanting to be as far away from Duncan as possible. And Jess made it clear that she was stuck to her father like sap on a windshield.

No one else is moving, so I head to the beach for a morning walk. Since we don't have access to any watches or clocks, I have no idea what time it is. The sun is still low, bathing the sky in golden hues. Just for fun, I've brought along Evelyn's fishing spear. Just in case.

My hope is that things will look different in the light of a new day. But they don't. What I need is advice from an unbiased observer. Maybe that's why I find myself walking up to the confessional.

There's a man at the camera today, but Ponytail is there, and I wonder if she's ever allowed to do anything else.

"Welcome back. Have a seat."

By now, I know better than to try to make myself comfortable. I just settle on the log and set down the spear.

"So what's new with you?" Ponytail asks.

"Oh, let's see . . . We're at the midway point of the game. My daughter still isn't talking to me much, and I'm being forced to socialize with the last man on earth I wanted to see. So, peachy."

She smiles. "You're a lot more open now, too."

I raise my hands in a shrug. "What can I say? I finally realized it was stupid to fight the system. The cameras are here, and if I want to build any kind of a relationship with my daughter, I'm going to have to talk in front of them."

"That's a good outlook. Do you want to talk about Duncan?"

"No." I purse my lips together and take a deep breath. "You know what really bothers me? The way he acts like the poor, injured party."

"He did just find out he has a grown daughter. That must have been a shock."

A sharp laugh bursts through my lips. "You want to talk about being shocked? Try finding out you're pregnant three weeks after the man you're in love with has left the country without telling you. He never knew about Jessica because I couldn't tell him. I had no idea where he was or how to get in touch with him."

Her eyes narrow, and for a second, I know Ponytail is empathizing. Then she regains her professional demeanor. "Is it awkward being around him now?"

"I really don't care about him one way or the other. What I care about is how he treats Jessica." I wave a hand in the air like I'm erasing a huge whiteboard. "Not that he isn't treating her well now. They're getting along great. But what happens when he just disappears from her life?"

"Like he did with you?" Ponytail asks quietly.

A fat, black beetle crawls across the log toward my thigh. A few weeks ago, the sight of it would have sent me screaming into the jungle, but now I flick it away with my fingernail, then smile at Ponytail. "Are you a psychologist?"

Her ponytail sways as she shakes her head. "We're talking about you, not me."

Well, it was worth a try. "I'm concerned that she'll get used to having him in her life, and then he'll disappear."

There it is. Besides the fact that I'm jealous of the time she's spending with him, this is what bothers me the most. That, as Ponytail said, he'll hurt her just like he hurt me.

The two-way radio clipped to her belt crackles. She pulls it off, presses a button on the side, and talks into it. "Go ahead."

A garbled voice, worse than what you'd hear from a drive through speaker, talks back, but I can't make out a word of what it says.

Radio still in her hand, Ponytail points with the antennae toward camp. "You'd better head back. They've already read the pail mail."

With a nod, I stand up, grab my spear, and leave the area. I decide to take the long way so I can walk along the beach a little more. It's a decision I quickly regret when I see Duncan hunkered down in the sand, letting the waves break around his legs.

I consider turning around and going the other way, but he notices me before I can. He rises, wiping his hands quickly on the sides of his cargo shorts, and stands in front of me. My fingers tighten around the long, sharp piece of wood I'm carrying.

"Good morning to ya, Nikki."

I ignore the smile and the crinkle of his eyes. And I ignore the pleasant greeting. "Don't call me Nikki."

"Sorry, Love. I can't think of you as anyone but Nikki."

"Then just don't think of me at all. You're good at that." I try to walk around him, but he reaches out and grabs my arm.

"Wait just a minute. Are ya saying ya don't think I've thought about ya in all these years?"

"That's exactly what I'm saying."

He looks down at the sand and slowly shakes his head. "Ya couldn't be more wrong, Nikki."

I wish he'd quit calling me that. It brings up too many memories, especially when he says it in that soft, drawn out way, like a gooey piece of caramel stretched between his fingers and his mouth.

"You left me. One day you were just gone. No explanation, no forwarding address, nothing."

His other hand reaches out, and now he's holding me by my upper arms and pulling me disturbingly close. "I had ta leave, but I didn't want ta. Ya have ta believe that."

"I don't have to believe anything you say." If I was smart, I'd poke him with the spear to make him let go, then I'd run off. But if I've established anything in the last few weeks, it's that I'm not always bright about things like this. "Fine. If you're telling the truth, then why did you leave? Why did you have to go?"

His eyes narrow. "It's complicated, Love."

Of course it is. "We need to get back for the next challenge. Please let go of me."

He does as I ask, and as I walk away, he calls after me. "I deserved to know about her."

I spin around so quickly, sand flies from under my feet. "You're right. You did deserve to know about her. But I didn't know where you were." I poke him hard in the chest with my finger. "I was alone and pregnant, so I dealt with it by myself."

There's a split second when his eyes change from angry to intense, and the muscles around his mouth soften, when I realize what's coming. But before I can stop it, he brackets my face between his palms, swoops down, and kisses me.

Thank God I have my stick. I hit the side of it hard against the back of his leg.

He yelps and jumps back. "What was that for?"

"What do you think?" I wipe the back of my hand hard across my lips.

The sincere confusion that comes over him is almost funny. "But I thought . . . You were so . . ."

Rolling my eyes like a teenager, I step back, putting more space between us. "I was angry, not turned on. You big dope."

I stomp away, but then another thought hits me. Turning again, I advance, spear at the ready, pointed straight at him.

"And if you ever, *ever* do anything to hurt Jessica, I will track you down and use this thing. Do you understand?"

From the twitching of his lips, I'm sure he's holding back a smile, but he has the good graces to at offer me a semi-serious look. "I understand perfectly. And I would never do anything ta hurt her."

"Good. Let's go." Feeling more pleased with myself than I have in a long time, I turn toward camp. "We've got a challenge to win."

24

Several eyebrows shoot up when Duncan and I walk back into camp together, but I don't bothering explaining. If anybody wants to know what happened, they can just watch it on television.

"What did the pail mail say?" I ask, dropping to the edge of the shelter.

Malcolm abandons the firewood he was chopping and sits beside me. "We've got an elimination challenge today." He slouches a little, leaning his head down so he can whisper. "Are you all right?"

I nod quickly, then move on. "Has anyone made breakfast?"

"There's a little problem with breakfast. We're out of food."

"Oh yeah." I forgot that I'd cooked the last of the beans two days ago, and after making breakfast yesterday, there was only a little rice left. Malcolm and Layla must have made it for dinner last night.

"We're not totally out of food." Layla walks forward with three rolls and a bunch of grapes. "I saved these from last night."

"Smart girl." I smile at her. "Looks like we'll have a continental breakfast today."

As we tear the rolls in half and split up the grapes, Malcolm chuckles. "This reminds me of the story in the Bible, where Jesus fed the crowd with the loaves and fishes."

"I wouldn't mind if He decided to multiply our food," Layla says.

The two of them joke about how Jesus also turned water into wine, so it would be great if he'd turn our grapes into medium rare steaks. Our food doesn't multiply, but as I pop a still-grape grape in my mouth, I send up a little prayer of thanks for what we do have.

About an hour later, we're tromping into the challenge area. Rick is already there. He looks at our group a little more intently than usual, probably wondering how many juicy sound bites Duncan and I have provided so far.

Most of the time, we can get a pretty good idea of what the challenge involves by looking at the playing area. But this time, there's nothing set up except a two-tiered set of benches, similar to the one in the final play area. The contestants are told to sit, while Jules and Duncan sit on a smaller bench near Rick.

"In honor of our special guests, today's competition is all about the relationships you've made on the island, and how well you know each other."

Jess and I look at each other. We may not know each other that well, but we've spent a lot of time talking to, or about, the others. There's a very good chance we can stay out of the bottom two.

Each team is given a dry erase marker and a small whiteboard with three tall sides around it to prevent cheating. "The game ends when a team reaches five correct answers. At that point, the two teams with the least number of points will be up for elimination tonight. In case of a tie, we'll play a sudden death round. Everybody ready?"

The game is harder than it sounds. Rick poses questions about everyone who played this season, not just those of us who are left. Jess and I know that Evelyn is the older of the two sisters and Malcolm is a pastor. We correctly guess that Maxie held the title Ms. Mega Muscle 1992. We have no clue that Bob is a physicist, Sal spent three years working in a malaria clinic in Africa, or that Payton spends his weekends teaching contemporary jazz at his local community center. Of course, we were all surprised about that last one.

After a few more questions, the score is close. Jess and I have four points, as does Bob's team. Malcolm and Trevor's teams each have three points.

"Next question," Rick says. "What was the name of Payton's teammate?"

It's obvious from the panic in Jess's eyes that she doesn't know. From the way the other teams are looking at each other, I don't think they know, either. That woman was so quiet, it's unlikely she offered up her name, and nobody had a reason to ask. Except me.

I start to write her name down, then stop. If I get this right, the game is over. Which means Malcolm and Trevor will be in the bottom two. If I throw this question, and we all get it wrong, that would give Malcolm a chance to get the next question right. But that could backfire, too.

"Five seconds," Rick says.

Jess elbows me. "Write something down!"

I scrawl a name, finishing just when Rick orders pens down. Then he tells us to show our answers. "Rhonda is the correct answer." He points at me. "Monica and Jess win with five points, and this challenge is over. Malcolm and Layla, Trevor and Wendy, you will fight for your lives tonight. See you then."

My odd foursome brings up the rear as we leave the area. I purposely lag behind, hoping to get a second with Rick. He's got some explaining to do.

But when I get close to him, he stops me before I can stop him.

"Monica, a word."

"Oh, I've got a word for you. Several, in fact."

He frowns, his forehead creasing up in that way it does when he concentrates. "Is Duncan behaving himself?"

"It's a little late to ask me that now, don't you think? Maybe we should have had this conversation, oh, I don't know . . . *before* you tracked him down and plopped him on an island with me!"

"I know you won't believe this, but I didn't have anything to do with him coming here." Rick rubs the back of his neck as he braces for my reaction.

"You're right. I don't believe you. This is your show. You know about everything that goes on. You're like the captain of the ship. Everything that happens is your responsibility."

He holds up his hand to bring a stop to my verbal landslide. "That's not entirely true. We have a whole team of writers and game technicians. Their job is to come up with new twists for the show. I think they came up with this one while you and I were on our way here in the jet."

I haven't known Rick all that long, but I've come to like him. So I really want to believe he's telling me the truth. But how can I? People lie to each other all the time in this game. Why should the host be any different?

"I'm sure you'll get great ratings, just like you wanted."

Before I can walk away in my intended huff, he catches my wrist. "I don't care about the ratings."

My heart sinks and I jerk my arm away from him. "Now I know you're lying. See you at the elimination."

This time, he doesn't stop me.

———

The mood around camp is somber, just like it always is before an elimination. Not even the ebullience of Jules and Duncan is enough to lift the spirits. Most of them, anyway. Jess is the exception, sitting near the fire with her father, chattering away.

Jules welcomes me back with a hug. "What was all that about?"

"He wanted to make it clear that he had nothing to do with bringing Duncan here."

"Do you believe him?"

"No," I say with a snort of derision. "Do you?"

She shrugs her shoulders. "What reason does he have to lie?"

"I don't know. To raise my opinion of him."

"But why does that matter? He doesn't usually give a flying fig whether or not the contestants like him."

"Maybe he wants me to join his Wolff Pack." Oops. That was the wrong thing to say.

Jules's eyes grow wide, and her smile grows to match. "You've been paying attention to his personal life, huh? Do I sense a budding romance?"

"Sh!" I swat her playfully on the shoulder while I look around for the steady-cam guys. I don't see any, but that doesn't mean they're not close by. "There's nothing romantic going on between us. Are you crazy?"

"What's crazy about it? He's single. You're single." She laughs and shakes her head. "I mean, you are really, *really* single. An innocent attraction might do you some good."

I cock my head to the side and stare at her. "Who are you, and what have you done with my best friend? There could never be anything innocent about any kind of relationship with Rick. You know his reputation."

She nods half-heartedly. "Sure. And I also know you can't always believe a reputation, even when it's plastered all over the entertainment super highway."

"Well, I'm not interested in Rick any more than I'm interested in Duncan." Her eyes get big again, so I shut her down before she can take us down this new dead-end street. "And I am absolutely, positively *not* interested in Duncan. Not in any way, shape, or form. Got it?"

"Got it."

"Good."

A rustling in the bushes on the edge of our clearing draws my attention. I don't see anything, but I'm pretty sure I hear a sound that doesn't belong in the tropics.

"Did you hear that?" I whisper.

"Hear what?"

"Clucking."

She leans away and looks down at me. "You think you hear a chicken?"

"It finally happened. I'm hearing things. Next thing you know, I'll start seeing things."

Jules tugs on the sleeve of my t-shirt and points. "You mean, like that?"

A fat chicken with black and white feathers struts its way into camp. I hear the rustling again, and a brown chicken scurries out from the bushes. Without taking my eyes off it, I call out to the others. "Hey, guys. If we work this right, we may have dinner."

One sure way to cause pandemonium in a camp full of half-starved people is to point out the existence of poultry. It's a mad dash as we try to keep the chickens from disappearing into the jungle at the same time we try to catch them.

The possibility of fresh meat has also broken down the wall of separation between us and the Singletons. Trevor, Bob, Tracy, Duncan, and I are chasing the brown chicken. Wendy, Layla, Jess, Malcolm, and Jules are stalking the other one. You'd think these foul would be no match for ten full-grown, intelligent, hungry adults. But the birds are wily, and I'm pretty sure we look like total idiots chasing them.

"Around that way!" Bob yells, pointing at a gap in our perimeter.

I fill in the space, and we move in closer. The chicken is dodging like a prizefighter, its head bobbing and turning, little clawed feet moving so fast they're almost a blur. Then it stops, and I could swear it looks me dead in the eye. Right then, I know exactly what it plans to do. It's as if I've been given the gift, just for a moment, to see into its itty-bitty peanut of a brain.

It's going to make a run for it.

I dive at the bird. From the corner of my eye I see movement. My fingers close around feathers. The chicken squawks as I roll onto my back, clutching it to my chest like a football. The next moment the wind is forced out of my lungs as a heavy weight lands on top of me.

Duncan looks down at me, his chocolate eyes narrowed with concern. "I'm sorry, Nikki. Are ya okay?"

"Chicken," I gasp.

Trevor squats down next to us. "It's kind of squashed between the two of you." He reaches to pull it away, then laughs. "You might want to let go now."

I relax my fingers and he extracts the bird, which is oddly calm. Bob takes a step closer. "Well, we don't have to worry about someone ringing its neck."

"We killed a chicken," I whisper.

Duncan smiles. "That was the idea, Love."

What is he doing stretched out on top of me? "Don't call me 'Love.' And get off."

"I call everyone 'Love.' And I'm sorry about tackling ya." He stands up and extends a hand, helping me to my feet. "Guess we both had the same idea. Ya were just a wee bit faster."

"Lucky me."

On the other side of camp, a shout goes up. They got their chicken, too. I feel my ribs, which thankfully don't seem to be broken, and look at the men. "Would you be game for having a meal together?"

Bob grins. "If it means you'll do the cooking? Sure."

Walking over to our side of camp, I smile to myself. Yeah, I'll do the cooking, but wait till they find out who has to pluck and clean these birds first.

25

This is the best chicken ever." Trevor moans as he licks his fingers.

It's really not that good. He's just been influenced by two weeks of very small portions of very boring food.

"Thank you for pitching in with the leftover spices." I salute him with a drumstick.

"And thank the good Lord for providing the meat," Malcolm adds.

I have a sneaking suspicion the chickens are another one of those game twists Rick was talking about. But considering what a good surprise they turned into, I definitely think there was some divine guidance behind it.

"What do you think, Jess?" Jules asks. "Can your mom cook or what?"

Jess looks up slowly. "What? Oh, yeah. Great chicken." She wiggles her hips and scoots closer to Duncan, then leans her cheek against his shoulder. Without hesitation, he plants a kiss on top of her head.

My chest tightens. She's been more quiet than usual, and now I know why. Such a sweet, normal, father/daughter moment, and it's about to come to an end. He's leaving tonight, and who knows when, or if, they'll see each other again?

I think about the two of them as we clean up. I should be thinking about Malcolm and Layla as we walk to the final challenge area, but I'm not. Once more, I'm behind Jess and her dad, a friendly stalker taking in every move, word, and glance they exchange. Duncan's arm lies casually across her shoulders, and her arm snakes tightly around his waist.

"I'm going ta give all my contact information to Julia," he tells Jess. "Phone, email, address, everything. If ya need anything, ya call me. If ya don't need anything, I'd still love ta have ya call."

Jess nods. "Thanks." Her voice quivers, and I'm pretty sure she's crying.

Maybe Jules was right. Jess obviously needed this time with Duncan. I should be happy for them both. And tomorrow, when he's gone, perhaps she'll be more open to me.

When we're sitting on the benches and the other two teams stand in the middle of the playing area, Rick comes out to announce the challenge. It involves balancing cups, plates, and saucers on the end of a thin, flat stick. The first team to have both its members drop their plates is the loser.

As challenges go, this is the most nerve-wracking one yet. It doesn't take long before sweat is rolling down their faces as they concentrate on balancing their tower of plates. I look over at Jess, who is sandwiched between Duncan and me. She bites her lip and leans forward, as if willing her friends to keep their sticks steady. Then Rick goes into motivational mode.

"Focus on what you're doing. Those sticks are getting heavy. The heavier they are, the more fatigued your muscles become. Hold them steady."

Wendy blinks rapidly, as if she has something in her eye. Then she gives her head a hard shake, which also shakes her stick, and her plates come crashing down.

"Wendy is out," Rick says. "Now it's down to three."

They add another plate, then another cup. They must have close to two feet of dishes balanced on those sticks, which is too much for Layla. One sharp jerk of her bicep, and the whole thing teeters and falls.

Rick nods as Layla walks away. "It's down to Trevor and Malcolm."

Trevor's eyes dart toward Malcolm, but Malcolm doesn't take his eye off his stack. The man is fully in the zone.

Another plate joins the tower. Then another cup, and then, the last saucer.

"There are no more dishes to stack," Rick says. "Now it's a matter of endurance."

Twenty minutes later, both men are still balancing their dishes. Every now and then, one will have a slight wobble. But they always recover.

"How long do you think they can keep this up?" Jules whispers.

I shake my head. "No idea."

If it were me, I'd be out by now. But those two aren't giving up.

A growl comes out of Trevor. Without looking at anybody, he says, "Cramp."

From where we are, you can see the knot forming in his arm. Just looking at it is painful. Jess sucks in a deep breath, then squeezes the spot on my leg just above the knee. Apparently, being on the edge of her seat makes her forget that she doesn't want to interact with me.

"Come on, Malcolm," she whispers.

Another guttural noise comes from Trevor, his arm shakes violently, and the dishes slide off.

"We have a winner!"

The moment Rick makes the pronouncement, Malcolm lets go of the stick and flexes his arm. He steps to Trevor and shakes his hand. "Good game, man." He makes his way to the benches, kneading the muscle in his arm as he goes.

Rick joins Trevor and calls Wendy back up. "Trevor, Wendy, you won't be the last family standing. Grab your things and go."

They wave, then walk away. Rick turns to us, and I feel Jess stiffen next to me. "And now, it's time to say good-bye to our special guests." He smiles, and it's one of what I'm starting to think of as his "real" smiles, not the kind he pastes on for the camera. "Take a few minutes to say good-bye."

We jump up and I wrap Jules in my arms. "I don't want you to go."

"It's not forever." She squeezes me tight. "Just think of all the coffee stories you'll have to tell me when you get back."

"I'm glad you were here for a little while."

Duncan and Jess hug quietly, gently, then separate. She moves to Jules, which means there's only one good-bye left to be said.

I extend my hand. "Good-bye, Duncan."

His lip quirks up as his brows draw down. "Oh no, Nikki. Not a handshake."

He pulls me into a hug, and this time, I let him. "It was good to see you again, Duncan." The surprise is that I really do mean it.

"Ya just remember, call me anytime. For anything. Will ya remember, Love?"

Taking a step back, I nod. "I'll remember." Though I doubt I will ever take him up on it.

Rick claps his hands. "Duncan, Julia, I'm afraid your time on the island is up."

They wave to everybody as they walk toward the steps that will lead them out of the play area.

"Wait!"

Jess runs to Duncan and hugs him so tightly, he just might have bruises tomorrow. "I'm glad I met you."

He lays his cheek on top of her head and sways with her. "Ya have no idea what it means to me, knowing ya exist." After one more squeeze, he pushes her gently at arm's length. "Now, ya go win this with your mother. All right?"

She nods and comes back to the benches, arms crossed, hands clutching her sides as if she's hugging herself. I want to reach out to her, finish the hug that Duncan started, but she won't have any of it. She stands beside me, but not close enough to touch. She doesn't even look at me.

But Rick does. And for a second, I think he really understands how much this hurts. With a blink, that understanding is gone, and he's once again the impartial host of the show.

"Three families are left, but only one will still be standing at the end. Head on back to camp."

Jess turns to Layla for comfort, and they stay close together all the way back to camp. A hand pats me on the shoulder. I turn, expecting to see Malcolm, but I get a surprise.

"Bob."

Our resident physicist walks beside me. "I owe you an apology."

"For what?" There are so many things . . . I need clarification.

"For being a jerk. When we first got here, I was jealous, so I acted pretty badly."

He has almost shocked me speechless. Almost. "Jealous of what? My innate klutziness?"

"No," he says with a laugh. "Of the relationship you have with your daughter."

Okay, that stops me dead in my tracks. "You do know our backstory, don't you?"

"I do. But you still have a better relationship than I have with Tracy." He sighs, and we start walking again. "You and Jess may not be best friends, but at least she respects you. She doesn't put you down and call you names."

No. Instead, she doesn't talk to me at all. But I get his point. "Has it always been like this between you two?"

He shrugs. "More or less. Her mom and I divorced when she was six. She got custody, and I had the typical every-other-weekend visitation. It didn't take long to figure out my ex was using Tracy as a way to vent all her frustration at me."

"I'm sorry. That must have been awful."

We walk in silence, until I have to ask a question. "How did the two of you end up on the show? I mean, considering her feelings, I'm surprised she asked you."

"She didn't. I asked her." Bob puts his head down and stuffs one hand in the pocket of his shorts. "She loves this show. So I applied. And when we were chosen, I told her if we won, she could have all the prize money."

"So you bribed her."

"You could say that." He frowns. "Do you think that was a bad idea?"

I wave a hand between us. "Hey, I'm not one to give parenting advice."

"But you do have an opinion."

"Well . . . . my opinion is that handing over a big wad of money will probably backfire. What you really need to do is spend time together and talk about your relationship. Which, I know, is easier said than done."

"It is."

Back at camp, we go our separate ways. But I call out to stop him.

"Thanks," I say.

He smiles. "You too."

Looking up at the moon, the stars, and the bats, I can't help but think how amazing God is. Whether it's something big, like the moon controlling the tide, or something small, like an apology at just the right time, He knows what we need.

If only He'd share some of that knowledge with me. Because right now, I know what I want, but what I need is a total mystery.

26

There is no challenge the next day. The pail is empty, which means we can do anything we like.

It appears Bob's apology last night was an indication of a total attitude reversal. He invites Malcolm to try out the fishing gear, and I hear them laughing as they head down to the water.

Layla scoots off the shelter and stretches her arms over her head. "Guess I'll try to strike up a conversation with Tracy."

She saunters off, leaving Jess and me alone. This is as good a time as any to do some laundry.

Because our clothes get so dirty, and we have so few of them, we've taken to washing them in a pot over the fire. The term *washing* is used loosely, because we have no soap. It's just stirring clothes in near-boiling water with a stick. When I'm done, I lay my semi-clean clothes over the bushes to dry, putting my four pairs of underwear in a spot where I hope the camera will miss them.

Over at the shelter, Jess is curled into a ball on the floor with her back pressed into the corner. I know she's in a funk. Maybe this is our time, the window during which we can have the heart-to-heart I've been waiting for. But where to start?

"Looks like it might rain." I cringe at my inane conversation starter.

An affirmative grunt comes from the corner.

"I'm going to get some water. Before it rains." Could I sound any lamer? But I push on. "Do you want to come with?"

She lets out a long, low sigh as she slowly sits up. "Sure."

We grab our canteens and head down the path to the fresh water station. Desperate to fill the silence, I fall back on trivia. "You know, they used to make contestants get water from a well, but after a few nasty cases of dysentery, they decided it was safer to provide clean water."

"I know."

I laugh nervously. Of course she knows. After all, Jess is the one who got us here. She's probably been watching the show for years.

A twig snaps behind us, reminding me of the ever-present camera operators who trail our every move. As much as I don't want to have my conversation recorded, I can't let that stop me. This may be the only time Jess and I are alone. Maybe, if I make normal, casual small talk, it will lead to something else.

"I didn't realize how much I missed home until I saw Jules. We live on the same block, so her family is dog sitting for me. Man, I really miss Ranger."

Jess freezes in place, and turns her toward me so slowly, it reminds me of a scene from a horror movie. "Your dog? You miss your *dog*?"

What did I say now? "Well, yeah. He's very lovable."

"Unbelievable."

This is the most emotion Jess has displayed with me. Her hands clenched into fists at her sides, eyes narrowed into angry slits, her entire body is a compressed mass of negative energy. And she's about to blow.

"Jess, I'm sorry. I don't know what I did, but—"

"I'll tell you what you did." She steps closer, and her voice grows louder with each word. "You gave your child away and never gave her a second thought all these years. But after sixteen *days*, you miss your dog."

Her words sting as much as if she'd slapped me across the face. "That's not fair. You have no idea what I went through."

"No, I don't. Because you never told me. You never tried to find me. You just handed me off like the mistake I was."

"It wasn't like that at all." There has to be a rational way to explain this to her so she'll understand, but my heart is such a tangled mess of emotions, my head can't think straight. "I did what I thought was best for you."

She huffs out a breath. "Sure you did. And I'll bet you've thought about me every minute of every day for the last twenty-five years."

"Of course not." The truth spills out, shocking both of us. "That didn't come out right."

Her hands go up, palms facing me, as if erecting a force field between us. "No, it came out loud and clear. This whole thing was a big mistake. I never should have asked them to find you."

Heat ignites my cheeks. "Why did you want me here? If you're so sure I'm such a horrible person, why would you want to meet me?"

The force field drops. The iron set of her jaw loosens. The stony glare of her eyes softens and the tears begin to fall. "Because you're my mother."

There it is. The irrefutable tie between us that can't be denied, no matter how much time has passed. I step forward, arms open, wanting nothing more than to comfort her.

"No." She backs away, shaking her head wildly. "You don't get to do that. You may be my mother, but you'll never be my mom."

I watch her running toward camp, growing smaller and smaller, until finally, she rounds a corner and she's gone. What do I do now? She doesn't want to have anything to do with me, and I don't blame her. When it comes to Jessica, all I do is make one mistake after the other. Now, for once, I'm going to try to give her what she wants.

Just like Jess, I run. But in the opposite direction.

I run from my failures.

I run from my pain.

I run from the daughter who deserves so much more than me.

The jungle darkens as clouds obscure the sun. Behind me, a male voice calls out.

"Monica! Stop!"

I keep running. Even when the sky opens and the rain pours down, forcing its way through the thick growth, I run.

I run until I break out of the trees and there's nowhere left to go. I stop short on the edge of a precipice, about six feet up. Then, as I stand there gulping in air, the rain soaked ground gives way beneath my feet.

"I knew you wouldn't make it to the end of the show without another injury."

That familiar male voice floats into my aching head. Slowly, I open my eyes. "Hey, Bruce."

"Hey, yourself." Despite his casual attitude, I can tell he's concerned. "Can you sit up?"

"Maybe." I try to push up, but the pain knifing through my wrist stops me cold. "If you help me, I can."

With one hand under my elbow and his other arm around my back, he gets me into a sitting position. I look around, trying to figure out where we are. It's still raining, but we're fairly well protected by a canopy over us.

I point up. "Where did that come from?"

"Emergency tarp. Super thin, super strong. We all carry one."

Then I look down at my legs. "I'm all muddy." I look at Bruce. "So are you."

He frowns at me. "Yeah. Thanks for that. When you went sliding down the hill, I had to follow you."

"Why were you following me in the first place?"

"You're on a reality show, remember? Someone's always following you."

I roll my eyes and immediately regret it because of the pain that shoots across my forehead. "No. I mean, why you instead of one of the other guys? I hardly ever see you around camp."

"Blame Rick. He was concerned how you and Jess would do after the Scotty left."

Bruce's obvious dislike of Duncan is comical, but Rick's concern is downright laughable. "Of course. Nothing boosts ratings like a mother/daughter argument."

"That had nothing to do with it. In case you haven't noticed, Rick likes you."

Poor Bruce. I actually laugh in his face. "I doubt Rick has met a woman he didn't like. No, thank you. I have no desire to join the ladies of the Wolff Pack."

He mutters something under his breath. "There is no Wolff Pack. That's just a name the press made up."

"Well, they didn't make up all those women he's dated." I saw pictures of the women. All those gorgeous, skinny, well-dressed women.

"Sure, he's dated a lot of women. But most of them were set up by his publicist and the woman's publicist. When you're in the entertainment biz, who you're seen with is almost as important as how good you are at what you do." Bruce shrugs. "He doesn't like it, but it's part of his job. That's why I stay behind the camera. No one cares about my personal life."

So the Wolff Pack is just a way to get publicity. If I believe Bruce, which I have no reason not to, it explains some things. Like why Rick appears to have had so many brief flings, and why he has a different persona when the cameras are off.

"You know, you're committing the cardinal sin on the island." I smile. "We aren't even supposed to acknowledge each other's existence."

He looks from his filthy clothes to mine. "Once you've slid down a mud bank to rescue someone, you just can't ignore her anymore."

"Good point."

"Besides, I've known Rick since we were kids, so I feel the need to defend his honor. I'll tell you this. He's not a womanizer."

Outside our protective canopy, the rain is letting up. "Do you think we should head back to camp?"

"Nope. After that fall, I'm not taking any chances. We're staying put until the rescue team finds us."

I start to panic just a little. "But we have no food, no water. What if they don't come looking for us right away? What if we're stuck here overnight? And how will they find us in the first place?"

His answer is to unclip the two-way radio from his belt and wave it like a pendulum in front of me.

"Oh."

"Don't worry. They'll get to us before dark." He leans back against a tree, stretching his muddy legs out in front of him. "But since we have some time to kill, do you want to talk about what happened with Jess?"

Jess. I've made such a mess of things. Running from the problem certainly didn't work, so why not talk it out with Bruce?

He listens and nods while I give him the condensed version of the story. When I'm done, he scratches the coarse hair along his jaw. "It must hurt to have her accuse you of not caring."

I nod. "It does. I can understand why she would make that conclusion, but it's just not true. I agonized over my decision to give her away. And I didn't blindly hand her over to an agency without having a clue about who would get her. I *chose* the Becketts. She said she had a great childhood and she loves her parents. Well, the only reason they're her parents is because of me."

Even to my own ears, I sound slightly hysterical. Bruce leans over and pats my shoulder, then speaks in the soothing voice of one who works with the mentally disturbed. "I'm sure you did what you thought was best for her."

"Yes! That's what I tried to tell her, but she doesn't see it. She thinks I popped her out, gave her away, and never thought about her again." I make the mistake of motioning with my hands. I'm now certain that wrist is broken.

"Of course you didn't forget her. Who could do that?"

Shame winds itself around my heart. "She isn't totally wrong." At his questioning look, I go on. "At first, I thought about her all the time. Mornings were the worst. I'd wake up, and for a moment, I'd think I was still pregnant. But then it all came back to me, and I'd remember hearing her cry in the delivery room, and how I caught a glimpse of her red hair before they took her away." My eyes burn, my nose tingles, and I'm terrified I'll lose it and start blubbering all over Bruce. But he doesn't look worried, so I keep talking.

"It was like that for the first month. Then I got to where the mornings weren't so bad, but I still thought about her. I don't know when it was exactly, but one day, I realized I hadn't thought about my baby in two days."

I bite my lip, remembering the tug of emotions, the desire to forget and be free of the pain, but the equally powerful need to remember. "If I had thought about her every minute of every day, the grief would have killed me. The only way to survive was to move forward, bury myself in school, then work."

"You don't sound like a woman who doesn't care." Bruce is unusually serious. "You sound just the opposite."

"What's the use?" I close my eyes and lean my head back against the tree. "Jess is so upset with me now, I doubt she'll talk to me again."

"She might surprise you."

"I don't think I can take one more surprise."

As if on cue, I hear someone call my name. Either the search party has found us, or I'm on the cusp of death and the angels are calling me home.

"Did you hear that?" I ask.

Bruce cocks his head, then grins like a boy with a rubber band gun. "They found us."

A few minutes later, Rick leads in a team of rescuers. He claps Bruce on the back. "You all right?"

"Oh sure. Nothing that a long, hot shower won't take care of."

Rick nods. "I'll take it from here."

Bruce turns to go, but before he leaves, he picks up something from under a bush. It's his camera, a red light blinking on top of the lens.

It was right there the entire time. But had it been on? Was that red light a good or bad thing? If it was on, I'm in trouble. Because while I spilled my guts, Bruce's camera could have caught every word I said.

27

As one of the medics wraps my wrist, he says he thinks I have a compression fracture, which is much better than a total break and will heal more quickly. But we won't know for sure without an X-ray, and we can't get an X-ray until we get off the island.

The medic gives the bandage a final check. "Stay put. I have to take care of something, then we'll get you out of here."

He walks away and joins Rick and the other medic, who are looking over some kind of grid on a piece of paper. Rick points at one of the boxes, shakes his head, then leaves them and comes to join me under the canopy.

"What were you looking at?" I ask as he hunkers down beside me.

"Just figuring out who won the pool."

"What pool?"

"There was a pool about when you'd hurt yourself again."

Huffing out my disgust, I shake my head. "I can't believe you bet on when I'd have an accident."

"Hey, I bet that you *wouldn't* have another one." He smirks. "I see now that was wishful thinking on my part."

"Thanks for your support," I mutter. "Does this mean I'm out of the game?"

His shoulders rise and fall in a casual shrug. "That depends on you. How does your wrist feel?"

I hold it up carefully. "Better since they wrapped it. But it still hurts."

"The medical team cleared you to stay and compete, if you want to. Your injuries aren't life threatening. But the last two challenges are already set to go. We won't be changing them to accommodate your wrist."

"I wouldn't expect you to. It's just . . . I want to do what I can to get Jess to the end. She deserves it."

The smile vanishes, and he becomes serious-Rick. "What about you, Monica? What do you deserve?"

I laugh, but it's not a happy sound. "I hope I never get what I deserve."

He touches the back of my unbandaged hand with his fingertips. "You're much too hard on yourself."

"That's sweet of you to say." Gently, I move my hand away. "But you really don't know me."

An odd look crosses his face, one I haven't seen before. "I shouldn't be talking to you personally like this. But when the game is over, remind me to talk to you about what I know."

Before I can pin him down and demand to know what he's talking about, he stands and goes to the medical team.

"Let's get her back," I hear him say.

Despite my protests that there's nothing wrong with my legs, the medics strap me onto the gurney and carry me back through the jungle. It's slow going as we jerk and dip along the uneven ground, and it brings to mind every stranded-and-struggling-to-survive movie I've ever seen. Unfortunately, the undulating motion of the gurney begins to emulate the movement of the ocean, bringing on a bout of nausea. I cover my eyes with the crook of my good arm, breathe deeply through my nose, and take my mind somewhere else.

Naturally, my thoughts go straight to Jess. I'm determined to stay in this game for her, but what if she wants out? She said coming here with me was a mistake. Does that mean she's done? On one hand, it would be a relief to walk away from this island while I still have use of my legs. But the end of the game effectively signals the end of my interaction with Jessica, and I'm just not ready for that.

The sound of several voices talking at once is my first clue we're nearing camp. I lower my arm and raise my head, trying to prepare for whatever I've got coming.

As soon as my litter-bearers deliver me into camp, I'm surrounded. Five faces hover over me and jostle the medics as they struggle to set the stretcher on the ground. Then, they all start talking at once.

"What did you do now?"

"We were really worried."

"Are they taking you off the island?"

"Can you still cook?"

"You scared me."

The only voice I pick out of that tangle is Jess, saying that I scared her. Where is she? I look on one side of the stretcher, then the other. Finally, I focus on her, standing by the right side of my head.

I smile at her. "Sorry." Then I struggle to sit up using my one good hand. As soon as I hold up the bandaged wrist, Jess and Malcolm, who's on the other side of the stretcher, reach out to help me.

"Thanks. Um, would you guys mind giving Jess and me a minute alone? We need to talk." Everyone looks so concerned, even the usually self-absorbed Tracy, that I hate to ask. But there's no way around it.

"Sure." Malcolm squeezes my shoulder and I think he winks at me. Either that, or something flew in his eye.

As they walk away, Jess sits cross-legged on the ground facing me. She extends a finger toward my wrist, but stops just short of touching it. "Is it broken?"

"Maybe. We can't know until it's X-rayed."

She nods. Looks away. Sucks in a shaky breath, then looks back at me. "I'm sorry."

For which part? Not that it really matters. We both have plenty to apologize for. "Me too."

The silence stretches out between us. On the other side of camp, I see Rick talking to the remaining four players. There's a lot of expressive hand movements and pointing in our direction. They must be talking about the possible scenarios.

"We have a decision to make," I blurt out. "If you don't want to be here anymore, I understand. This wrist thing is the perfect excuse for us to leave." Her head lowers and she flicks at the sand with one fingernail. I've given her an out. Now I need to give her an actual choice. "But I don't want to leave."

Her head jerks up. "You don't?"

"No."

"But what about your wrist? If it's really broken, you need to have it set."

"I think I just sprained it. It'll probably be back to normal by morning." Of course, it won't. Even a bad sprain will take the rest of our time on the island to heal. But I've got on my happy game face, and I'm using it for all I'm worth.

"I don't know . . . "

"Look, even if we stay, it may not be for very long. We could lose the next challenge and end up going home anyway. But I want to give it my best shot." My eyes meet hers and I refuse to look away, hoping she understands what I'm about to say. "I'm not going to give up."

She blinks and turns her head. I imagine all the different things she must be thinking, the pros and cons she must be weighing. Because this moment is about more than just the game. This moment, right now, will determine whether or not we have any kind of relationship in the future. And we both know it.

"Okay." Jess looks back at me, and she has that Mona Lisa smile like the first time I saw her on television. "Let's stay."

"Great. Now please help me off this stupid stretcher."

No more looking like an invalid. I've got a game to play, and a daughter to win over.

28

Rick doesn't seem at all surprised when Jess and I tell him we plan to keep playing. I am required to sign a medical release, stating that I'm aware of the fact I may have suffered a serious injury and I will not sue the production company should complications develop. Then one of the medics produces a nifty brace to keep my wrist immobile, just in case.

Finally, the crew exits our camp, leaving behind only the ubiquitous steady-cam guys. There are two with us now, and neither one is Bruce. Either Rick is no longer concerned about Jess and me tearing each other apart, or Bruce wants to stay away from me so I can't grill him about whether or not his camera was on.

Layla strides over and sits next to me in the shelter. "In honor of your decision to stay in the game, we're going to cook for you tonight."

"That's great," I say with a laugh. "What's on the menu?"

Bob walks up with his hand behind his back. "While you were off rolling around the island, we had a little excitement back here." With a flourish, he produces a string of beautiful fish.

My excited squeal can probably be heard by every bat within a one-mile radius. "That's awesome. You caught all those?"

"Malcolm and I did."

Oh, how I want to get my hands on those babies. But right now, with only one good hand, I'm fairly useless. "Does anybody here know how to clean fish?"

They silently question each other, then Tracy pipes up. "They were really sandy, so I washed them with canteen water."

I nod seriously, vowing not to laugh at the poor girl. "That's a great start. Now the scales need to be removed." A thought occurs to me. Maybe this is a chance to help someone else. "Hey, if you and your dad want to be in charge of cleaning, I'll talk you through it."

She doesn't look too thrilled about the idea of working with dead fish. So I try a different tactic. "Or I can show someone else. It's pretty detailed work. Not everybody can do it."

Tracy lifts her chin a bit. "I can do it."

"I know you can. That's why I suggested it. But I totally understand if you don't want to try. It can be daunting."

"You just tell us what to do."

As she and her father get ready to work on the fish, I notice Jess standing off to the side. Obviously, she watched the whole exchange. Now she smiles and nods, which I think means she's impressed with my amateur attempt at reverse psychology.

Tracy and Bob do a very nice job, especially considering it's their first time cleaning fish, and probably the first time in years that they've truly worked together. I make sure to give them lots of praise and encouragement. After they're done with the fish, we skewer them on sticks and hold them over the fire, roasting them like big, fishy marshmallows.

Sitting around the fire, a chorus of satisfied moans goes up as the fish is consumed. For me, eating is a challenge. I have a big, waxy green leaf on my lap, almost like a place mat.

Keeping the fish on the stick, I anchor the end with my brace, and pick off the meat with my other hand.

"This is the best fish I've ever eaten." I display terrible manners, talking with my mouth stuffed. "And I've eaten some amazing fish."

"I wish we had dessert," Tracy says in a dreamy voice.

Layla nods enthusiastically. "I could go for a gooey chocolate brownie topped with vanilla ice cream and hot fudge."

"Warm cherry pie, a la mode," Bob says.

Malcolm holds up a finger. "Chocolate chip cookies, fresh from the oven. With a glass of ice-cold milk."

We all groan, and I swear, I can smell those cookies.

"What about you, Jess?" I ask. "What's your guilty pleasure?"

She doesn't even need to think about it. "Crème brûlée."

Perfect. "You're in luck. I make a mean crème brûlée."

"Cool." She smiles as she takes the cap off her canteen. "Maybe you can make it for me sometime."

My heart jumps in my chest at the thought of Jess in my house, sitting on a bar stool at the kitchen counter, the two of us talking and laughing while I whip up dessert. Instead of losing my cool and scaring her off, I nod and stay calm. "I think that could be arranged."

I can't sleep. Lying on the bamboo floor of our shelter is never what you would call comfortable, but we're all usually so exhausted that sleep comes pretty quickly. Tonight, my wrist is throbbing, and I know my declaration that it would feel better by morning was nothing more than wishful thinking.

Careful not to disturb anyone, I scoot from the shelter and make my way to the beach. I want to sit, but I'm afraid if I do, I won't be able to get back up. So I stand there, listening to the waves crash against each other as they run to shore. And just like that, I'm transported back to another time, another ocean.

It's a spring evening on a deserted California beach, the air damp and chilled. Duncan and I, fingers intertwined, walk barefoot through the surf, our shoes hanging from the fingertips of our free hands. He'd rolled up his pant legs, but I let my skirt hang free until the hem was soaked, and when we strolled under the pier, the material clung to my calves. We'd only known each other for a month, but I was so happy, my heart so full of love for this amazing man, that when he took me in his arms, I was home. When his fingers threaded through my hair and he brought his lips down to mine, I melted into his kiss. And when that kiss grew, wiping all rational thought from my mind, I gave myself to him. Because this was real, everlasting love.

Except it wasn't. Because a week later, he was gone. No explanation, no tearful good-bye, no promise to return. He left me totally alone. Or so I thought.

A ragged sob escapes my lips and is carried away on the salty breeze. For so many years, I've thought of my life as two different parts: Before Duncan, and After Duncan. There were times when I considered being so gullible, and falling for his pretty words spoken in his lilting accent, as the biggest mistake of my life. But how can I think that anymore? If not for that time in my life, there would be no Jessica. The Becketts wouldn't have had the joy of raising her into the fine young woman she is, and I wouldn't be getting to know her now.

Yes, I made a mistake all those years ago, but look what God did with it. He turned it around and kept His hand on all of us until we ended up in this place. Of all the things He could have used, He decided a reality show was the perfect place for reconciliation.

My sobs turn to laughter as I consider the divine comedy of it all.

Something touches my shoulder, and I jump.

"Easy, it's just me." Jess stands next to me, layered in every piece of clothing she brought along in an attempt to ward off the cold. "What are you doing out here?"

I could dodge the issue, make up some story, but I don't want to hide anything from her anymore. "I was thinking about your father, and how glad I am you were born."

She laughs and crosses her arms. "Yeah, I'm pretty happy about that, too." We both stare out at the ocean. "Did you ever think of . . . did you ever consider not having me?"

"Yes, I did." It pains me to say it, but it's the truth. "It was an option. And when you find yourself in that position, you look at all the options."

"It would have made your life easier," she says. "One appointment, an hour or so out of your day, and there you go. Problem solved."

I look at her, her face silhouetted in the moonlight, and my heart breaks. "You sound like you have experience with it. Have you . . . ?"

"No." She shakes her head, but still doesn't look at me. "A friend of mine. I went with her, hoping if I was there and she could talk through her feelings, she'd change her mind. She didn't."

"I'm sorry. It's a terrible decision to be faced with."

"Why didn't you do it?" Now Jess turns to me, her eyes speaking volumes even in the darkness.

"I just couldn't. I always knew the life inside me was exactly that. A life. What right did I have to end it?" Thinking back on that time, even though it was filled with confusion and fear, it also brings warm feelings. "And then there's the fact that my maternal instincts kicked in. I know it's hard to believe, but I loved you from the moment I found out about you."

Her lips purse and her brows pull down. "Then why did you give me away?"

"Because I wanted you to have a better life than what I could give you. I was a twenty-year-old in culinary school with no way of making a decent living. I wanted you to have a stable family with a mother and father who loved you."

"That part worked out." One corner of her mouth lifts, just a little. "My parents are great. Very loving."

"I knew they would be. When I read their information sheet and saw their pictures, I knew. That's the family you were meant for."

She shakes her head as she squeezes her arms tighter across her chest. "Then why do I feel this way? I love my parents. I wouldn't have wanted to grow up any other way. No offense."

"None taken."

"So why do I feel this resentment because you gave me away? If I was meant for them, then I should be grateful, but I'm not." Her teeth begin to chatter and her body shakes. "Why am I so mad at you for abandoning me?"

In a spontaneous reaction, I open my arms to her. This time, she walks into them, letting me hold her while she pushes her face against my shoulder and cries.

A really good mother would have the answers to all her questions, but I don't. All I have is my own confusion and my own feeble attempts to explain things that don't make any sense. "I don't know why all this works the way it does. But I can't imagine anyone would be happy about their mother giving them away, no matter how great their life turned out."

Her body jerks, and I'm not sure if she's laughing or crying harder. Then she pulls back and wipes the back of her sleeve across her nose.

"You know what the worst part has been? All the unanswered questions." Her arms are crossed again and she's put more distance between us. "Not knowing anything about you, or why you did what you did. Even little things like capers."

"Capers?"

"Yeah. My parents hate capers. We never had them around the house while I was growing up. But the first time I tried them, I loved them. So I've wondered if that was something I got from you."

I can't hold back my smile. "Yes, I'm a caper fan. And a crème brûlée lover. It sounds like you may have inherited my love of food."

"Maybe." Her eyes dart away and she stares at the ocean, as if she's embarrassed by the show of emotion.

"I'll tell you what. From now on, if you have any questions, I want you to ask me. Anything, no matter how big or how small. Will you do that?"

She nods. "Man, life is weird. Last month, I didn't know a thing about my birth parents. Now I've met you both and I have an open invitation to contact either one of you whenever I want."

There's nothing to do but agree. "Yep. Life sure can be weird. And there are times when life can be wonderful."

No doubt about it. This is one of those times.

29

Morning comes much too early, and with it the announcement that we have pail mail.

"Come on, Monica." Layla encourages me to follow as she leaves the shelter.

"Don't wanna," I grumble. "You come back and tell me what it says."

"Ladies. A little help here."

Three sets of hands start pushing and pulling to move me out of my semi-comfortable spot.

"Watch out for her wrist," Jess says.

"Okay, okay." I swat at them with my good hand. "I'm up already."

Layla and Tracy hurry ahead, but Jess stays back as I shuffle along.

"Aren't you tired?" I ask.

She shrugs. "A little. But I'm more excited to see what the challenge is today."

"Oh yeah. Me too." My flat delivery isn't fooling anyone, not even myself. Yesterday's can-do attitude has been beaten into submission by a night of restless half-sleep and a near-constant throbbing in my wrist, cut only by the occasional slice of knife-like pain. If it weren't for Jess, I'd turn in my resignation right now. But after our heart-to-heart last night, and her enthusiasm this morning, quitting is out of the question.

At the mail pail, Bob has already removed, untied, and unrolled the scroll that holds the clue to today's festivities.

"Well, this is interesting. It's a limerick." He clears his throat and reads. "Three weeks you've spent together, in every kind of weather. Prepare today, to go the way, that may seem quite familiar."

I'm in no mood for riddles. "What does that mean?"

"It's not good," Jess mutters.

"It's a challenge mash up," Tracy says. "They take pieces from previous challenges and put them into a new, bigger challenge."

Jess was right. This isn't good at all.

"And since we're down to the last three teams, this isn't a prize challenge." Layla speaks with such authority, even if she's dead wrong we'd all believe her. "This one's a biggie."

Chewing on my lip, I mull over what this all means. The result of today's challenge will send two teams to the elimination challenge. Whoever loses there goes home, leaving two teams. And at that point, the challenges are over. That's when everybody who watches the show votes for who should win.

"So this is it," I say. "One way or another, the game's over in a few days."

That proclamation has the same effect as pulling a plug from a socket. All the energy seems to have leached out of the group.

Finally, Malcolm claps his hands together. "Well, let's get ready."

Getting ready usually doesn't take more than a few minutes. But using one hand to put on a dry pair of socks is awkward. More than once I end up rolling on my back like a disoriented turtle. Then I roll back up and start over. After I conquer the donning of the socks, shoes are next. One look at the double-knotted laces, and I want to cry.

Jess plops down in front of me and picks up a shoe. "If we want to get there today, you'd better let me help."

From the lilt in her voice, I know she's teasing me, and that just makes me want to cry even more. "I don't know how we're going to do this."

"Easy. I'll untie your shoes, then—"

"Not *this*." I wiggle my finger at my feet. "The challenge. You know it's going to have a ton of physical stuff in it."

She nods as she picks open the knot in one of my shoelaces. "It probably will. So?"

"So? So I have a wee bit of a handicap." Looking down at my braced wrist I wonder how I ever thought I could keep playing this game.

"We'll figure it out." She puts the shoe down where I can slip my foot into it, then works on the other one. "I'll do the physical parts, and you can do the puzzles."

"What if there are no puzzles?"

Frowning, she sets down the second shoe. "I don't know. Let's just do one thing at a time, okay?"

"Okay." I push my feet into my athletic shoes and lean forward, then stop. "Would you tie my laces, please?"

"Sure." As she ties knots and makes loops, a smile blossoms on her lips. "I couldn't tie my own shoes until I was seven."

"Really?"

"Yep. Something about it never clicked. Then one day, my dad realized that when they sat in front of me and showed me how to tie it, I saw the process backwards. So he sat behind me and reached his arms around me. By that night, they couldn't get me to stop tying my shoes." She finishes with a flourish and squeezes my foot. "And look at me now."

I give her a thumbs-up. "You've come a long way."

Malcolm and Layla walk up, each carrying two canteens. "We got you some water."

"Thanks." Jess puts both straps around her neck. "Let's head out."

Layla and Jess lead the way, with Malcolm and me trailing. He leans sideways slightly and talks under his breath.

"Did I really see her helping you with your shoes?"

"You did." I cradle my arm as we walk, but every step jars it and increases the ache. "Things are going way better, but I'm worried about the challenge."

"All you can do is your best. She knows that."

Watching Jess up ahead carrying our canteens like belts of machine gun ammo, I wonder what she's really expecting from me today. I don't want to let her down, but the chances of us making it through to the final two is almost zero.

I smile at Malcolm. "Thanks. Whatever happens, I'm pulling for you and Layla to make it to the end."

My entire arm throbs by the time we reach the playing field, and my heart drops when I see it. It's pretty sad that I identify each mini-challenge with an injury.

Rick greets us as we go to our colored mats. Then he explains the course while two staffers walk through it to demonstrate. After they're done, and my mind is whirling, he instructs us to take a minute to strategize.

I pivot sharply toward Jess. "What do we do?"

"Okay . . . I'll be blindfolded this time and you can guide me to our poles."

Thankfully, there are only two poles and two bags to retrieve. "Then I'll put together the puzzle."

"Right. And I'll break the pots with the slingshot."

"Great." It's a sensible plan, one that might actually get us through to the end. If it weren't for one thing. "What about the obstacle course?"

Even Jess can't put a positive spin on that. "It's the hardest part, for sure. I'm just glad the Tarzan ropes are gone."

"We wouldn't have a chance with those ropes. But there's still the mud to crawl through."

"And the wall to climb over." Jess puts her hands on her hips as she surveys the course with a critical eye. "I think we can do this. The wall is definitely the biggest problem, but I'll help you with that." She turns to me. "The most important question is, do you really want to do this?"

"Yes."

"Are you sure?"

"Yes."

"Because I don't want you to get hurt any worse than you already are."

"Jess." I put my good hand on her shoulder. "I want to do this. After all we've gone through to get to this point, and all the injuries I've suffered, do you really think I would quit now?"

"I know you don't want to, but—"

"No buts. I'm here and I'm ready. Besides," I say with a grin, "it would be a shame if you did all that lace tying for nothing."

"You got me there. I can't fight logic like that."

We're both laughing when Rick tells the teams to take their places. I scramble onto the platform while Jess settles the face mask over her eyes.

"Families get ready," Rick calls. "And . . . go!"

Remembering how I panicked when I was the Seeker, I take a moment to make sure Jess can hear me before I tell her which way to go. It helps that mine is the only female voice calling out directions. Bob and Malcolm both have deep, booming voices that sound oddly similar when they yell at their daughters, and it appears to be confusing Tracy and Layla.

"Jess! Turn ninety degrees to the left!"

She turns, stops, and waits.

"Five steps forward!"

We go on like this until she finds the first pole and retrieves the bag. I guide her back to me, she tosses the bag toward my voice, and I send her out again. It's all going smoothly, until I see Tracy barreling straight at her.

"Jess! Stop! Now!"

She jerks to a stop as if her shoes have been nailed to the ground, and Tracy sails past, barely missing her. A relieved breath puffs out of me.

"Straight ahead, Jess! Three steps!"

It doesn't take much longer to get her to the pole and then back to the platform. Once she tosses me the last bag, she rips off the blindfold.

"Go!"

Grabbing the bags, I jump down from the platform, yelp when the impact of hitting the ground jolts through my arm, then run to the puzzle tables. When I go to dump the pieces out of the bags, I realize they're tied shut.

"More knots," I mutter.

Using my right hand and my teeth, I undo the bags and get the pieces out. These aren't your run-of-the-mill, flat puzzles. They're three-dimensional instruments of torture, designed to turn the brain into Swiss cheese. Laying the pieces out, I look them over, trying to make sense of how they could fit together.

Focus, Monica. You can do this.

I tune out everything and just stare at those oddly shaped pieces. And then, somehow, they start to make sense. There are two that I know belong together. And there are another two. And this piece fits over there on top of those two. My fingers fly as I assemble the puzzle sculpture mostly with one hand.

Then I'm done. I did it. I look at Rick for verification.

He comes to the table. "Monica thinks she has it . . . and she does! She and Jess move on to the next part of the challenge with an incredible lead!"

Jess is already standing in front of the pots, holding the slingshot, but she can't start shooting until I'm there too. I run over, and as soon as my feet hit the mat, she sends the first marble flying.

"Bob and Malcolm are working on their puzzles now." Rick yells. "Come on, guys! You're still in this!"

Silently, I urge Jess to hurry. The slingshot takes some getting used to, but once she does, it's like she's been using one her whole life.

"With incredible aim Jess makes quick work of all three pots." Rick points to the obstacle course. "On to the last, and most difficult, part of this challenge."

We run to the obstacle course. As she fastens the leather belts around both our waists, Jess takes a moment to make sure I'm okay.

"We can stop right here."

"No." I look over my shoulder and see Bob and Tracy sprinting to the slingshot area. "We're not giving up. Let's go."

The net over the mud pit is about ten feet long. It's so low, the only way to get to the other side is to do a kind of frogman crawl, pulling yourself forward with your arms. It was hard enough the first time. But now, with my latest injury, it's nearly impossible.

Jess moves ahead of me, but the rope connecting our belts stretches tight, holding her back and yanking me forward. Which gives me an idea.

"Pull me."

She pulls on the rope. I dig in with my right hand, and push forward with my legs. It's slow, but it's working.

By the time we get to the end, the other two teams have reached the mud and are diving under the net. It won't take them long at all to get through.

Jess looks at me with worried eyes. I move toward the wall. "Come on."

The wall is about eight feet tall. It has six knotted ropes hanging about three feet apart, and small spaces between the wooden slats that are too thin to use as handholds. How am I supposed to do this one-handed?

"Get on my shoulders."

"What?" Is she crazy? I tug on the belt rope. "This isn't long enough."

"It will be." She sucks in her stomach, grabs her belt, and hikes it up until it's right below her chest. Then she pushes mine lower so it sits on my hips. Then she squats down in front of me. "Get on."

I hesitate. Behind us, the other teams shout as they emerge from the mud pits nearly at the same time and run for the wall.

"Now!" Jess yells.

We're close enough to the wall that I use it to steady myself as I straddle my daughter's neck like I'm preparing to ride an ostrich. "Please don't hurt yourself. If you get a hernia picking me up—"

"Stop talking."

As she straightens up, she growls. The higher I go, the louder she growls, until she sounds like an injured Wookiee.

"Can you hold on to the top with your good hand?"

"I think so." The wall shakes as everyone tries to climb it. I reach up and manage to hook my elbows over the top of the wall. "I'm hanging on!" I yell back down to Jess.

She moves away from my legs, and the weight of my body pulls me down. Instinctively, I clutch at the wood with both hands, which was a bad idea. Biting my lip to keep from yelling, I tighten my grip with my right arm.

Since I'm hanging with my head facing away from her, I can't see what Jess is doing. But from the grunts and the way the belt keeps jerking down on my hips, I think she's trying to climb up by using the knotted ropes.

Then I hear her yell. The rope on my belt yanks down hard. I try to hold on, but the weight pulls me down, scraping the undersides of my arms along the wood. I've fallen enough times that I should know better than to fight it, but instinct is a pretty powerful thing. My fingers catch on the top of the wall, holding on for a split second, but it's no use. As I make that sickening, slow motion fall, I have the presence of mind to tuck my hands in instead of reaching back to break the fall.

As soon as my body meets the ground, all the air is pushed from my lungs. I thrash from side to side, gasping for breath, and thinking this must be what a fish out of water feels like.

Then I look at the wall and realize no one is on it anymore.

We lost.

30

I'm not sure what hurts more: my almost-certainly broken wrist, or my splinter-infested fingertips. Once more, Jess and I are under a canopy, having our wounds tended to.

"I don't remember ever seeing one person so many times." The medic chuckles to himself. "Depending how much makes it on air, I might get my SAG card out of this."

I grimace. "Great. It thrills me to help further your acting career."

With a sheepish grin, he undoes the closures on my muddy wrist brace. "Tell me if anything hurts. Okay?"

Before I can agree, he pulls the brace away and a firey-hot pain shoots through my arm.

"That hurts!"

He nods. "I gathered as much. You need a new brace, but first I've got to clean off your arm. Are you ready?"

In other words, I'm in for more pain. Gritting my teeth, I close my eyes and brace myself. "Go for it."

The man may be gunning for more airtime, but he certainly is gentle. Even though it does hurt, it's not nearly as bad as I expected. A few feet away, Jess isn't having such good results.

From the way she's groaning and complaining, I think her medic took lessons from Nurse Ratched.

"That bandage is really tight," Jess says. "It's cutting off my circulation."

The gal working on her sighs. "Do you feel it when I do this?"

"Ouch! Yes, I felt that."

"Then the circulation to your foot is fine."

If Jess wasn't so feisty, I'd be worried about her. But other than a sprained ankle, she doesn't seem any worse for wear.

"Of all the medical tents in all the world, she had to limp into mine." Rick swaggers in, looking back and forth between the two of us. "How are the patients?"

My medic speaks up first. "This one has splinters, bruises, and increased aggravation to her previously injured wrist."

Rick nods, then looks at Jess. Her medic barely acknowledges him.

"Sprained ankle. No big deal."

Jess glares at her. "It might be a big deal if it were your ankle."

Rick laughs. "In other words, they'll both live."

"Yes." The medics answer together.

"Good." Rick comes closer and hunkers down by my side. "Tell me, is this a ploy to get attention?"

"Of course not." The medic slowly turns my arm so he can clean the underside, and I breathe in a gasp of air through my teeth. "Bet you're really glad I signed that release, huh?"

"No doubt." He smiles. "I have to ask, though. Do you want to keep playing?"

If ever there was a time to roll my eyes, this is it. "What do you think?"

"Like I said, I had to ask." He squeezes my shoulder before standing up. "Just try to keep out of trouble, okay?"

Jess, who's been listening to the entire conversation, barks out a laugh. "Stay out of trouble? What fun would that be?"

Shaking his head, Rick looks over at her. "Just make sure you can walk into the elimination challenge tomorrow night."

He starts to leave, but I call out to stop him.

"Rick, wait. Who are we competing against?"

Tilting his head, he looks confused. Then he gets it. "That's right. You didn't see who won today."

"No, I was too busy falling off a wall."

"Bob and Tracy won."

My heart sinks. "Then we're going up against Malcolm and Layla."

"Yes." From his lack of a dimple-bracketed grin, it seems Rick realizes how much I don't want to compete against them. But it is what it is.

Before Rick can make his escape, there's one more thing I need to bring up. "I haven't seen Bruce since we got stuck out there in the rain."

Rick doesn't say a word.

Okay, acting casual won't work. I'll have to use the direct approach. "Do you know if, uh, he filmed anything . . . interesting lately?"

"Try to get some rest before tomorrow." Completely ignoring my question, he turns and walks away.

The medic makes a sound I interpret to mean, "You should have known that wouldn't work." And yeah, I knew it was a long shot. But you can't blame an injured woman for trying. The information he did give me wasn't good. Even though we've been playing against each other this whole time, I hate the idea of a one-on-one battle against Malcolm and Layla.

"One more challenge," I mutter to myself.

"Let's hope there's no mud involved." My medic tightens the Velcro straps on my clean brace. "How does that feel?"

"Good. Thanks."

He pats my shoulder. "Hey, I was kidding before. I'd be perfectly happy not to end up on camera again."

"I'll do my best."

He walks away and I close my eyes. My best. Not much of a promise, really. Because lately, my best has been just short of abysmal.

The rain starts as we walk back to camp, which takes twice as long as it should due to Jess's limp and my overall achiness.

"I'm going to need a visit to the chiropractor when this is over."

Jess glances at me, using her hand to shield her eyes from the rain. "Didn't falling off that wall pop some of your joints into place?"

"Oh yeah, some of my joints popped all right. Just not into the right place."

"I'm sorry I pulled you off." She shakes her head, whipping her waterlogged ponytail from side to side. "You were right about those ropes. They're hard to hold on to with muddy hands."

Like mother like daughter. "No problem. We sure did great up until that point, though."

"We did. If not for the obstacle course, we would've won."

But we didn't. And now I don't feel like talking anymore.

By the time we reach the shelter, we're soaked. Thanks to the rain, there will be no fire to dry us out or keep us warm. I just hope somebody thought of cooking something before the deluge started.

I'm surprised, but glad, to see Bob and Tracy joining us in the big shelter. Two more people taking up the small talk slack are exactly what I need right now.

Standing in front of the shelter, Jess and I try to squeeze out or shake off as much water as possible, but it's an exercise in the impossible. Finally, she crawls in, dripping her way across the floor. "Pardon our puddles."

"No worries," Malcolm says. "Every time the wind shifts, it blows the rain inside. I don't think any of us are going to stay dry tonight."

We all look out at the same time, and I know they're hunting for the same thing I am. There he is, one lone cameraman, covered head to foot in a variety of rain gear, his camera perched like a big, plastic-wrapped blob on his shoulder.

"Is it wrong that it makes me happy to see him sharing our pain?" Tracy asks.

We all chorus, "No," except for Malcolm. His lone "Yes" draws looks from all of us.

"It's not his fault we're out in this miserable weather," Malcolm says with a shrug. "We all asked to be here."

Bob nods. "You're right. By the way, why did we do that?"

"Temporary insanity?" Layla says.

I raise a finger. "Hey, I didn't ask to be here, I was invited."

Lying on her back, Jess speaks to the roof. "Bet you're sorry you said yes, now."

"Nope. I wouldn't have missed this for the world."

She turns her head, her eyes narrowed. "Seriously?"

"Okay, I wouldn't have minded missing out on all the injuries. But the rest of it . . . " Just as Malcolm predicted, the wind shifts and the inside of our snug shelter is pelted with rain. But I refuse to let my attitude become as damp as the rest of me. "If I could do it over again, I'd still say yes."

We spend the next hour or so eating tepid mashed taro root and bananas, and trying to take our minds off how cold it is.

Layla has her arms wrapped around her knees, pulling herself into as tight a ball as possible, and leaning against her father. "The first thing I'm going to do when I get home is take a long, hot shower."

Jess shakes her head. "Not me. I'm going to soak in a tub full of bubbles."

"I need a manicure." Tracy holds up her hands, fingers spread wide as she inspects her ragged nails. Then she glances at her feet. "And a pedicure."

"Coffee." Bob's one word produces a chorus of approving moans.

I toss my banana peel onto the pile that's formed by the side of the shelter. "You know what I look forward to most?"

It's a rhetorical question, but Jess jumps in to answer it. "Hugging your dog?"

My head snaps in her direction, needing to see if she's still upset about that. But her grin puts me at ease. "Well, yes. But besides that, I can't wait to get in my kitchen and cook something real. Something that requires multiple pots and pans and more than two ingredients."

Malcolm waves his hands like he's shooing away an angry wasp. "No. Stop. If you start talking about food again I'm going to walk out of this shelter, lay on my back with my mouth open, and drown myself."

Laughter wraps around me, not quite enough to keep me warm, but at least enough to make me not mind the cold as much. We've come a long way since the first day on the island when trust was hard to come by. Now, I feel an unusually strong bond with these people. It's probably because of the isolation and the extreme conditions we've been exposed to. There's a part of me that wants to stay in touch, invite them over to my home, cook them dinner, but I know the chances of that happening are slim. Once we leave the island, and our shared experience is over, we'll go back to our individual lives. This will be nothing more than a story we tell at parties.

With the exception of Jessica.

She's sitting up, her chin resting on one knee, while her other leg is straight out, her wrapped ankle propped up on her canvas bag. Tracy is telling her something that requires animated hand movements and sound effects. Jess laughs, and the music of it pierces straight to the center of my heart.

The relationship we've forged is fragile and tentative, but it exists, which is more than I could say a month ago. I have no idea if we'll keep it going, I just know that we have to. Because now that she's in my life, I can't let her go.

Not again.

31

Annie lied. The sun doesn't always come out tomorrow. And even when it does, that doesn't mean it will do you any good.

The day is gloomy, filled with clouds that are an endless source of rain. It's so bad, even the cameraman has given up and left. So we sit in the shelter, without anyone to document our misery, only leaving it long enough to run to the Porta-Potty area when we just can't wait any more.

It isn't until well into the afternoon when the rain finally stops. An hour later, one of the staffers comes to tell us it's time for the elimination challenge. As we slog our way to the play area, I remember what Kai said about dry shoes being a distant memory. If I ever see her again, I think I'll compliment her on her talent for understatement.

Rick greets us as soon as we walk into the play area. Bob and Tracy go to the benches, and the rest of us stay standing.

"That was some storm last night," Rick says. "Glad to see you all made it through."

I'm sure that's a coded message for me. Maybe he means that only an act of nature could keep me in one spot long enough not to hurt myself. I look down at my fingertips, wondering just how long they'll resemble prunes. When I look back up, a steady-cam operator has moved into my line of sight. It's Bruce.

Rick comes closer and stands between our two teams. "Let's get right down to the challenge. Tonight will be a test of balance, strength, and stamina."

Terrific. Three things I have zero of at the moment.

A staffer trots in and demonstrates how we will stand on a narrow piece of wood while at the same time, pulling down on a handle hanging above our heads.

"As long as you hold the handle and stay on the wood, you're in the game. But if you let go of the handle, it releases a flag." Rick nods to the staffer, who releases the handle. Behind her, a large black flag with a yellow sad face in the middle pops up. "If you fall off the wood, or if your flag goes up, you're out of the game."

It's a straightforward concept, and on a good day, I'd think we had a chance. But with Jess's sprained ankle and my mangled wrist, we might as well say good-bye right now. When I turn to her, it's obvious she's thinking the same thing.

"Let's go out giving it our best," she says.

I nod and am about to step on the balance board, when Rick makes another announcement.

"One more detail to make this more challenging." He points at our feet. "Take off your shoes. You'll be balancing on the wood barefooted."

This doesn't seem like a big deal until my shoes are off and I step on the beam. It's about a foot high, but less than an inch thick, so the edges dig into the tender soles of my feet. Rick gives us a chance to balance, then reach up and grab the handle, which is thankfully positioned to the right.

Once we've all stopped wobbling, he gives the word. "And this challenge is on."

It's probably the quietest challenge we've had. There's no yelling, no encouraging each other. There isn't even any moving. At least none I can tell. Jess is to my left, and on the right is Malcolm and then Layla. I can kind of see them, depending on how far I swing my eyes from one side to the other, but there's no way I'm moving my head for a better look. I'm barely even breathing, because I know the slightest movement or shift in weight will throw my balance right off.

"We're five minutes into this challenge." Rick speaks with the soft breathiness of a golf announcer.

"Only five minutes?" Layla's voice is stretched tight. It sounds like she's in pain.

And if she's hurting, I can only imagine how Jess feels. I want to tell her to walk away and elevate her sprained ankle, just like I want to stop the torture being inflicted on the one part of my body that didn't hurt prior to this challenge. But she doesn't want to go out that way, and neither do I. I'm going to stay on this stinking beam, with my fingers around the handle and all the blood draining from my arm, until I can't stand anymore.

"Ow!"

It takes all the control I have not to look in Layla's direction and see what's wrong.

"What's going on, Layla?" Rick asks.

"My arm. Muscle cramp." She yelps again.

Out of the corner of my eye, I see movement. Then I hear the whoosh of her flag going up, and Rick confirms what I think just happened. "Layla is out of this challenge."

Wow. I didn't suspect one of them to drop out before Jess and me.

"Monica." Jess says my name in a hissed whisper. "My foot really hurts. I don't think—"

She grunts and stumbles forward. Her flag goes up.

"And just like that, we're down to two players."

The frustration comes off Jess in waves, so I take the chance of speaking.

"You did great, Jess."

"I lost."

"No. We're a team, and our team is still in this."

She doesn't respond, but I hear her shuffle away through the sand.

Beside me, a deep chuckle rumbles from Malcolm. "Well, you wanted to go to the end together. How do you feel now that we're here?"

"We're not at the end. We're final three."

"Close enough."

The minutes tick by and the silence stretches. My muscles ache and my feet feel like they're full of porcupine quills. This is simultaneously the most boring and most painful challenge ever.

A low groan comes from Malcolm. Shifting my eyes as far to the right as possible without moving my head, I detect movement. Could he be faltering? Malcolm's a big guy, which isn't helping him in this challenge. His feet are supporting far more weight than mine are. If I'm hurting, he must be in agony.

If I can just hang on a little longer, maybe—pain shoots through my leg, taking my breath away. Teeth clamping down on my lip, I try to remain calm as my calf muscle contracts into a rock-like ball, and my toes curl in on themselves.

No, no, no. Not now. Not when I'm so close.

None of this escapes Rick's scrutiny. "Malcolm is struggling to regain his balance. This could be Monica's game. No, wait. It looks like she's in trouble, too."

"No, I'm not." The words hiss out through clenched teeth. I've endured so much physical pain over the last however-many days, there's no way I'm going to let a muscle cramp take me down. For once, my best is going to be more than good enough. For once, my best is going to be better than everyone else's.

"She may not be in trouble, but I am." Malcolm barely puffs out the words before he falls off the beam, landing on his hands and knees in the sand.

"Monica wins!" Rick has abandoned his golf voice and moved straight on to you-won-the-Super-Bowl yelling. "Monica is the last person standing!"

It takes a moment for it to register that the challenge is over. My fingers are still tight around the handle when Jess tackles me in a hug and knocks me off the beam.

"You did it! I can't believe you did it!" We continue to stumble backward until we land in the sand, alternating between laughing and saying "ouch."

When we calm down and struggle to our feet, I see Layla hugging Malcolm, patting his back and telling him it's all right. He smiles at me over her head, a sad little smile that says he wanted to win for her, but he's still happy for me. Which is exactly how I would have felt if he'd won.

Rick walks over to them and puts a hand on Layla's shoulder. "Malcolm and Layla, you won't be the last family standing. It's time to pick up your things and go."

Tears well up in my eyes as they leave the play area. Who would have thought I'd become so attached to the people who were supposed to be our competition?

Bob and Tracy leave the benches and stand next to us. Then Rick does his summation.

"This is proof that you never know what's going to happen until it happens. The four of you have beaten every other team to get where you are, but now, it's out of your hands. Tomorrow, your former opponents will have the chance to ask you why you deserve to win. After that, the vote goes to America, and they will decide who will be the last family standing." He takes a dramatic pause while making eye contact with each one of us, then smiles. "Head on back to camp."

Jess and I are both limping now but, despite the pain, I feel lighter than I have in a long time.

32

There's a surprise waiting for us when we wake up the next morning. A large table has been set up on one side of camp, and it's loaded with food. Fresh fruits, covered bowls of scrambled eggs, sausage, bacon. Baskets of croissants and muffins, and tall carafes of chilled orange and cranberry juices. But the best thing of all sits on a table all its own.

"Coffee." Bob nearly hugs the thermal pot in his excitement.

"This is so great," I say, ripping the top off a blueberry muffin. "I guess they figured there's no point in starving us anymore."

Jess shakes her head. "Nah, they want us to have plenty of strength for tonight's inquisition."

Tracy stops in mid-pour as she fills her juice glass. "How bad can it be? The physical challenges are over."

"Thank God." I do a little raise-the-roof movement with one palm pointed heavenward.

"No kidding," Tracy says. "All we have to do tonight is answer some questions. Piece of cake." With a grin, she bites into a slice of coffee cake for emphasis.

Jess spears a chunk of pineapple with her fork and brandishes it in the air. "This Q and A can be brutal. Remember when they were in the Seychelles? When Tina accused Big Al of being a racist, which he wasn't. And then she grilled him about what he did for a living, and he finally admitted he was a hair stylist?"

Tracy wrinkles her nose. "Oh yeah. I do remember that. Poor guy."

"Do you really think anybody in this game would be that vindictive?" I look to Bob, hoping to get the opinion of the other mature—aka, old—person on the island.

His hands are wrapped protectively around his coffee cup, which he holds inches away from his mouth, as if he can't bear the thought of being separated from the hot, brown liquid any longer than necessary. "I don't think so. I mean, what would they have to gain from acting like that?"

"More airtime," Jess says. "Tina ended up in almost every clip montage they put together."

Another excellent point. When it comes right down to it, even the tiniest bit of fame can be a powerful motivator. Or there could be people who are mean-spirited, simply because they didn't get to the end. There could also be people who find Bob and Tracy more deserving, so they'll bash Jess and me. Which could go the other way, too. It all comes down to one thing.

"We won't know what to expect until we get there, so let's not ruin our amazing breakfast by stressing over it." I point near Bob. "Would you pass the strawberries, please? And the whipped cream?"

As I dip succulent red berries into light-as-air whipped cream, I do my best to heed my own advice. Nothing we do now will make one bit of difference tonight. Still, I can't help but go over the possible scenarios. Have I made anybody angry? Have I given anybody a reason to want to embarrass me? Until the last week, Bob was my biggest problem, and if I'd been asked to pick someone I thought would treat me badly, it would have been him. But now, not only have we come to an understanding, we're heading into the questioning together. Bob has just become the least of my worries.

After breakfast, I go to the latrine area. I'm about to return to camp when I change my mind and head over for one last trip to the confessional.

Ponytail greets me with a huge smile. "I cannot believe you made it to the end."

I look at her sideways as I plop down on the familiar log. "Are you really supposed to tell me things like that?"

She shrugs. "Today's the last day. I'm feeling a little loose with the rules."

"Okay then." I skooch myself around until I feel semi-settled. "To be honest, I'm beyond shocked that I made it to the end without some serious head trauma."

"That comes tonight, Hon," she says with a wave of her hand.

"Yeah. Back at camp, they're all talking about how brutal tonight will be. But I just don't see it."

"Why's that?"

I shrug. "Because, for the most part, we all got along. And I don't think any of those people are mean-spirited." When Ponytail doesn't say anything, I continue. "I'm trying not to worry about it."

"And how's that working for ya?"

Laughing, I shake my head. "It's not. I can't stop obsessing and playing out worst-case scenarios in my mind."

"What do you want people to know?" Ponytail is serious now. "If you could make sure they leave here knowing one thing about you, what would it be?"

"That winning doesn't matter to me. I came here to be with my daughter, so we could start building a relationship. And we have. Whether we win or lose doesn't mean a thing to me."

"Yet here you are, making it all the way to the end." Ponytail laughs to herself. "That alone is enough to make some of them dislike you."

"Great. I'm offending people by my very existence." I push up off the log. "Guess this will be the last time I see you. Take care."

Ponytail nods. "You too."

I'm walking away when I hear her call me back.

"Hey, Monica!"

I look over my shoulder.

"Good luck."

Smiling, I give her a nod of thanks, then continue on. In just a few hours, the grilling will begin.

The final play area has been made over so it feels more like an amphitheater. Four chairs sit on top of a bamboo-looking stage that fills the center space. The two-tiered benches are empty, but ready. And around the whole thing are blazing tiki torches. It's ironic how hard we've worked all this time to maintain fire, and now we're surrounded by it.

The four of us file in and take our seats as Rick offers a greeting.

"Bob, Tracy, Monica, Jess . . . congratulations on being the final two families standing. And now, let's welcome everyone you had to beat to get here."

They file in, entering in the order that they left the game. Some of them, like Sal and Gracie, smile when they see us. Others, like Maxie and Marcy, wear expressions that are impossible to read. But they all have clean hair and are wearing clean clothes, which should put them in a good mood. I hope.

Once they're all sitting, Rick resumes. "America will vote which team deserves to be the last family standing. But we want to give them plenty of information to base their decision on. So a spokesperson from each team will now address the group." He turns pointedly toward the benches. "You can make a statement or ask a question to either or both teams. Sal, you're up first."

Sal bounds up to the stage, still grinning. "Hey, guys. First, congratulations." He glances back at Gracie, then continues. "Since we left the game so early, we didn't get a chance to experience a lot. So what Gracie and I want to know from each one of you is, what was the biggest challenge you faced?"

I smile back at Sal, hoping he knows how thankful I am for that question. "For me, it was trying to stay away from the medics."

Laughter breaks the tension. The others provide their answers, and we move on to Evelyn. Another friendly face, another nonantagonistic question. This is turning out to be much easier than I expected.

Then Maxie steps up, and even before she opens her mouth, I regret letting myself relax.

"Monica, you're the only one I need to speak to."

Uh oh. I lean forward slightly, just to show her I'm paying attention.

Standing straight as a marble pillar, her white hair moussed and spiked into an intimidating configuration, she lets me have it. "You came in here as the celebrity contestant. The big-time chef from Sin City."

I shake my head, because surely, I'm hearing her wrong. "I'm not a—"

She holds her hand up like a cop stopping traffic. "I get to talk now. You just listen. You've done plenty of talking over the last few weeks, ordering people around and acting like you're better than everyone else."

None of this makes any sense. Maxie and I hardly had any kind of interaction, which is probably why she's describing a person who absolutely cannot be me. I want her to give me examples of the terrible things I did, but she's keeping her rant pretty general.

"The only reason you made it this far is because you've been flirting with the host." She jabs a finger in Rick's direction. He frowns at her, but doesn't offer a rebuttal. "Not that anyone should be surprised. A woman like you, who would give away her own flesh and blood, would do anything to come out on top." Maxie turns her head, spits—she actually spits on the ground—and then stalks back to her seat.

My eyes burn, and I know that if I make eye contact with anyone or try to speak, the waterworks will start. So I look down at the bamboo floor, concentrating on a black mark near the toe of my shoe.

Beside me, Jess rises slowly to her feet. "You're way out of line, Maxie." Her voice is low and controlled, full of contained energy like a lion just seconds before springing on its prey.

"And you're an idiot," Maxie shoots back.

Now I jump out of my seat. "You can't talk to her like that."

Maxie takes a step back toward the stage. "I'll talk to her anyway I like, and you can't do a thing about it."

I may only have one good hand, but right now, that's all I need. We move toward each other. The only thing that stops the argument from getting physical is Jess grabbing me, Marcy holding back Maxie, and Bob jumping in between us.

"Okay, folks. Let's settle down." Apparently, Rick has seen worse, or at least just as bad, because he doesn't sound overly concerned.

My legs are shaking as I move back to my chair. Jess squeezes my hand and leans over to whisper. "Ignore her. She doesn't know what she's talking about."

Still not trusting myself to say much, I just nod.

Payton is up next. He looks at Bob and thanks him for the time they spent talking about the origins of the universe. "I didn't understand most of it, but it helped distract me from how darn much my bug bites stung."

Then he looks at me. "Monica, you shared fire when you didn't have to, so you're obviously not all bad." He winks, then goes back to his seat.

He goes back to his seat, passing Trevor along the way. Trevor crosses his arms tightly over his chest, his feet planted apart. He reminds me of Mr. Clean, only not as happy, and with more hair. I brace myself to be blasted, but to my surprise, he ignores me.

"Bob, the plan was for us to go all the way together, which obviously didn't happen. And now that I'm here and you're there, I can tell you that I never liked you. Not one little bit."

Without another word, he turns and walks away. Leaning forward in my chair, I look over at Bob and raise a questioning brow. He shrugs, then says in a low voice, "I guess I won't ask him to be president of my fan club."

Tracy snorts back a laugh, but sobers when Malcolm walks up on stage.

"Hi, guys." He's relaxed, standing with his hands clasped behind his back. "Being on this island and participating in this game has had a profound effect on me, as I'm sure it's had on you. So my question for each of you is this: What will you do differently when you get back to civilization?"

Leave it to Malcolm to ask the deep question.

Tracy speaks up first. "I've gotten to know my dad a lot better through this experience. So I think, when we get home, I won't automatically assume he's wrong about everything."

Bob rubs her back quickly. "Thanks, kiddo. As for me, I'm not going to take anything for granted. That goes for big things, like my relationship with Tracy, and small things, like a hot, fresh cup of coffee."

Malcolm smiles, then looks at Jess and me. "Your turn," he says.

Jess turns her head toward me. "You go first."

"Okay." Here we go. Malcolm has given me the perfect opportunity to make sure everyone knows exactly what my motivation was for coming. But now that it's right in front of me, I choke. Literally.

In one of those bizarre moments when you inhale and accidentally suck a drop of saliva down the wrong pipe, I begin to cough and sputter. Jess pounds my back with the flat of her hand.

Someone calls out, "Do you need water?"

Another voice says, "I think she swallowed a fly."

"Serves her right."

I manage to stop choking long enough to glare at Maxie.

From his place at the podium, Rick looks on in concern. "Are you going to be all right, Monica?"

Nodding, I hold up one finger. Breathing slowly and deeply, I finally am back in control. "I'm fine," I croak out in a gravelly voice. "Sorry."

"No problem. As soon as you're ready, continue."

All that hacking interrupted what could have been a great, heartfelt moment. Now, I do my best to regroup and get back on track.

"This show has given me a new identity. Before I came here, I was a woman, a chef, a friend . . . but I never saw myself as a mother. I didn't even think I had maternal instincts. But now, after meeting this amazing young woman, I know that's not true.

"You all know, the only reason I came on this show was to meet Jess. I had no expectations beyond that. And now, I hope she'll allow me to continue to be part of her life. Because I can never go back to the way things were. I'm a mother, pure and simple."

"Thank you," Malcolm says. "Jess? What about you?"

Fingers laced together, she exhales a shaky breath. "I can't lie anymore. Everyone thinks I came on this show because of a burning desire to find my birth mother. But that's not true."

The chair seems to dissolve beneath me. What is she saying?

"I needed to get on the show, and I knew that searching for the woman who gave me up was my best shot."

"Jessica." Rick interjects, his face hard and not a trace of a dimple in sight. "Are you saying you lied?"

She looks up from her hands. I start to reach for her, but there's something in her face that stops me. It's a look of resignation, but also regret. As if she doesn't want to divulge this information, but she has no choice.

"I never lied about Monica being my birth mother. She is." She turns her full attention to me, her eyes brimming with emotions. "I just lied about coming on the show so I could meet you."

"Why?" I shake my head, trying to shake off the betrayal I'm feeling. "Why was it so important that you get on the show?"

"Because of the money. I need the money."

No. It can't be something so crass. "For what? How could you need money so badly that you'd put us both through all . . . all . . . *this*?"

She squeezes her eyes shut, as though the truth is too ugly to look at. "My mother . . . my real mother . . . is dying. I need the money for her."

33

After the inquisition, everyone is taken straight to a hotel on a nearby, larger island. Everyone except me. I'm hustled off to a clinic where my wrist is X-rayed and, after confirming that I do in fact have a compression fracture, is put in an honest-to-goodness cast. All of this is done with very little interaction on my part, since I'm still in a fog of confusion and denial.

When my escort finally gets me to the hotel, I'm met by the concierge.

"A pleasure to have you here, miss," he says with a solicitous smile. "Our kitchen closes at midnight, but if you tell me what you'd like, I'll make sure it's delivered to your room."

I look around blankly, still not quite used to being inside a building with electric lights. "What time is it?"

"Eleven forty-five."

Huh. I didn't realize so much time had passed since Jess dropped her bombshell and left me with a crater where my heart used to be. Right now, the thought of food makes my stomach lurch, but as long as he's offering, it would be smart to take him up on it.

"A roast beef sandwich, please. With fries. And iced tea."

"Very good, miss. And for dessert?"

"Chocolate cake." I may skip the sandwich and go straight for the cake. The idea of drowning my sorrows in sugar and frosting holds some appeal.

"Wonderful. Cameron!" The name is barely out of his mouth when a young man appears at his side. Cameron, as his name tag confirms, wears a crisp uniform of a colorful tropical shirt, beige slacks, and a thousand-watt smile. The concierge motions to me. "Please see Miss Stanton to room 223."

"My pleasure, sir." Cameron turns to me. "Right this way, miss."

I follow the man to the elevator, trying not to think about where Jess is or what I'll say if I run into her. Thankfully, my destination is only a few rooms down the second floor hall. The bellhop opens the door and hands me the key card.

"Your things have already been brought inside. But if you need anything at all, just call down to the front desk."

What a sweet guy. I wonder what he would do if I told him what I really need is a daughter who wants to be in the same room with me, and does he have one of those behind the desk?

"Thank you." My hand automatically reaches to dig out a tip, but I don't have my purse. "I'm sorry. I don't have any money."

He holds up his hand. "Not a problem. Everything here is covered by the production company, including gratuities. All you need to do is relax and enjoy." With another smile and a barely detectible bow, he bids me good-bye and heads back down the hall.

I shut the door, then lean back against it as I take in the room. Done in shades of brown, yellow, and green, it has an artificial tropical feel that seems too bright after a month in the real thing. Walking further in, I see a suitcase on a collapsible stand against the wall. As I lift the lid, I see all the items I wasn't allowed to bring on the island, including my purse, as well as a clean change of clothes and a blue cotton nightshirt. For the first time in hours, I think of something other than Jess. I turn slowly and sigh at the sight of the king-size bed. Covered in a soft, white spread and three plump pillows leaning against the headboard, it looks like a little piece of heaven. I reach to pull back the covers, then stop when I catch sight of my fingers. So much dirt is embedded around my nails, I may never get it all off, but it makes me realize a bath is essential before I get in this bed.

I trudge into the bathroom, feeling worse than I ever have in my life and quite sure it's the worst I ever will feel. But that's until I catch sight of myself in the mirror. At first, I yelp, thinking someone else is in the room with me. When I realize I'm looking at my own reflection, I yelp again. Since there were no mirrors on the island, I never really knew how my body was being affected by the game. I saw what it did to the others, but for some reason, I didn't transfer the effects to me. Yet another case of Monica living in her own little dream world.

My skin is a mottled mess of blues, purples, and yellows from bruises in various stages of life. The numerous bug bites that litter my arms and shoulders are red and irritated. My hair hangs in stringy clumps around my face, almost resembling dreadlocks. And, to top it all off, I've lost so much weight that my collarbones appear ready to rip through my skin. This is the hollow shell of a woman America will see on their television sets.

I'm pulled out of my funk by a knock on the door. Expecting room service, I pull it open, only to find Rick standing on the other side.

He smiles. "I just wanted to make sure you got in okay."

"Sure. I'm great. I just took a look in the mirror and discovered the island turned me into the Crypt Keeper."

"Don't feel bad. It happens to everybody."

His honesty is oddly refreshing. "Thanks for not even trying to pretend I don't look hideous. I've had about all the deception I can take for one day."

"About that." He stuffs one hand in his pants pocket, and leans against the doorjamb with the other. "I want you to know, I had no idea about any of that with Jess. I believed she wanted to find you. Period."

"I know. It was pretty clear from the look on your face." Trying to lighten the mood, I shrug. "Hey, it's going to make great television when the editors get done with it."

"No kidding." He straightens up and rubs the back of his neck. "To be honest, I haven't figured out what to do with it yet."

"What's to figure out? You have to use it."

He cocks his head slightly. "You'd be okay with that?"

"It's part of what I signed up for."

His eyes are warm and understanding as he nods his approval. "How's the wrist?"

"Busted." I hold it up between us. "Not a total break, just a compression fracture. I'll be good as new in about six weeks. My biggest problem will be brushing the knots out of my hair with one hand."

Rick glances down the hall. "I can send Jess over to help you."

"No." It comes out hard and sharp, like a slap to the face, but it doesn't faze Rick.

"You're going to have to talk to her eventually."

Oh really? I managed to go twenty-five years without talking to her. It shouldn't be hard to go twenty-five more. But instead of spewing my frustration all over Rick, I force myself to be pleasant. "Is Kai here somewhere?"

"She is. Would you like me to get her?"

I sigh with relief. "That would be so great. I just don't feel up to seeing any of the contestants right now. I hope that makes sense."

"It does. Total sense."

"Excuse me, sir." Cameron comes up behind Rick, pushing a room service cart.

Rick moves out of the way and starts peeking under the silver plate covers. "I'm glad they got food for you. I'll let you eat in peace. Expect Kai in about fifteen minutes."

"Thanks, Rick."

He's almost to the elevator when he turns back and winks at me. "Eat the cake first. It's good for your soul."

Cameron pushes the cart into the room, while I stand in the doorway and watch the elevator doors slide shut. *Eat the cake first.* Rick Wolff may just be a man after my own heart.

I am determined to stay in this bed as long as possible. That's why, when someone rudely ignored my request to "do not disturb" and knocked on my door at 8:00 a.m., I rolled over, snuggling deeper under the covers. And when the phone rang an hour later, I sandwiched my head between two pillows and luxuriated in the softness of them.

Now, the phone is once again trilling, doing its best to pull me out of my blissful cocoon. With a sigh, I reach to the nightstand, past the phone, and pull the clock closer. 11:15. As good a time as any to start moving back toward real life. But that doesn't mean I'm answering the stinking phone.

I sit up and swing my legs over the side of the bed. My bare toes curl into the carpet, marveling that it's neither wet nor sandy. With my good hand, I push off the mattress, groaning as I extend my aching muscles and joints. You'd think that a night in a normal bed would make me feel better than ever, but apparently, my body has become accustomed to bamboo.

"Don't get used to it," I mutter as I shuffle into the bathroom.

The mirror reveals a much cleaner version of the woman I discovered last night. It took Kai a good twenty minutes to liberate my hair from all the snarls and knots it had worked its way into. Then she took another fifteen minutes to scrub my hands, going carefully around my fingernails with a small, stiff brush. At that point, I thanked her, and said I could do the rest by myself. It had been challenging to wash my hair with one hand and hold my cast up and out of the water, but I'd done it.

Today, though . . . today calls for a nice, long soak in the tub. After rummaging through my bag of toiletries, I find a butterfly clip to pin up my hair and a small bottle of bath bubbles. Perfect.

When the tub is full, I step through the bubbles and carefully lower myself in, hissing as the hot water covers my skin. With my cast resting on the side of the tub, I lean back until my neck sits just right against the cool porcelain and close my eyes.

"Thank you, God, for hot water heaters and indoor plumbing."

As I lounge there, determined to relax, there's a knock on the door. Somebody certainly is persistent. I wonder . . .

And there I am, back to thinking about Jess.

My real mother is dying . . . I need the money for her.

How could she? How could she act like meeting me was a major goal in her life, when all the time, it was just a means to an end? I understand about being desperate. I've certainly been there myself. But there had to be another way for her to get money. A way that didn't include dragging me through several circles of hell, and breaking my wrist—and my heart—in the process.

Of course, I'm not the only one in pain. I think of Jess's parents the way they were so many years ago. Their pictures displayed a happy, loving couple. In most of them, Susan's long, golden hair was swept back, either in a ponytail or a French braid. It told me she was practical, and her smile told me she enjoyed life. And Robert. There was a picture of them at a picnic, and the way he looked at her made my heart hurt. Because I so desperately wanted someone to love me the way he obviously loved her.

How are they dealing with Susan's illness? What does she have? I have so many questions now, but no right to ask any of them. I thought I'd been invited into my daughter's life, but I really wasn't. Instead, she was using me to do what she had to for the mother she loves. As much as that hurts, I really can't blame her.

A tear runs down my cheek and plops into the now-tepid, bubbleless water. My soak is done.

After carefully drying off, I wrap a towel around my torso and leave the bathroom. On my way to get clean clothes from my suitcase, I notice a piece of paper on the floor by the door.

"Instead of pail mail, I'm getting floor mail."

It's a note from Rick. At 12:30, there's a lunch and final group meeting with all the cast and crew before we go to the airfield and head our separate ways. Funny, now that the game is over, we're not contestants anymore, we're "the cast."

I check the clock. There's just enough time to get dressed and head for the meeting room. Looks like my self-imposed isolation is coming to an end.

34

Monica! You look great." Layla runs up to me and wraps me in a hug. Gracie is right behind her.

"I love your dress. Come sit with us."

They lead me over to a table where their dads are sitting. Both men stand up and we exchange friendly hugs.

"You've cleaned up quite well," Malcolm says with a grin.

I can't help but laugh. "Thanks. After a month of gritty shorts and wet athletic shoes, I had to put on a sundress and sandals." Before anyone can get me to talk about something more personal than my clothes, I turn to Sal. "So, have you and Gracie been staying at this lovely hotel all this time?"

"We have." He winks at his daughter. "Being the first off the island has its advantages."

Gracie rolls her eyes. "I don't know that I'd call it an advantage. All of you lost weight, but they've fed us so great here, I think I gained ten pounds."

I shake my head. "You're talking to the wrong people if you expect sympathy."

Layla snatches a roll from the basket in the middle of the table and lobs it at Gracie. She dodges just in time for it to sail past her head and hit Sal right in the chin. The three of them are quickly embroiled in a good-natured argument that I'm praying doesn't evolve into a food fight.

Malcolm leans over, his voice low. "How are you? Really?"

"I am really, really conflicted."

"I'm sure." He looks across the room and motions slightly with his head. "She's over there."

She's sitting with Bob, Tracy, Evelyn, and Jasmine. "I'll bet Bob doesn't envy me anymore."

"You haven't talked to her about it yet?"

A waiter leans between us to put down salad plates. After thanking him, I look back at Malcolm. "What's there to talk about? She loves her mother, she did what she had to do."

His forehead creases in a frown. "But what about you? What about that relationship you wanted to build?"

"I don't want to anymore." I try to spear a cherry tomato with my fork, but the tines bounce off the slick skin and send it skittering off my plate. "I don't want, or need, a one-sided relationship."

He scoops up the tomato with a clean spoon and drops it back on top of my lettuce. "You might change your mind later."

"Sure, I might." Nodding my head in an overexaggerated manner, I paste on a smile. "After my skin clears up, and my body stops aching, and my wrist heals so I can go back to work again . . . maybe then I'll feel warm and fuzzy and change my mind. For now, I want to enjoy this lovely, crisp salad."

Malcolm takes the hint and we eat in silence. And for the record, the lettuce is wilted and the dressing is far too heavy on the vinegar.

When the salad plates are cleared away, Rick walks to the center of the room. Even he looks different now. Instead of the short-sleeve safari shirts and khaki shorts that were his signature island style, he's wearing blue jeans and a Star Trek t-shirt that's so thin and faded, it must be one of his favorites.

People start clapping when they see him. He breaks out his dimpled smile, which hasn't changed one bit, and holds his hands up for silence. "Congratulations, everybody, on finishing another great season of *Last Family Standing*."

More clapping, accompanied by cheers, whistles, and a few *woot woots*. I slap the palm of my uninjured hand against my thigh, just so I won't stand out as the one sourpuss in an otherwise enthusiastic group.

"I'm sure you all want to know what happens next. Crew, you guys already know how this works, but bear with me while I break it down for the cast." He turns toward the three tables we're all gathered at. "Our crack editing staff has been working on assembling episodes since your first day on the island. So by the time you get back home, the first episode will already have aired."

The first episode. Funny, despite all the cameras, the challenges, the confessional visits, I'd kind of forgotten that the show really isn't over. In fact, it's just beginning.

"A word of caution to all of you," Rick continues, his voice and expression now serious. "As soon as that first show hits, there won't be any question about who the cast is. Everybody, your friends, your family, even strangers, will grill you for information. It is imperative that you don't give away anything that happened on the island. You can discuss events after they air, but do not hand out spoilers." Then he grins. "And if you have any trouble keeping mum, just remember the confidentiality agreements you signed and the penalty for breaking them."

Nervous laughter ripples from our tables. Now Rick addresses the entire group, telling us that we'll be receiving a schedule of when our flights are leaving. Then he thanks us all for a great season and tells us to enjoy our lunch. As he walks over to one of the crew tables, the waiters come back out with plates of grilled chicken, garlic dill baby potatoes, and green beans.

I don't know what possesses me to glance at Jess, but when I do, she's staring right at me. Our eyes meet and she sits a little straighter, her mouth curving up the tiniest bit. I try. I try to feel empathy for what she must be going through. Try to move my face into something warm and pleasant. But I can't. Instead, I turn away and look down at my plate, even though it holds no interest for me at all.

After all that time on the island, sleeping outside and being exposed to the elements, I thought I'd never again want to leave the comforts of a climate-controlled roof and four walls. But here it is, my second night in the hotel, and I feel as though I'm suffocating. The air in my room is too cold when the AC is on, but stuffy and stale when it's off. I've got to get out of here. I grab my sweater and my room key and head out the door.

The hotel is small, but exclusive, and our group has taken over the entire thing. It's nice to know that, at the very least, I have a level of anonymity here. Strolling down a paved walking path, the breeze from the ocean ruffles my hair. I pass two men talking to each other, one leaning against a palm tree, and both smoking. They look vaguely familiar, and I think they might be camera operators. Now that they're off duty, they smile and wave when they see me, then dive back into their conversation.

I follow the path around a curve and find a small cluster of beach chairs facing the ocean. Picking the nearest one, I stretch out, pulling my sweater close around me as I put my head back and close my eyes. This is exactly what I needed. It feels so good to be close to the sand but not on it, to be clean and dry as a gentle breeze caresses my skin, and to enjoy the sounds of the tropics while not being terrified that a monkey will chew off my face in my sleep. Wow, I really was a pitiful mess. Remembering how scared I was those first few days makes me laugh.

"Is this a private party, or can anybody join?"

The laughter flees as I open my eyes and see Jess standing next to me. Either this is a big nasty coincidence, or she followed me out here. Either way, there's no point in me being rude. "It's a free beach." A casual wave of my hand indicates that it won't bother me if she sits down.

"Thanks." She sits in the chair to my right, but instead of stretching out like me, she sits cross-legged, leaning forward with her elbows on her knees.

She doesn't say anything else, and I wonder if she's thinking about the last time we were out on the beach together at night. That had been such a great night. I really thought it was a turning point for us. But now, I know it was simply how she chose to play the game.

This would be the perfect time for a waiter to materialize with a tray of refreshments. What I wouldn't give for a skewer of pineapple chunks and cherries in a tall glass of brightly colored punch, topped with a festive paper umbrella. At least that would take my mind off how totally and utterly awkward this situation is.

"I'm sorry."

Slowly, I turn my head toward Jess. The way her shoulders are hunched and her head tucked in, she reminds me of a hedgehog rolling itself into a protective ball. Without my permission, that maternal instinct asserts itself again. I can't just ignore her, not even if I wanted to. Which I don't.

"Why did you do it?" I ask.

She won't look at me. "I told you."

"I know, but . . . Why didn't you tell me the truth from the beginning? If I'd known—"

"You wouldn't have come."

"Yes, I would have."

Now she looks my way. "Seriously? You would have come if you knew the only reason I was doing this was for my—"

She cuts herself off, and it touches me that she seems to be considering my feelings. "For your mom. Yes. I would have done it for you and for her." I shift in my chair, bracing my cast on my hip and looking straight at Jess. "I don't understand, though, why you saw this show as a way to help her."

"What do you mean?"

"Well, the application process takes a long time. And there was no guarantee that once they saw your application, you'd get on the show."

A sad little smile settles on her lips. "This wasn't my only plan. I did everything I could think of, including applying to every game show and reality program known to man."

Why, oh why, couldn't we have been accepted to a cooking show? I pull my attention away from my battered body and back to my battered daughter. "So this show was the first one that answered you."

She nods.

There's still so much I don't understand. "How is this going to help, though? We won't even know if we've won until the last episode. That's three months away."

"They still pay us for being contestants."

Something else I'd forgotten about. Or else I was so preoccupied with more important things, I totally missed it in the first place.

"And the longer you stay on the show, the more money you make." Jess finally looks me in the eye. "Thanks to you, we made it all the way. You have no idea how much it will help."

"I don't. But I'd like to." For the first time since her shocking admission on the island, I reach out and touch her, resting my hand on her shoulder. "Tell me."

She looks away, but I don't move my hand. When she looks back at me, her eyes and nose are red from everything she's holding back. "Okay."

As Jess shares her story, I feel worse and worse. And by the time she's done, all my anger and frustration are gone, replaced by resolve.

My daughter's mother is in crisis, and I'm going to do what I can to help her.

35

I wave behind me as Jules's husband backs their car down the driveway, then I push the button to close the garage door.

"Honey, I'm home!" I call out as I pull my suitcase into the kitchen. Nails clattering on the tile, Ranger barrels around a corner, barking and doing a mad welcome dance that's part jumping, part thrashing, and all excitement.

Dropping to my knees, I throw my arm around his neck while keeping my cast tucked tightly against my chest. "How's my boy?" His response is several sloppy, slobbery kisses to my face. "I missed you, too, buddy."

Jules's laughter comes around the corner before her body does. "So much for hoping he'd choose to stay with me over you."

"Never." I ruffle the fur along his back and plant a kiss on top of his head. "I know who loves me." Then I stand up and almost throw myself into her arms.

"Welcome home, conquering hero."

I melt into the familiarity of her vise-like hug, glad to have found two constants in the world: my best friend and my dog.

"Thank you for sending Jackson to pick me up."

"No problem. Now that you're a celebrity, we can't have you standing on the curb waiting for the shuttle. Although," she waggles her eyebrows, "it wouldn't have surprised me at all if Rick had brought you home himself."

"Don't be silly. He doesn't have time to deliver all the contestants to their front doors."

"Of course not. But I got the feeling he doesn't think of you as just another contestant."

A slow smile takes over my lips. After my jungle heart-to-heart with Bruce, I opened myself to the possibility that maybe Rick really was fond of me, in a noncontestant kind of way. And the more I thought about it, the more I liked the idea. Especially after the lingering good-bye hug he gave me at the hotel taxi stand, not to mention the kiss on the cheek. But for now, that's a memory I prefer to keep to myself, so I change the subject.

"I caught a few people staring at me in the airport, but I thought it was just because I look like I've been run over by buffalo."

"Oh no, my friend, people are going to start recognizing you." She holds me at arm's length and inspects my face and arms. "Although, the lovely bruising probably helped them pick you out of the crowd."

I don't even want to ask the next question. "Did you see the first episode?"

"Of course! You were great. Especially when you ran into the pole."

"Oh great." Cringing behind my hand, I let my shoulders slump. "I'm sure they made me look like a huge idiot."

"Don't worry, I recorded it for you so you can see for yourself. Now come on." She leads me into the living room. "I want to hear everything."

Ranger follows close on my heels, and when I plop down on the couch, he settles on the floor, resting his head on my sandaled foot. I look blankly around the room. A month is a long time to be away from home, and I find I don't quite feel settled yet. It's all my stuff, but it doesn't seem like my stuff. "You know what's weird?"

"What?" She tucks one leg under her and sits beside me, leaning in.

"Every now and then, I find myself looking for the machete."

Jules laughs. "Oh man, you should have brought one home as a souvenir."

"I tried, but I couldn't sneak it past security. Seriously, I do have a couple of mementos. My bandana, which is filthy. A flint." I hold up my arm. "This nifty cast."

"Very stylish," she says with a nod. "But I want to know about Jessica. What happened with her?"

Normally, there's nothing I don't tell Jules, especially something this big. But now, I've got a problem. "Oh man, so much happened with her. But I can't tell you any of it."

"I don't want to know game secrets." Her expressive face contorts in irritation. "I want to know the personal, relationship stuff."

"I know. And I want to tell you, but it's all tangled together. I can't tell you about the personal stuff without talking about the game." I puff out a sigh. "Darn confidentiality agreement."

"Yeah, that thing's pretty serious."

I'm chewing on my lip when I process what she just said. "Wait a minute. When you came on the island, did they have you sign one of those?"

"Sure. I don't think anybody gets out there without signing."

"Then you can't tell anybody anything about the game either. Which means that I can tell you about Jess, because we're both covered by the same agreement."

Jules grins, her eyes twinkling. "Good thinking. And since nothing you say to me will leave this room, there's no problem."

"Exactly." And with no further delay, I dump all my emotional baggage right in her lap. I tell her about the challenges and my many injuries. I tell her about the argument with Jess and how I ran off in the rain and slid down the muddy hill. I tell her about the talk Jess and I had on the beach after Duncan left, and how I felt we'd made huge progress that day. And then I tell her about the inquisition, when Jess made her final statement and pulled the palm-frond carpet out from under me.

I stop talking. Jules is staring at me, her eyes wide, jaw slack. Finally, she responds.

"Wow."

"Yep. That about sums up the entire experience."

"So . . . I'm confused." She shakes her head and wrinkles her nose. "What happens now?"

"Well, that's where it gets really interesting."

"It gets more interesting? Hold that thought." She holds up one finger and walks to the kitchen. "I need a Dr. Pepper."

"I don't think I have any."

"Yes, you do," she calls with her head in the fridge. "I restocked the essentials for you."

Now that's a true friend. She comes back with two open bottles of Dr. Pepper—because we both insist that it tastes better when it comes from a glass bottle.

"Okay." Jules hands me a Pepper as she returns to her place on the couch. "I'm ready for the really interesting stuff."

"Well, our last night at the hotel, Jess and I finally had a long talk. When she said she needed the money for her mother, I thought she meant for medical bills. But she didn't mean that at all."

"What did she mean?"

"Susan, that's her mom, was diagnosed with ALS a year ago."

Jules reels back slightly, much like I did when Jess told me. "Oh man. That's Lou Gehrig's disease, right?"

I nod. "I need to do some research on it, but from what Jess told me, it's terrible. The usual life expectancy is about five years from the time of diagnosis."

"How is Jess taking it?"

"Hard. Of course. The family is very close." Jules's eyes crinkle with concern, and I smile at her. "I'll admit, I was jealous of that at first, but not anymore. It's the whole reason I gave her up in the first place: so she could grow up in a loving, two-parent family."

She raises her bottle in agreement. "Amen to that. Now, back to Jess. If she doesn't need the money to help with medical bills, then what does she need it for?"

"Something pretty amazing. When Susan found out she was sick, she and Robert and Jess sat down and made a list of things they wanted to do together while they still could. I think they did one thing, and then Robert realized that, even with their insurance, most of their money was needed for medical expenses." I have to pause and take a drink, because even now as I recount the story to Jules, it chokes me up. "Jess needs the money so her family can complete that list."

Jules puts her fist to her mouth and bites one knuckle. "Incredible. That's some daughter you have."

"She is. Not that I can take any credit for her compassionate nature."

"I don't know about that. Some stuff must get passed through the genes."

"It doesn't matter," I say with a shrug. "The point is, we made peace before going our separate ways. And we made plans to see each other again."

Sitting up straighter, Jules reaches out and slaps the top of my good arm. "I can't believe you waited to tell me that part. That's awesome! When are you going to see her?"

"Next week. I can't get back to work until my wrist heals, so Ranger and I are taking a road trip to California." At the mention of his name, Ranger looks up and whines, leaning all his weight against my leg. "By the way, did Duncan leave you his contact info like he said he would?"

Her eyes narrow. "He did. Why?"

"Because I need to get in touch with him. He doesn't know it yet, but he's coming to California, too."

Whether he wants to or not.

By the time Jules heads back home, I'm exhausted. It's only 7:00 p.m., but between stress and jet lag, I barely have enough strength to drag my suitcase upstairs to the bedroom. At the sight of my own bed, I sigh and touch the corner of my quilted spread with my fingertips.

"I've missed you so."

Ranger cocks his head to the side, as if he finds it strange to hear a grown woman speaking to bedroom furniture.

Even though I want nothing more than to throw back the covers and slip into the sweet oblivion of sleep, I don't. Instead, I toss my suitcase on the mattress and force myself to unpack. All my clothing goes straight into the laundry hamper on my closet floor. As I toss in an armful, I catch a flash of the orange bandana. Picking it out of the pile, I hold it aloft between two fingers. It's dirty, it's sweaty, and I think there's even a little blood on it. After all it's seen, all it's been through, it seems almost disrespectful to wash it.

But then I inhale, and the stench coming from it convinces me I have two choices: wash it or burn it. I'll try washing it first.

A high-pitched trill comes from the general area of my suitcase, and for a moment, I don't know what it is. Then I realize it's my phone. Shaking my head, I mutter to myself as I tromp out of the closet.

"You'd think I was on that island for a year, not a month." I wag my finger at Ranger. "If I start talking to a volleyball, go get help. Quick."

He yawns. Apparently, the novelty of having me back is wearing off.

The notification on my phone is a text from Jules with all of Duncan's contact information. I'm tempted to call him now, but if I'm remembering the time difference correctly, it's about three in the morning in Scotland. Besides, I'm so loopy at the moment, there's no telling what I might say to him.

The challenge will be reaching out to Duncan to help Jess without giving him the impression that I'm reaching out to him for myself. Seeing him again on the island was a shock, but it showed me that he hasn't really changed all that much. He still has those qualities I fell in love with—the warmth, the charm, the heart that reaches out to others because it makes him feel good. But he's also self-absorbed. If he can help someone without it causing him personal discomfort, then he will. But he will always put his own welfare first. Now that I see how he really is, and not my idealized version of him, I have a much better idea of how to deal with him.

As I stumble toward the bathroom, Ranger sits up and pokes his nose at me. Laughing, I sit on the floor and hug him.

"I envy you, Ranger. It is so easy to make you happy."

Tongue lolling out of his mouth, he lies on his side. He's so soft and cuddly, I decide to lie down too, and use him as a pillow. Beneath my cheek, the rhythmic beating of his heart reminds me of the tide rushing in and rolling out. Just for a minute, I'll lie here and relax.

Just for a minute.

36

I wake up the next morning curled on the floor, and Ranger has made his escape. How I could fall asleep down here is beyond me, although, it's ten times more comfortable than that bumpy bamboo floor in the shelter.

Twenty minutes later, I've showered and faced the challenge of getting dressed. Since I lost so much weight on the island, all of my pants are too big. The only thing I could find that would stay on was a pair of drawstring shorts, tucked in the back of a dresser drawer.

Downstairs, Ranger is prancing in circles by the front door, reminding me that life goes on as usual, whether I'm ready for it or not.

"I get the hint."

I grab his leash and snap it to his collar. Ranger and I have gone for a morning walk almost every day since I brought him home from the animal shelter. There's no reason not to keep that up.

It's just a little after eight, but the morning air is already hot and dry. A quick check of the sky reveals a smattering of puffy, white clouds and not the slightest chance of rain. The neighborhood is quiet, but what movement I do see is totally normal: two women jogging, a man working on a car in his driveway, another woman pulling weeds from the planter around a tree. There are no bats, no monkeys, no cameramen lurking around every corner, no game show host. Funny how I actually miss some of those things. Not that I'd admit which ones.

"Monica!"

Now there's a familiar voice. I turn and smile. "Good morning, Mr. Williams. Good to see you."

"And you." He and Caesar rush up to me. As I scratch the big dog behind one ear, Mr. Williams stares at my bare legs. "Goodness, you really took a beating out there."

Oops. By finding shorts that fit, I've inadvertently put every bruise, bump, and bite on display. "I guess you watched the show, then?"

"Oh yes." He nods with such vigor, I'm afraid he may pull a muscle in his neck. "When I saw you walk out on that beach, I almost tossed my popcorn."

I sure hope that's not a euphemism for something else. "I haven't seen the episode yet."

Caesar strains on the leash, but for once, Mr. Williams stands his ground. "How do they get so much on film? There must be cameras everywhere."

"Pretty much." If only Ranger would give me an excuse to walk away. But he's so busy sniffing Caesar, he couldn't care less if we stand here all day.

From the way Mr. Williams is scratching his chin and looking at me through narrowed eyes, I can tell he's deep in thought. Then he points a finger at me. "You made it to the end, didn't you?"

"What? Why would you say that?"

He points at my legs. "Some of those bruises look quite new. The only way you'd get them is if you were playing right up until the end."

Oh man. It's no problem to keep myself from blurting out game details in casual conversation. It's another thing altogether to be asked a direct question and have to evade it. I can't lie to the man's face, so I try to throw him off with humor.

"You know, I could just be naturally clumsy."

"You could, but I've never seen you bruised up like this." He grins, obviously proud of himself. "No, ma'am, I believe you played all the way to the end."

I underestimated Mr. Williams. He doesn't just watch the show, he's a fan. And there's no way he's letting go of his theory. So I tell him the truth.

"We're not allowed to discuss details. But you already know that, right?"

He laughs. "Right."

"Besides, what fun would it be if I told you now how it all works out? It would take all the suspense out of watching."

"Good point." He reaches out and pats my shoulder. "I'll be seeing you. And I'm rooting for you and your daughter."

Sensing this is his moment to move, Caesar jerks on the leash again. This time, Mr. Williams pays attention and waves good-bye as they walk on.

I've been home for less than twenty-four hours and only the first episode has aired and already I've been grilled by a friend. Suddenly, my relaxing little walk around the neighborhood has taken on an element of stress.

Anticipating some resistance, I wrap Ranger's leash more securely around my good hand and turn back toward home. Sure enough, he pulls back, probably thinking of all the bushes and flowers and paving stones he hasn't had a chance to sniff yet.

"Sorry, buddy." He looks up at me with soulful eyes and wags his tail like a feathery flag. In his own doggy way, he gets it. "It's time to go home. We've got a road trip to plan."

"Ah, Nikki, I knew ya couldn't stay away from me for long."

Chuckling, I lean back on the couch. Duncan is nothing if not predictable.

"Believe me, I can go a very long time without talking to you. But now I need to talk to you about Jess."

"What about her?" His tone turns completely serious. "Is she all right?"

I hurry to assure him that she's fine. "But her mother, Susan, is not."

With the exception of making affirmative noises here and there, he doesn't interrupt until I finish telling him the story. When I'm done, his response is immediate. "When are ya leaving for California?"

"As soon as I can get things tied up here. Probably in the next two or three days."

"Can ya hold on, Nikki?" Without waiting for an answer, he starts talking to someone on his side of the phone, but the voices are muffled. He's probably covering the speaker with his finger. A few minutes pass before he comes back on. "Are ya still there?"

"Of course."

"I can be in Las Vegas on Wednesday, and we can go ta Jess together."

His statement is so completely beyond the scope of what I'd been planning, my mind goes blank for a moment. "You want to drive to California with me and my dog?"

I must sound as dense to him as I feel, because his laugh booms through the phone. "Sure, we could drive, Love, but we'll get there a lot faster if we take my plane."

"If we . . . *your* plane?"

"Yes. My plane." He pauses, and I realize he's surprised by my surprise. "Ya don't know what I do for a living, do ya?"

"No."

"And you didn't know back when we dated, did ya?"

Now I'm getting frustrated. "I didn't think you had a job. Isn't that why you were at culinary school? To become a chef?"

A garbled sound comes from his end, which I'm pretty sure is some not-very-nice Scottish sentiment. "Seems we have a lot to talk about. For now, give me your email address and I'll have my secretary send ya all the flight information."

"You have a *secretary*?" He's just one surprise after another.

"As I said, we'll talk." The tension is still in his voice, but I can almost hear a smile come on. "And yes, Love, ya can bring your dog along."

By the time we hang up, my head is spinning. Duncan has a secretary. And a plane. What else does he have?

I jump up and hurry into the spare bedroom I use as a home office. Twenty-six years ago, it wasn't commonplace to Google everyone you met, and in the years since, I hadn't thought about Duncan enough to care. But now, I need answers, and I can't wait until Wednesday to start getting them.

I type slowly, making sure I spell his name correctly. *Duncan McAllister.*

Enter.

No . . . that can't be right. I double check the spelling. Hit enter again. And fall back into my chair.

About 1,800,000 results.

Which isn't all that surprising. There are obviously lots of Duncan McAllisters in the world. What *is* surprising is the first entry, which has a picture next to it. A picture of the Duncan I know. And a link to a website.

McAllister International.

My finger hovers over the mouse button as I brace myself for what I'm about to read. Then I take a deep breath, and jab it with my fingertip.

It's a slick website with multiple tabs for each division of the company. But what interests me most is the "About Us" tab. One click, and there he is, looking handsome and professional in a dark suit, his hair still too long for the corporate world, but his smile so charming that you forgive him for the hair.

Duncan McAllister, CEO.

No way. The carefree man I knew, the one who breezed in and breezed out, wasn't serious enough to run a corporation. And if he worked for this company back then, what was he doing at culinary school?

Typing as fast as I can with one hand, I go back to Google and do another search. After a little digging, I come up with his biographical information. He's forty-eight years old, married once, divorced, with two children, both boys. Oh wow. I wonder, during those times when he and Jessica talked on the island, did he tell her that she has half brothers?

Moving on, I come to the part about McAllister International. Patrick McAllister, Duncan's father, ran the company until 1988 when he suffered a massive heart attack and died.

1988. The year we met. The year he left.

I put my hand to my mouth, and for a moment, I feel the pain again. I was convinced that Duncan chose to leave me and that everything he'd told me had been a lie. It never crossed my mind that he might have had a good reason for leaving.

Would things have been different if I'd known? If he'd been able to tell me why he was leaving, would I have kept the baby?

Shaking my head sharply, I close each window with a click of the mouse. I know everything I need to know for now. If I keep going over it, I'll just drive myself crazy with what-ifs and whys. He'll be here Wednesday, and then he can tell me his side of the story.

I pick up my cell phone and dial Jules as I walk back to the living room. She isn't going to believe this.

37

Why didn't you tell me you'd be gone for over a month?"

"Nice to talk to you, too, Mother."

For the last two days, I've been avoiding the phone, but when I saw it was Mom calling, I had the urge to talk to her. Maybe it's because she and I have something in common, now that I'm just past being a mother in name only. Maybe being away for so long made me miss her. Whatever the reason, as soon as she barks at me without so much as a hello first, I regret the decision.

"Don't avoid the question, Monica. Why didn't you tell me?"

"Because I couldn't." With a sigh, I open the sliding glass door and step out onto the patio. After my time on the island, I have a new appreciation for being able to sit outside and enjoy the dry, desert air. "All the contestants have to sign confidentiality agreements. Nobody was allowed to talk about it ahead of time."

"I'm surprised confidentiality is something that concerns you."

"Excuse me?" I have no idea what she's talking about, but the tone in her voice warns me to prepare for a scolding.

"You obviously have no problem exposing our family's secrets to the world."

Here we go. "I never kept my pregnancy a secret. There was just never a need to discuss it before."

"And now there is?" Her voice takes on a shrill, brittle pitch. "What would possess you to do such a thing?"

"She asked me to."

Silence.

"She wanted to meet me. I couldn't say no."

"Of course you couldn't say no. But you could have met her somewhere else. A coffee shop, a mall. For heaven's sake, you could have met her on top of the Empire State building if you had to be dramatic. But on a reality show?"

Despite the tension between us, I have to hold back a laugh when she accuses me of being dramatic. This from the Queen of Drama herself.

"Mom, you knew I was going on the show. You gave them my information. You even told them about Duncan."

"Yes, but I didn't fully realize what that meant. I didn't expect you to be so open about why you were there. I don't understand it," she continues. "It's bad enough to have that shame in your past, but to flaunt it on television, well, it's undignified, to say the least."

My cheeks start to burn, and I no longer find any of this amusing. "I didn't *flaunt* anything. But I'm not ashamed, either. I made a young, impulsive mistake, but now that I've met Jessica, I don't regret any of it."

"How can you say that? Especially now that you've met her, can't you understand how wrong you were?"

"Jessica is a warm, lovely young woman. I will never regret having her."

Mom's rapid-fire response halts. Then she sputters a bit before continuing. "That's not it at all . . . you are completely misconstruing my words. Your mistake wasn't having her, it was giving her away."

The anger recedes. At least now, we're back to the same old argument. "Mom, I know you never agreed with my decision, but it was for the best. Really."

"But if you'd raised her—"

"Then she'd be a different person today. Believe me, she had a happy childhood. Her parents love her. How can I be anything but happy now for her?"

Whether she's pondering the answer or keeping her consternation to herself, I don't know. But I'm more than happy to take advantage of her silence.

"The day she was born, when you gave my picture to her parents . . ."

"I suppose you're going to yell at me for that, again."

I haven't yelled at her yet, but that's beside the point. "No. I want to thank you. Because if you hadn't given them the picture, Jess wouldn't have found me."

"Well." Her voice shakes, just the tiniest bit. "I'm glad."

It's not an apology, but it's a start.

There were times when I thought Wednesday would never come, but now that it's here, I want to turn the clock back a bit. About a month and a half would be good.

"Thanks for driving us to the airport."

Jules smiles without taking her eyes off the road. "You couldn't have stopped me if you wanted to. I need to get a look at this private plane." She jerks her thumb over her shoulder, pointing to where Ranger is curled up on the back seat. "You sure you want to take him along? He may not enjoy the ride."

"Yeah, I promised Jess. She wants to meet him."

"I predict they'll fall in love with each other."

"Of course they will. And Ranger will fall in love with Duncan, too, just like Jess did." I shut my eyes as I lean back against the headrest. "It's going to be a regular love fest."

"Sounds like you're not feeling much love right now."

My head lolls in her direction. "I'm nervous."

"About?"

"All of it. Seeing Jess again. Seeing Duncan again. Meeting Jess's parents." I wrinkle up my nose. "How weird is that? I'm going to meet my daughter's parents."

Jules laughs. "You've got the material there for a whole other reality show."

"Don't say that. Rick might think it was a good idea and send out his army of steady-cam dudes."

"Rick, huh?" Her voice drips insinuation. "Sounds like you got to know *Rick* pretty well."

"I don't know him any better than any of the other contestants. Well, maybe a little better, but that's just because we flew to the island together." There's also the fact that Bruce told me Rick likes me, which sounds so much like something straight out of grade school, there's no way I'm mentioning it to Jules.

"Whatever you say." She turns her attention to the airport signs. "Which terminal are we going to again?"

"Terminal three. Private flights." I shake my head. "I never thought I'd be flying on a private jet twice in two months."

"Watch out. People will start thinking you're too good to fly coach."

I frown at her. "If you weren't my best friend, and you weren't operating a vehicle, I'd slap you for that."

"Ah ha! The diva behavior begins!"

Before I can show her just what a diva I can be, we arrive at our destination. And there he stands, Duncan McAllister, former collegiate bad-boy turned current corporate executive bad-boy. Not that he looks like a CEO. His shadow of stubble, tousled hair, Hawaiian shirt, and cargo shorts emphasize his casual approach to most things in life.

I open the door and he steps forward, extending his hand to help me out of the SUV. "Good ta see ya, Nikki. And my island friend, Julia." He goes to her as she walks around the vehicle, and pulls her into a hug.

Yep. Everybody loves Duncan.

She hugs him back, then she pushes him away and pokes him playfully in the chest. "I should be mad at you. All that time we spent talking, and you never said a word about owning Scotland."

"Ah, now you're exaggerating," he says with a wink. "I only own about half of Scotland."

I clip the leash to Ranger's collar and let him hop out onto the tarmac. Just as predicted, he goes right to Duncan, who squats down to ruffle his fur.

"This is Ranger," I say, even though the introduction is unnecessary.

Since the two males are bonding, I hand the leash to Duncan and head to the back of the SUV where Jules is pulling out my luggage. "You should have let me get those."

She shrugs her shoulders and slams the hatch shut. "No problem. It's part of Julia Braemer's all-inclusive chauffer service. And your stuff smells a whole lot better than the sports equipment bags I'm used to hauling around."

Between her three sons, Jules is a fixture at just about every junior sports event in the valley. She's the kind of mom I like to think I would have been, if not for the circumstances. But now, I'm a different kind of mother altogether. I'm a mother who will do just about anything to support her daughter.

Jules shakes a finger at me. "You're overthinking again. I can see the wheels turning." Then she hugs me. "Call me when you get there. And if you need anything, even if it's just someone to make you laugh, you call. Promise?"

"Promise."

A casually dressed man in dark blue jeans and a pale green polo shirt with an embroidered M.I. logo approaches us. "We're ready for takeoff whenever you are, Mr. McAllister."

"Thank ya, Bradley. Would ya stow these bags, please?"

Bradley nods and snatches up the luggage. I try to take Ranger's leash from Duncan, but he points at the stairs leading up to the plane.

"You'll need that one hand to hold on ta the rail."

"Are you insinuating that I'm clumsy?"

"Ah no, Love. I'm saying it straight out." His laugh is a hearty boom that brings a responsive bark from Ranger. The traitor.

Rather than encourage him, I accept his offer to board first. As I put my foot on the first step, I can't help but think it would serve him right if I fell and sent us both tumbling backwards. Of course, that would prove him right, something I hate doing. So I hold on tight, determined to keep my balance, no matter what happens.

38

The flight from Las Vegas to Irvine is only about an hour, so once we're in the air, I don't waste any time.

"Why did you leave?"

"I haven't gone anywhere, Love." Duncan stretches out his legs and grins. "I'm right here."

"Quit playing games. You know what I mean."

"Yes, I do." His grin dissolves, as if it takes too much energy to hold it in place. "That was my sad attempt to put off talking about it."

I uncross my arms and lean forward. "I'm not crazy about digging into the past, either. But don't you think we should discuss it before we see Jess?"

He looks out the window, probably hoping he'll see something to divert my attention, like a smoking engine, or an odd little troll dancing on the wing. But no such luck.

"I left because I had no choice."

"Your father's heart attack."

His eyebrows go up in surprise as he nods. "You know about that?"

Shoot. Now I have to admit that I Googled him. "After we talked the other day, I looked you up on the Internet."

"Then you know."

He looks relieved that he doesn't have to tell me, but I'm not letting him off the hook. "I know why you left, but I don't understand why you didn't tell me. You acted like we had something special, but then you were just gone."

"I handled it badly."

"You think?" I want to say more, but instead I clamp my lips together and lean back. There's no point losing my cool now about something that happened so long ago. But I still want to know why.

"The day I left . . . My father's assistant called and said he was critical. And I knew. I knew he was dying." He sighs. "I wish I could say my first thought was ta tell ya good-bye, but it wasn't. All I could think of was getting ta my father before he died."

"Did you?"

"Just barely. And then I was thrown into his role. I had ta see ta my mother, and I had ta take over his company. There was no time ta think about myself. Suddenly, I had no choice but ta be responsible."

"And all this time I thought you were being exactly the opposite." I soften my response with a smile. "I get it now."

He leans forward, hands out, and for a moment I think he's going to touch me. But he stops just short of my knee. "Ya have ta believe me, when I finally realized what I'd done to ya, I was so angry with myself. I wanted to call ya, but after acting like such a complete . . . if I'd known ya were pregnant, well, I would have come back for ya."

I reach out, bridging the gap between us, and take his hand. "If you'd come back for me, that would have been one more mistake on top of the pile of mistakes we both made. And if I'd chosen to keep the baby and raise her alone, that would have been another mistake. Neither one of us was ready to be a parent back then."

His smile is sadly sweet. "And now?"

"I think we're ready now to give Jessica what she needs." After what I mean to be a comforting squeeze, I release his hand and sit back. "I don't know that I believe everything happens for a reason. But I *do* believe that God uses everything we do, even our mistakes, and turns them into something good, if we let Him."

He sits back, too. Then he looks out the window again and says, almost to himself, "I hope that's true."

Twenty-six years ago, Duncan and I didn't discuss our faith. Now, I wonder what he believes in. I thought we were going to California to help Jess, but I'm starting to get the feeling we're going to get some help for ourselves, too.

When we land, a car is waiting for us at the airport. I'm relieved to see it's a simple sedan, not a limo of any kind. After Bradley transfers our baggage from the jet to the car, he opens the back door for me.

"Thank you." I climb in and slide over on the seat, making room for Ranger to jump in after me. Bradley shuts the door, which is followed by the sound of a second door slamming. I look to my left and there's Duncan, smiling like he's about to spill some delicious secret.

"Why aren't you sitting up front?" I ask.

"And leave ya alone back here? That wouldn't be very gentlemanly, would it?"

Now he worries about manners. "Your chivalry is boundless."

Up front, the driver leans over and looks into the rearview mirror. "To the Beckett house, sir?"

"Yes. Thank ya." Duncan turns his attention back my way. "We're going straight to Jess's. After we see her, then we'll go to the hotel and get checked in."

At the mention of the hotel, my breath catches in my chest. We never talked about sleeping arrangements. He doesn't think—

The laughter that bursts from Duncan is so hearty and loud, it makes Ranger sit up and take notice. "I wish ya could see your terror-stricken face, Nikki. Give me a little credit for common sense. We'll be in separate rooms."

"Oh." Man, it's hot in the back of this car.

"We can even request different floors, if ya like."

I wave my hand in front of my face. "No, no, that's not necessary." I chance a look at him from the corner of my eye. "Sorry. I guess I'm more nervous than I thought."

"No need ta be sorry." He pats my knee in a gesture so quick and casual, there's no way to misconstrue it as anything but platonic. "Considering my track record, ya have good reason to be cautious."

I turn my body on the seat and look at him dead-on. "You're a good man, Duncan. The past is just that. Past."

He nods, his lips pursed. "That it is. Until the past shows up on your doorstep and says, 'Hello, let me introduce you to the daughter you never knew you had.' "

I glance at the driver, but from the unmoving position of the back of his head, it seems he's diplomatically ignoring our conversation. "That must have been some shock for you."

"Ah, that's a mild way of putting it." This time his laugh is short, hard, brittle. "The jerk from the show told me I was going out there to see ya. He made no mention of a long-lost child."

What a startling way for him to find out. It was hard enough for me to meet Jess for the first time, and I knew she existed. "Well, you two sure hit it off right away."

"I always wished I had a daughter. Not that I'd trade my boys. The little hooligans are just enough like me ta be interesting, but not so much ta keep me up at night." He leans forward on one hip and takes his cell phone from his back pocket. After a moment of tapping and scrolling, he hands it to me. "That's William, on the right. He's in his second year at Cambridge. And Daniel is taking a year off from school, deciding what to do with his life."

I laugh at his description of them as *little*. The two are tall and muscular, just like their father, but their hair, eyes, and skin are much lighter. They must get that from their mother. I want to ask about her, but then the conversation would invariably turn to me and my lack of a love life. That's one road I have no desire to go down.

"They look like fine young men. You must be very proud of them."

He nods as he takes back his phone. "That I am."

We stay silent for the rest of the drive. Ten minutes later, we've come into a lovely neighborhood with wide streets and sidewalks you just know were designed for health-conscious young mothers with jogger strollers. The homes are pristine, all with fresh paint, neatly manicured yards, and colorful flower beds.

"A planned community," Duncan says, his tone less than complimentary.

"You don't approve?"

"Strikes me as cold. There's no room for individuality." He shrugs. "But that's just me. I still live in the same wee cottage me Da bought for Ma."

"You do?"

He smiles, and his eyes twinkle with mischief. "Well, now, it's updated, of course. And there have been a few additions over the years."

"A few additions?" My eyes narrow. "Like what?"

"A few bedrooms and bathrooms. A better kitchen." He rolls his eyes upward, as if reading some invisible list on the car roof. "Oh, and the game room."

I laugh. "Yes, because what traditional Scottish cottage would be complete without a game room?"

"Exactly. Ya should visit some time. I remember how much ya loved the Centipede game."

When we first met, we spent hours playing at our favorite pizza joint. But the classic arcade game was almost impossible to find now. "I haven't seen a Centipede game in years. You really have one?"

"I do. And I have a big bowl of tokens for guests." He smiles warmly. "You're welcome any time."

The car slows, and the driver pulls over, parking in front of a two-story white house with dark green shutters and a deep-red door.

"Here we are, sir."

Duncan looks at the house, then looks at me. "Are ya ready?"

This shouldn't be so hard. Jess invited us, so I know she wants us here. But this time around, we're on her turf. No cameras, no TV host to guide us through awkward moments. And the thought of meeting her real parents, the parents of her heart, terrifies me.

"Nikki?"

"No, I'm not ready. Are you?"

His head moves slowly from side to side. "Not even close."

All right then. I hold out my good hand, palm up, and he takes it in his. Then I give his fingers a squeeze and take a deep breath. "Let's go."

It's time to see our daughter in her natural habitat.

39

We're halfway up the flagstone walk when the door opens and Jess bursts out of the house.

"Hey!" She dashes to meet us halfway, then stops short just before we collide.

We stand looking at each other, not quite sure how to handle this moment. Finally, I raise my hand in an awkward hello wave. "Hey, Jess."

Duncan isn't as controlled. With one stride he's by her side, his arm around her shoulder, pulling her close against him. "Good ta see ya, Love."

She smiles up at him, and I can already see a difference between Jess-on-the-island and Jess-at-home. A week back to real life with easy access to food, water, and a dry bed has softened the hard-edged, stress-filled look we all acquired by the end of our adventure.

"You look good," I say.

"Thanks. So do you." She points at my cast. "Other than that, you look injury-free."

"I'm glad the bruises went away. They were pretty hard to explain." Ranger tugs on the leash, whining and straining to get closer to Jess. "Sorry. He's not going to calm down until you say hello to him."

With a grin, she goes down on one knee and sinks her fingers into the ruff of fur around his neck. "Nice to meet you, Ranger."

As he licks her face, Duncan chuckles. "Obviously, ya passed his test. Now ya belong to the pack."

After one last scratch to his back, she stands up and looks behind us. "Where's your luggage?"

"In the car," Duncan says. "We wanted ta see ya first before going ta the hotel."

Jess frowns. "Don't you want to stay here?"

I glance at Duncan who's as surprised by her question as I am. "We didn't know that was an option." I look over her shoulder at the house. "Do your parents have room?"

"Of course. We've got two rooms ready for you guys. Ranger, too." Her smile is tentative, guarded against possible rejection. "We really want you to stay here."

We. She and her real parents talked together, worked together, to welcome her technical parents into their home. *What am I thinking?* If I could do it without causing a scene, I'd smack myself across the face right now. I have *got* to get over this petty jealousy.

"In that case, we'd love to." With a smile that's 90 percent genuine, I look at Duncan. "Let's get our bags."

"No need." He gives Jess another squeeze and kisses the top of her head. "You gals go inside. I'll handle the luggage. And perhaps I should take Ranger to the backyard?"

"That would be great." Jess points to the gate in the tall, white fence surrounding the yard.

As he walks away with Ranger in tow, I have a powerful urge to run after him, grab his arm, and force him to come with me. But I control myself. After all, I'm not walking into an enemy compound. I may feel like it's three against one, but really, we're all on the same side.

Shoulders back, attitude positive, I give Jess a nod. "After you."

I did a lot of research on ALS since Jess told me about her mother's illness. But no matter how many articles and blogs I read, nothing prepares me for seeing Susan Beckett face-to-face.

Jess led me down a ramp, which I'm sure wasn't part of the home's original design, and into the living area. A man and woman sit together, he on the end of the couch, she in a wheelchair beside him. As we enter the room, he stands and comes to me, hand extended.

"Miss Stanton, I can't tell you how happy we are to see you." His smile pushes up cherubic cheeks as he surrounds my hand with both of his and pumps for all he's worth.

"The feeling is mutual. And please, it's Monica."

"Monica. Of course. I'm Robert. And this is my wife, Susan."

He steps aside, releasing my hand and motioning toward the woman in the wheelchair. The short cut of her sandy-blonde hair, while easy to manage, emphasizes her sunken cheeks. In an involuntary movement, her left index finger taps on the armrest of her chair. But when she smiles, the movement slow and deliberate, her eyes light up. Susan Beckett's body is frail, but there's no hiding the strength inside her.

"Hello, Monica." Her words are thick, like molasses making its way through the neck of a bottle.

"Susan." Tears prick the back of my eyes, demanding to be let loose, but I refuse to cry in front of this brave woman. I take Robert's former spot on the couch and then, even though I'm clueless to the etiquette of the situation, I gently place my hand on top of hers. "Thank you."

There are many ways to interpret my thanks, and from the look on her face, I believe Susan understands all of them.

Duncan comes into the room and says something to Jess.

"Mom, Dad. This is Duncan."

In a moment, Robert has captured Duncan's hand in the same rapid-action, pumping shake he gave mine. Watching the two of them, I can't help but smile. Robert is a good five inches shorter than Duncan, with a hairline that has receded all the way to the back of his head. Duncan is, well . . . he's Duncan. But there's a mutual respect between the two men that transcends appearances.

I look over at Jess. She leans against the doorjamb, arms crossed, watching her two sets of parents meeting each other for the first time, and there's no way to misinterpret what she's feeling.

Pure, unmistakable joy.

"Let me get this straight. You and Duncan are staying at their house?"

"Yep."

As soon as Jess showed me to my room and told me to take some time to settle in, I called Jules to give her a status report. Now, I'm stretched out on the twin bed, leaning against the pillows wedged between me and the headboard.

"Jess has an apartment nearby, but she's staying here for the next few days. And I'm pretty sure the room they gave me is Jess's old room."

"How can you tell?"

"It's pink."

Jules makes a strangling sound. "Flamingo pink or Pepto pink?"

"Both. And then some."

The walls are a very pale shade of pink, like melted vanilla ice cream mixed with a spoonful of strawberry syrup. Frilly, bubble-gum pink curtains frame the windows. The carpet is deep red, like the inside of a red velvet cake. The whole room is starting to make me hungry.

I've never been a girly-girl myself, but somehow, this room feels right. It's no surprise that the girl who grew up in this room became a fashion designer, or that her parents would want to keep it just like it is for as long as they could.

"It's not how I'd decorate, but I like it."

"That's what matters. And how are things going with Duncan?"

"I told you, we had a good talk on the plane and on the ride over here. We're getting along fine."

"Just fine?"

Uh oh. Jules has just switched into matchmaker mode. "I'm not interested in getting along with him any other way."

"That's right. You're saving yourself for a certain reality show host."

I'm glad she can't see my stupid grin. "I'll admit, the idea of seeing Rick again has crossed my mind. But for now, dating needs to take a backseat."

We chat a few more minutes, then, with a promise to call her back when I have something new and interesting to share, I hang up and drop my phone on the bed. Running my fingers over the bedspread, I wonder who picked it out. Jess or Susan? The fabric is an abstract pattern of bright pinks, purples, yellows, and greens, and is something a teenager would be likely to choose. They probably picked it out together. It's good to know Jess grew up in a house where her creativity and flair were not only accepted but encouraged.

A knock sounds and I sit up quickly, swinging my legs over the side of the bed. "Come in."

The door opens and in walks Jess. "Are you hungry? Mo–uh, we thought you might be ready for lunch."

I smile at her attempt to be diplomatic. The funny thing is, even though I've been battling unnecessary jealously, her need to be sensitive to my emotional needs doesn't make me feel better about myself. It makes my heart go out to her.

"Jess, you don't have to avoid calling her Mom. It's sweet of you to consider my feelings, but it's not necessary. She's your mother. I know that."

Her eyes dart away for a moment. "It's just a weird situation, you know? I'm still trying to figure out how to act when we're all in the same room."

"I know exactly what you mean. But we're all rational, well-intentioned adults. We'll get there." I pat the mattress beside me. "Can we talk for a minute?"

"Sure." She perches on the edge of the mattress, and I imagine she wants to be able to make a quick getaway if the conversation becomes uncomfortable.

"Someone in this house sure loves pink."

She laughs and relaxes a little. "That would be me."

"That's what I thought."

"I've always loved pink. Maybe because I can't wear it."

"Why not?"

She pulls a lock of her long hair over her shoulder and waves it between her fingers. "Red hair and pink clothes do not a pretty girl make."

I chuckle and nod, understanding her point. "You strike me as the type who wouldn't let that stop you. I'd expect you to find a way to make pink work."

"Oh, I tried. But not many times. Mom . . ." She hesitates, but when I smile at her, she continues. "Mom said to me one day, 'Just because you *can* wear something, doesn't mean you should.' Her point was that part of a woman's personal style is being comfortable in her own body and understanding what works with it."

"Good advice."

"It was. And it's why I became interested in fashion. I started to see clothes not as mere decoration, but as a way for a woman to express who she is. I began to understand that I could empower women through fashion that flattered their true selves. Oh boy." A red tinge creeps up her neck. "There I go again. I kind of get carried away when I talk design."

"Feel free to get carried away with me anytime."

She laughs and stands up. "You say that now, but after a few hours of listening to my thoughts on beachwear and the power of the maillot, you might want to stuff cotton in your ears."

"Highly unlikely." I stand up too, and glance at the clock on the nightstand. "But now, we probably should go downstairs for lunch before they wonder where we are."

40

It's so nice to sit at a table and eat a sandwich." Jess is savoring her BLT, holding it with gentle reverence in both hands.

"I'm just happy to eat food with no sand in it." There's nothing reverent about my one-handed sandwich grasp. The bread is falling apart, and as I take a bite, a piece of tomato falls out and splats onto my plate.

"Da ya want some help with that, Nikki?" Duncan leans closer, holding out a napkin.

I shake my head. "It's okay." I look across the table at Robert and Susan. "As you can see, I really get into my food."

Robert smiles as he wipes his hands on a napkin. "Jess tells us you're a chef. I'm sorry we didn't have something more exciting to offer you."

"Please, there's nothing to be sorry about. Even simple food becomes elevated when you eat it with the right people."

"I agree." Susan says.

In the short time we've been around her, I've come to realize that speaking is difficult for Susan, so when she chooses to speak, she doesn't mince words. Trying to watch without staring, I marvel at the care Robert takes with his wife. In between bites of his own lunch, he dips a spoon into the bowl near Susan, and feeds her what looks like vanilla pudding. His movements are loving, but matter of fact. He doesn't baby talk her, like so many people would be tempted to do. He acts like it's the most natural thing in the world to spoon-feed his wife, and Susan receives his actions with quiet dignity. It's quite possibly the most beautiful thing I've ever seen.

"Don't forget, Monica." Jess talks around a mouthful of sandwich. "You promised to make crème brûlée for me."

At the mention of the dessert, Robert and Susan look at each other and smile, making me think it has some special meaning to them. Which gives me a great idea.

"Why don't I make it for all of us?"

Jess finally puts down the sandwich remains. "Really?"

"Sure. If you have all the ingredients, I'll make it tonight."

"If we don't have all the ingredients, I'll just take you to the market." Jess pushes back her chair and hurries to the pantry. "What do you need?"

Conveniently, I know the recipe by heart and can count the ingredients on one hand. "Eggs, granulated sugar, heavy cream, and vanilla extract."

"Eggs are in the fridge. Sugar is right here. Hmm." She hums to herself as she shifts cans and bottles. "I don't see any vanilla." Stepping back, she puts a hand on her hip and looks at Robert. "How can you not have vanilla?"

He shrugs his shoulders. "When was the last time anyone in this house cooked from scratch?"

"Good point," she says.

"Besides, we don't have heavy cream, either." He points the spoon at me before scooping up another portion for Susan. "Looks like you're going to take a trip to the market. We'll pray for you."

Before I can ask what he means by that, Jess walks up behind him and hooks her arm around his neck. "That's Dad's gentle way of saying I'm unsafe behind the wheel." She kisses the middle of his bald head, then straightens up. "I don't know how he got that idea. It's not like I've ever been in an accident."

Robert winks at me, then says with a straight face, "Her mother and I have done a lot of praying since she turned sixteen."

Susan nods. "Cars, boys. Lots of prayer."

"Okay, that's enough. If you keep talking like that, Monica won't want to ride with me. Then nobody gets crème brûlée. Is that what you want?"

"No," they say together.

"Na way," Duncan adds.

Like anything would keep me from spending time with Jess. They could tell me she's been in an accident every day for the last year and I'd still get in the car with her.

She turns to me. "Ready to go now?"

"Sure." I stand up and grab my plate, intending to help clean up before we go.

"Ah no ya don't." Duncan takes it from me. "Ya two go on. I think Robert and I can handle the kitchen."

Robert nods. "Absolutely. Have fun, girls."

I turn to remind Duncan to check on Ranger, but when I do, I catch Susan's eye. She smiles at me, but there's something else there now. It's a look of longing, and I try to put myself in her place. Even the simplest outing, like going to the store for groceries, must be a major production for her now. And as the disease progresses, it will only get worse. To watch Jess and me casually going out the door together can't be easy. My insecurities suddenly pale in comparison to what Susan has faced every day since her diagnosis.

"We'll be back in a bit." Jess calls out to anybody who's listening, then leads me out through a door in the kitchen that leads to the garage.

There are two vehicles parked side by side. One is a minivan, the other is a lime-green compact. It's not hard to figure out which one to get in.

As we drive down the street, I figure this is as good a time as any to talk. "Your parents are great."

She smiles. "Thanks."

"Does Susan have any food restriction? Like dairy or sugar?"

"No."

"Great. Then she should be able to eat the crème brûlée. The consistency is similar to the pudding she was eating."

Jess glances at me. "It's sweet of you to think of that. She's had problems swallowing for the last six months. It finally got to the point where she couldn't get down anything that had to be chewed. Now, she lives on pudding, ice cream, Jell-O, and protein shakes."

Despite her attempt to keep things light, I see how tightly her fingers curl around the steering wheel. Susan may be the one with the disease, but the entire family has been affected by it.

The grocery store is huge, which is good, because that means they might have a brûlée torch, something I'd totally forgotten about needing. If they don't, I can still make dessert, but it will just be a yummy baked custard.

Since Jess knows her way around the store, she pushes the cart. In the dairy section, I grab the heavy cream.

"How many eggs do you have at home?"

She shrugs. "I didn't think to look. I just know we have some."

I grab a dozen eggs. "Better to have too many eggs than not enough."

"Sounds like something you'd read in an Amish fortune cookie."

"Is there such a thing?"

"I don't know, but wouldn't it be cool if there was?"

As we stroll down the aisles to collect vanilla and a bag of just-in-case sugar, we laugh and come up with more Amish fortunes. In an aisle marked "Kitchen Equipment" we find one brûlée torch. It's low quality and high priced, but it will work.

When we get to the checkout, Jess hands the woman her Preferred Shopper card.

"Thank you, Miss Beckett."

She scans our items, and since I want to reserve my cash, I swipe my debit card. When the little screen reads, *Please show card to cashier*, I do.

"Thank you very much Miss . . . Stanton. Wait a minute." She looks from me, to Jess, and back to me. "Monica Stanton. And you're Jess! I saw you two on *Last Family Standing*!"

Uh oh. I never stopped to think anybody might recognize us. "Thank you," I say politely. Jess scoops up our bags and motions for us to leave, but the cashier is still holding my card.

"I can't believe this!" With every word, her smile gets bigger, and her voice grows louder. "I've been watching that show for years, but you two are my favorite contestants so far."

Other people are starting to look now. In the line behind us, expressions are changing from irritation at having to wait, to interest in who the famous people are and what they'd come to the store to buy. We've got to get out of here.

"That's really very sweet of you. If I could just have my—"

"Oh, you broke your arm! You did that on the island, didn't you?"

"I really can't talk about it." I bite my lip and reach for the card. "Please, we really need to go."

From the neighboring check stand, an elderly woman squints in our direction. "For heaven's sake, it *is* you."

Behind me, another woman starts talking. "If you and Jess are together now, the reunion must go well. Did you two make it to the end?"

Jess slips her arm through mine and tries to pull me away. "Leave the card," she whispers in my ear. "Let's get out of here before the mob grabs their pitchforks and turns violent."

She's right, but I can't do it. It's my debit card, for crying out loud.

The woman is talking again, waving my card in the air to the beat of her animated, one-sided conversation.

"Is Rick Wolff as hot in person as he is on television? He must be if he dates all those gorgeous women."

It occurs to me that I may have no choice but to give up and run, when a man walks up beside the checker. I'm relieved to see he's a manager. "Is there a problem here?"

"We need to go," I say weakly. "She has my card."

He looks at the clerk. "Is there a problem with it?"

"No, sir. These two were on *Last Family Standing*. You know, the mother who gave her daughter away and—"

"Cecilia!"

I could kiss the manager for cutting her off.

He frowns at her. "Cecelia, give the woman her card. Now."

Cecilia is none too happy that her celebrity moment is coming to a close. She hands over the card and glares at me as if it's my fault she got in trouble. I think it's safe to say Jess and I just lost one viewer vote.

"I'm so sorry for the inconvenience." The manager looks around, taking note of the worked up onlookers. "Let me help you with your bags, ladies."

Normally, I would politely decline. But when Jess lets him take the bags from her and we follow him out the door, I'm relieved. And when he puts the bags in the trunk and stands a respectful distance from the car before we drive away, all without turning into a crazy psycho guy, I say a silent prayer of thanks.

"I think we screwed up."

Jess's voice shakes, and for a moment, I wonder if she's okay to drive. Then I realize I'm not in any better shape than she is.

I squeeze my forehead with my fingers. "It never occurred to me that someone might recognize us. Ever. All I wanted to do was make crème brûlée."

"What do we do now?"

"Find the nearest time machine."

"Very funny."

Well, at least I got a laugh out of her. But seriously, what is there to do? We can't undo it. We can't keep the people who saw us from talking to their friends. Or worse . . . posting on a blog. And I'd be willing to bet Cecilia hangs out at more than one fan site.

"I need to call Rick."

"You have his number?"

"Sure. Don't you?"

"Uh, no." Now she's smiling. "I'm pretty sure he doesn't make a habit of handing it out to all the contestants. Just the special ones."

"The only special thing about me is I'm always getting in trouble. Which is why he gave me the number. He knew I'd need it."

And right now, I wish I didn't have it. Because when I tell him what happened, he's going to kill me.

41

I overestimated Rick's reaction, but not by much. After muttering something I couldn't repeat to anyone in the Beckett house, he said sharply, "You and Jess stay put. Don't move. I'll be there in an hour."

There must have been traffic, because the doorbell rings an hour and a half later. After introductions to Robert and Susan, we all gather in the living room for damage control.

"Monica and I are so sorry," Jess says.

The rest of us are sitting, but Rick paces the room, as if the movement will help him think more clearly. "What was so important that you had to go to the market together?"

"Crème brûlée."

He stops and looks at me. "What?"

"I wanted to make crème brûlée. But I needed heavy cream and vanilla."

"And a torch," Jess adds.

"A torch?" Duncan asks me.

"Yeah. To brûlée the top. We found one, too. Not a great one, but—"

"Enough!" Rick's on the move again. "I get it. You needed groceries."

I nod. "And we just didn't think what would happen if anybody who watched the show saw us together."

"To be fair," Jess says, "no one ever told us not to go out in public together."

I hold my breath as Rick stops again, then stares at her.

"You're right. We should have made that clear. It's just never been a problem before."

The air whooshes from my lungs. At least he's not mad at us. "What can we do now? How can we fix it?"

"Honestly, I don't know." He scratches the back of his head and looks at the floor. "I know what you can't do. No more mother/daughter shopping trips." He looks at Susan, and I can tell he regrets what he said. "I'm sorry. I didn't mean that the way it sounded."

"Don't be sorry." She smiles. "It's true."

Robert pats her arm. "Mr. Wolff, we are thrilled to have Monica and Duncan here. They were Jessica's parents first. If it hadn't been for them, we would have missed out on the greatest blessing in our lives." He beams at Jess, who ducks her head in embarrassment. "There are no hard feelings here."

Just when I thought I couldn't respect these two anymore than I already did, he goes and says a thing like that.

Rick is equally impressed. "Thank you, sir. You can be very proud of your daughter. As you'll see on the show, she's quite a girl."

Beside me, Duncan tenses. He doesn't mind sharing Jess with her parents, but apparently he minds sharing her with Rick.

Then Rick addresses me. "Monica, may I have a moment alone with you?"

Duncan's leg slides over until his knee touches mine. Add me to the list of things Duncan doesn't want to share. As if he has any say in who I talk to.

"Sure." I stand up and look at Robert. "Where would you recommend we go?"

"Why don't you take advantage of the patio?"

"Great idea. Thanks." It will also give me a chance to spend time with Ranger.

Rick follows me out the sliding glass door. The backyard is just as beautiful as the front, with a water feature in one corner providing a calming gurgle. As we sit down at the round, glass table, barking cuts through the night air as Ranger runs around the corner. He pauses just long enough to give my knee a hello lick, then rushes to check out his new friend.

"Good to see you again, Ranger." Rick scratches him firmly behind the ears, rolling the dog's head from side to side.

"You remembered his name. I'm impressed."

"He's memorable. Just like his owner."

I ignore his compliment and give them another minute to bond, then call Ranger over to my side and motion for him to lie down. To say I'm shocked when he does it on the first try is an understatement.

"So, what did you want to talk to me about?"

Rick rests one elbow on the table. "What's going on with you and Duncan?"

No beating around the bush here. "We came out here to see Jess. He is her father, you know."

"Yeah, I know. I'm surprised that you and Jess aren't taking time for the two of you."

"This trip is about more than parental bonding." How much should I tell him? It's not like I owe him an explanation, but I find myself wanting to share what I've been going through. Considering the importance of not giving away show secrets, he's the only one I can talk to besides Jess and Duncan.

So I spill my story, telling him about Susan, about the list, about how rich Duncan is and how I hoped we could help this family. When I get to the end, he's smiling, and the ambient glow of a streetlight drops a shadow into one of his dimples.

"You are an amazing woman."

"I am?" To be honest, I thought the story I just told him was more about Susan than me.

"Yes, you are. And the fact that you don't know it makes you a little more amazing."

"Well. Thank you."

He laughs. "You're welcome."

The moment feels awkward, so I shift the focus elsewhere. "The list the family made is pretty cool. One of the items is to visit a genuine medieval castle. That's what made me think of getting Duncan involved. I mean, if a Scotsman can't get them to a castle, who can?"

Rick is nodding, but his eyes are looking just past me. Something is percolating inside that man's head.

"I'd love to see their list. Do you think Jess would show it to me?"

"Probably. Let me go get her." I go to the door, then look over my shoulder. "Would you like a soda or something?"

"A diet anything would be great."

"Diet? Seriously?"

"It's a job requirement." He pats his stomach. "You know what they say about the camera putting on ten pounds."

"Hey, you want to know a good way to keep your weight down? Try eating nothing but coconuts, bananas, and the occasional fish for thirty days. That'll take the weight right off."

His grin tilts. "Point taken. Now, about that diet soda . . ."

"Coming right up, oh camera-ready one."

When I walk back in the house, everybody is right where I left them. They all look at me, obviously expecting a report on my conversation with Rick. Feeling a little playful, I decide to make them work for it.

"Is there any diet soda in the fridge?"

Jess stands up. "We have Pepsi and Sprite. Which one do you want?"

"It's not for me, it's for Rick. He seems more like a Pepsi guy, don't you think?"

I head into the kitchen with Jess on my tail. When I turn from the fridge with the soda in my hand, she's standing right behind me. "What did you talk about?"

"He wanted to know how things were going. Why Duncan is here. And I told him about the list your family made and how we're going to do our best to work our way through it."

"Wait. Back up. He asked why Duncan is here?"

"Yes."

Her eyebrows waggle. "Did he sound jealous?"

"He kinda did. Yeah." Despite my earlier protests, I have to admit that I enjoy thinking he might want to pursue a relationship with me.

"That is so cool."

I nod. "But bringing this conversation back to reality . . . he wanted to know if you'd let him see your list. Would that be all right with your parents?"

"Sure. I'll go get it."

"Great. Meet us out on the patio. Oh, and Jess." I lower my voice. "Don't tell Duncan what we're talking about out there."

She giggles and runs out of the kitchen.

Two months ago, I was a forty-five-year-old woman with no romantic prospects and a predictably dull routine, and the only close relationships I had were with my best friend and my dog. Now, I'm a forty-five-year-old woman who's been on an island adventure, is forging a relationship with an amazing young woman, and may very well have two handsome, available men vying for my attention.

"Well played, God," I murmur as I leave the kitchen. "Well played."

42

F*our months later*

"Are ya ready, Love?"

"Aye, as ready as I'll ever be." I've spent so much time with Duncan over the last few months, I've fallen into the habit of copying his brogue.

He laughs and hugs me to his side.

Jess hurries up to us. "How do I look?"

Duncan turns his finger in the air and she twirls full circle. He moves his fingers into an okay sign. "Beautiful, as always."

She rolls her eyes. "Why do I even bother asking you? Mon?"

Jess may never call me Mom, but I couldn't care less anymore. The relationship we've built means more to me than any title.

I tap my lip with my finger and give her outfit a critical look. "The dress is gorgeous. Very flattering." And it's one of her own designs, which makes it even better. "But I'd lose the necklace. It's too heavy for the delicate neckline."

She nods as she undoes the clasp. "I was thinking the same thing. Thanks." She holds out the turquoise necklace to Duncan. "Would you hold on to this for me?"

"Of course." He slips it in his jacket pocket. "Are your parents here?"

"Yep. Right in the front on the aisle. They saved you a seat."

"Great." He puts an arm around each of our shoulders, draws us to his side for hugs, and takes turns kissing the top one head and then the other. "Go knock 'em out, gals."

As Duncan walks away, he passes Rick, and the two exchange waves.

"You two look great."

Rick pulls me into a hug and kisses my cheek, then turns to Jess and does the same with her.

"You look pretty great, yourself." I point to the Celtic cross hanging around his neck. "This is especially nice."

"It was a gift from a very special friend." He looks around to make sure no one can overhear him, then speaks in a low voice. "I have to admit, I'm thrilled that America cast the deciding votes tonight. Because if anybody accused me of being partial, I wouldn't be able to deny it."

I put my hand on his shoulder. "I've gotten so much more out of this experience than I ever dreamed I could. No matter what happens tonight, I'm one blessed, happy woman."

His lips move into his familiar grin. "Just the way I like you."

A production assistant calls out as he runs past. "Five minutes to showtime!"

Jess takes a deep breath. "Oh boy."

"You're going to be great. You both are." One more smile, and then Rick leaves to get into place.

"Let's go." I link my arm through Jess's and we walk around the dingy, unimpressive backstage area until we find the spot where all the contestants have gathered.

Even though everybody looks good, they all look so different than they did on the island that I have a hard time recognizing some of them. The men are clean shaven, the women have their hair and makeup done, and everybody put back on the weight they lost. Malcolm and Layla wave at Jess and me. We have just enough time to wave back when the music starts.

We're live.

Through the backstage monitors, we can hear Rick welcoming the audience. Then, he introduces the contestants in the order we left the show. Sal and Gracie are first, Jess and I are last. When we walk out onto the stage, I'm disoriented for a moment by the bright lights and the roar from the audience. Jess pulls me forward. I follow her, but don't see whatever it is my heel catches on. I stumble and almost fall but am able to pull myself up before doing any damage.

The crowd laughs. As we make our way to our seats, Rick ad libs with the moment. "This season, Monica visited the medics more than any other contestant in previous seasons. Jess, you're in charge of her tonight."

More laughter. I look out into the audience and finally locate Robert, Susan, and Duncan. Right behind them are Jules and Jackson, and beside him is my mother.

The show goes on. Rick talks to each family. There are some comical video montages, including one of my many trips to the medical tent, which ends with me gazing up at Rick and saying, "You have pretty eyes."

The crowd loves it. I still find it mortifying.

And that leads us into the part where Rick talks to Jess, and then to me, and then the big reveal about why Jess really wanted to be on the show. The story and the players are so familiar now, I didn't expect to get choked up talking about it. But I guess some things will always stir the emotions seeing them again.

When Rick finishes with us, he addresses the audience. "I know you're all anxious to find out which of our two final families is the last standing. But first, I want to share an exciting new project with you that spun off from this season of *Last Family Standing*. It's the first of what we hope will be many more."

The big screens on either side of the stage begin to show the prefilmed package. "For ten years, *Last Family Standing* has put families in survival situations and dared them to make it to the end. Now, in *The List*, we're taking a family that's going through a real-life survival situation and daring them to live out their dreams."

I've seen this several times already, so instead of watching the package, I turn my attention to all the people who've become so important to me.

The last four months have gone by in an amazing, bittersweet blur. After reading over the Beckett family's list, Rick shared his big idea with all of us. It would be a reality show, but it would be more than that. Not only would we work through the items on the list but also we'd participate in humanitarian events wherever we were. On top of that, we'd increase awareness of ALS, and let people share in the developing relationship between Jess, Duncan, and me. How could any of us turn down an idea like that?

We've already had our first amazing adventure. Duncan found us a castle to visit. Of course, it helped that the owner of the castle is part of the McAllister clan, which means Duncan isn't just rich, he's some kind of nobleman. Our stay there included reenactments of all sorts of medieval things, including a joust and a celebration ball that required us to be in historically correct costume. Rick still ribs Duncan about the unfortunate gust of wind that caught him in his kilt.

I've had the privilege of not only getting to know Jess, but getting to know her parents. To watch them together has healed a wound that was so deep inside me, I didn't even know it was there. There is no doubt in my mind that I did the right thing all those years ago. This family—Susan, Robert, and Jessica—

was meant to be together. And now, they've allowed Duncan and me to be part of it.

Jess and I have spent countless hours talking about how things work. Is it fate? Providence? Are our futures predestined? Does everything happen for a reason, or does God take everything we do, even the mistakes, and give a reason to them?

It used to bother me that I didn't know the answer. Now I know that the answer doesn't matter. What does matter is the life I'm living.

The clip comes to an end. The audience applauds. Rick's voice booms out.

"And now, it's time to find out who America has chosen as the last family standing."

Rick smiles at me, and I smile back. I never expected a reality show to change my life, but it has. It's given me my daughter and my extended family. It's given me adventures I never dreamed I'd have.

And it's opened me up to love. From the hints Rick has dropped the last few days, I'm fairly certain there's a proposal coming my way tonight. Some people might say it's too soon, but we've spent almost every day of the last four months together. Besides, I've wasted enough time being afraid to share my heart. Now, I'm beyond ready.

So when Rick says, "And the winner is . . ." I close my ears to it. I take Jess's hand in mine and look out at the audience, at Duncan, Robert, and Susan. The smile on Susan's face says it all.

I don't need to win the grand prize. I've got the best prize in the world: my family. And no one can take them away from me.

GROUP DISCUSSION GUIDE

1. Monica has no desire to compete in a reality TV show, but she'll do it to meet her daughter. Would you want to be part of a reality show? If not, what would motivate you to do so?
2. Jules helps Monica practice her survival skills before she heads off for the show. If you had to rough it on a tropical island, what would be your best skill? What would give you the most trouble?
3. Once on the island, the contestants have to decide whether to work together or tough it out on their own. How would you choose to play the game?
4. Some of the contestants believe it's okay to lie, cheat, or steal in order to win the game. Do you think it's all right to act in a way contrary to your moral beliefs in order to win a game that essentially has no rules?
5. When Jessica's birth father arrives on the island, Monica admits she never told him about having a daughter. What do you think of her decision? Considering that she was giving the baby up for adoption, should she still have tried to find Duncan and tell him he had a child?
6. Jessica has grown up happy and loves her adoptive parents, yet she still has issues with Monica. What kind of feelings do you suppose Jess struggles with?
7. Jessica's birth parents welcome Monica into their family. How would you feel if you were in their shoes?
8. Jess is helping her adoptive mother, Susan, work through a list of things she wants to do before her illness makes it impossible. If you had a list like that, what would be on it?
9. At the end of the story, Monica wonders, "Does everything happen for a reason, or does God take everything we do, even the mistakes, and give a reason to them?" What do you think?
10. We are never told who won the game. What do you think? Was it Bob and Tracy or Monica and Jess?

We hope you liked *Last Family Standing*, and we hope you'll check out Jennifer Allee's other books. Here's a sample of *The Mother Road* for your enjoyment.

1

I cannot get divorced.

"I want a divorce."

Tony repeats himself, speaking slower. Does he think I didn't hear him the first time? That somehow I missed his startling proclamation? Oh no, I heard every one of those ugly words. I just can't believe they came out of my husband. Not him. Not the man I've been so blissfully, ignorantly joined to for the last eighteen years.

"Natalie, say something."

I try to swallow, try to push down the shock that clogs my windpipe. This day started out so normal. How did it go so wrong?

When Tony arrived home from work, late as usual, I didn't complain. In fact, I had everything ready for a beautiful evening. Dinner warming in the oven, a special bottle of wine breathing on the table, and me, ready to celebrate. But when I greeted him at the door, my welcoming arms wrapped around a statue of a man, his arms hanging straight down at his sides, his torso cold and hard.

He's anything but statuesque now. Pacing like an agitated animal, he rakes his hands through his hair as he looks back at me. "Come on, Natalie. Don't give me the silent treatment."

Is that what he thinks I'm doing? Punishing him with my silence? What I wouldn't give for more silence. How I wish I could turn back time and press my hand against his mouth, forcing his lips closed so the words couldn't spill out.

But there's no going back. No undoing the news that all these nights I thought he was working late, he was actually getting cozy with his administrative assistant.

I stare back at him. What does he want me to say? What is there to say?

"When did it start?"

He stops pacing and sighs. I bet now he wishes he hadn't encouraged me to speak. "In Omaha."

Omaha? "I thought you went there alone."

"I was going to. Bringing Erin along was a last-minute decision. I needed a hand."

I'll bet you did. Facts bounce around my brain, banging into one another as I try to grasp what my husband is telling me. That trip was only three months ago. How can he already be certain that our marriage is over?

"We can get through this. We can go to counseling." The words squeeze out of me so thin and garbled it sounds like I'm talking through the speaker at a fast-food drive-through. Humiliation burns my cheeks, the back of my neck. Basically, I've chosen to ignore the fact that he's been unfaithful and am begging him not to leave me. If I have to swallow my pride to work things out, I will.

Because I cannot get divorced.

Tony closes his eyes, jerks his head hard to the left. "It's too late for that."

"It's never too late." I grab his arm, my fingers digging into his shirt sleeve, twisting into the cotton. Now that I'm touching him, I'm desperate. Desperate to keep contact. If I can just hold on, I can fix this. "We can work it out. Remember our vows? We're a threefold cord, you, me, and God. Together we—"

As soon as I say "God" his eyes cloud over and he yanks his arm away from me. "No. I can't do this anymore."

"But Tony, I—"

"She's pregnant."

Pregnant. That one word sweeps away anything else I might have said. Pregnant. And after only three months. I put my palm flat against my own stomach and sink onto the couch. Well, now we know.

There's no fight left in me. I can't look at his face, but I see his feet step closer.

"I'm so sorry. I didn't mean for it to happen this way."

This way? In other words, he did mean for it to happen, just in a nicer, more humane way. Finally, my mind clears and I know exactly what I want to say.

"You need to leave now."

He doesn't answer at first. But then his shoes back away and he says, "I'll have my lawyer contact you."

The absurdity hits me, jerking my head up, pulling me off the couch so I'm standing upright, hands balled into fists at my side. "You already have your own lawyer?"

His face is a mixture of sadness and pity. *Poor Natalie*, it seems to say, *how could you not see this coming*?

He scoops his car keys off the hall table and walks out the front door. He pulls it closed behind him so gently I barely hear the click of the latch.

So this is how it ends? Eighteen years of love, work, planning . . . over after a fifteen-minute confession.

The ding of the oven timer calls me to the kitchen. On my way there, I pass the dinner table, set so beautifully with our good china, a centerpiece of fresh flowers in the middle of a midnight blue tablecloth. And there, between Tony's seat at the head of the table and my seat to his right, is the reason I was so ready to celebrate. The contract for the next three books in the *Happily Married* series.

I cannot get divorced.

I'm a romance novelist. And not just any romance novelist. One of the top-selling Christian romance novelists in the country. I also write nonfiction books about—get this—marriage. I've put my life under a microscope and written about it, bared my soul, and now I'm considered an expert in the field. I make a living from couples who live happily ever after, or are at least trying to.

A cold numbness spreads through my body as I walk into the kitchen. I turn off the timer. Turn off the oven. Pick up the oven mitts from the counter. Open the oven door. Pull out the roast.

It looks perfect, but I pinch my lips together as the aroma sets my stomach to rolling. I don't even like roast. I only made this stupid thing because it's Tony's favorite.

So much boils up inside me—anger, grief, nausea—that I explode. I hurl the hunk of meat, roasting pan and all, against the wall and release a scream that comes from somewhere beyond my toes. Dropping to my knees on the floor, I weep as meat drippings and carrots and onions slide in slow motion down the wall and ooze across the floor.

My whole adult life has been about happily ever after. And now, it's over.

I'm getting a divorce.

Want to learn more about author
Jennifer Allee and check out other great
fiction from Abingdon Press?

Sign up for our fiction newsletter at
www.AbingdonPress.com
to read interviews with your favorite authors, find tips
for starting a reading group, and stay posted on what
new titles are on the horizon. It's a place to connect
with other fiction readers or post a
comment about this book.

Be sure to visit Jennifer online!
www.jenniferalleesite.blogspot.com